PRAISE FOR MARYBETH MAYHEW WHALEN

"*When We Were Worthy* is a startlingly clear look at life in a small town where the carefully crafted characters are neither heroes nor villains—they are simply real people wedged into an unimaginable situation. Heart-wrenching and vivid, this is a beautifully written novel about letting go and holding on, of family, of love, and, ultimately, of forgiveness."

—Karen White, *New York Times* bestselling author

"*When We Were Worthy* is a poignant, haunting story of truths and secrets—the power of tragedy to unravel an entire community, and then stitch it back together—I couldn't turn the pages fast enough."

—Amber Smith, *New York Times* bestselling author of *The Way I Used to Be*

"Not everyone who lives in Worthy, Georgia, lives up to the name. In *When We Were Worthy*, Marybeth Mayhew Whalen explores the spectrum of guilt and innocence in one small town after the tenuous connections between neighbors and friends are tested by a horrific accident. Told in alternating voices, this compulsively captivating novel weaves a tapestry of wrenching grief, love, anger, danger, and eventually hope."

—Ella Joy Olsen, author of *Root, Petal, Thorn* and *Where the Sweet Bird Sings*

"Fans of Lianne Moriarty and Jodi Picoult—this is an author for your favorites shelf. Marybeth Mayhew Whalen's taut, smart novel is a natural-born page-turner that doesn't sacrifice depth of feeling or character. Whalen knows this town, these people, and she lays them open for us with razor-sharp insight, wit, and empathy. Don't miss this one."

—Joshilyn Jackson, *New York Times* bestselling author of *Gods in Alabama* and *The Almost Sisters*

"What do you do when your whole life is turned around, crushed, and destroyed? Do you rise above it? Do you seek revenge? Do you run away? Do you blame yourself? *When We Were Worthy* is a brilliant, gripping novel that challenges the fabric of who we think we are, a story that speaks to both the fragility and strength of the human spirit in the wake of tragedy. I highly, highly recommend this novel!"

—Joy Callaway, author of *The Fifth Avenue Artists Society* and *Secret Sisters*

"In *When We Were Worthy*, MaryBeth Mayhew Whalen expertly weaves a haunting story of a small town ripped apart by tragedy. Narrated by four women—each with unique ties to the victims of a terrible car crash—each revealing secrets and lies that will make you second-guess everyone *and everything*. Written with heart and a splash of southern spice, *When We Were Worthy* is both charming and powerful."

—Liz Fenton & Lisa Steinke, authors of *The Good Widow*

WHEN
WE
WERE
WORTHY

WHEN WE WERE WORTHY

MARYBETH MAYHEW WHALEN

LAKE UNION
PUBLISHING

Text copyright © 2017 by Marybeth Mayhew Whalen
All rights reserved.

No part of this book may be reproduced, or stored in a retrieval system, or transmitted in any form or by any means, electronic, mechanical, photocopying, recording, or otherwise, without express written permission of the publisher.

Published by Lake Union Publishing, Seattle

www.apub.com

Amazon, the Amazon logo, and Lake Union Publishing are trademarks of Amazon.com, Inc., or its affiliates.

ISBN-13: 9781503941601
ISBN-10: 1503941604

Cover design by Rex Bonomelli

Printed in the United States of America

For my daughters.
May I never take for granted every day I get with you.

I am not what happened to me. I am what I choose to become.

—*Carl Jung*

The Girls

BEFORE

One thing everyone agreed on—it was the perfect night for football. There was a nip in the air—just enough to need a sweatshirt—and it smelled of popcorn and moldering leaves, was filled with the sounds of thundering cleats and the band's instruments mingling with the screams of excited fans, carrying as far out as the interstate, so that even people passing through caught a bit of our excitement. "Our boys really showed up tonight," we all said.

We were Worthy, a town and a team. The town was small, just 4,162 souls calling it home. And we knew just about all of them in one way or another. Small as the town was, we had at least one of every kind of church, and it didn't matter whether you were a good person or a straight-up heathen; you showed up in one of them on Sunday morning. If you didn't, we would talk about you.

Our few restaurants were passable but none of them especially good. Folks liked Chessman's for their fried chicken and barbecue plates. Tomasina's had decent pizza (so long as you'd never had really good pizza somewhere else and didn't know the difference). And of course there was the Subway and the Hardee's if we wanted fast food. There was also Stooges Pool Hall and Bar, but we weren't supposed to go out there, even though it was rumored that they served people under twenty-one. We knew if we even tried it, we'd get spotted by someone who'd tell our parents.

We had some stores—a Dollar General, a Rite Aid, an Ace Hardware, and Trout's Market, the town grocery store where we were sure to run into someone we knew, so we never went there if we weren't fixed up. (We always left Trout's with instructions to tell someone in our families that someone else said "hey.") But that was pretty much it for shopping, unless you counted Maxine's Finery, a place our mamas always wanted to take us because that was where they used to get their dresses when they were our age. But we preferred to go to Macon or, better yet, Atlanta for our clothes.

We had a swim club that practically everyone we knew was a member of. In the summer we went up there all the time to tan and swim and see our friends. There was a lake just outside town with a public beach, so sometimes we went there just to do something different. Once, late on a summer's night, we even skinny-dipped in that lake, shrieking and laughing as we slicked off our clothes and leaped into the dark water.

But it wasn't summer anymore. It was fall. And fall meant football in Worthy.

Once football season started, we were more the team than the town. And that season we were the team to beat in Bibb County. We had Webb Hart and Ian Stone and Seth Bishop as starters. It was Coach William "Fig" Newton's last year (after a Georgia record of 470 wins and counting) as head coach of the Worthy Wildcats. We were halfway through another winning season that promised to last all the way to the state championship. That night brought another victory: 28 to 7 against the Central Chargers.

At halftime they escorted Diane Riggle out onto the field, the only girl ever in the history of Worthy to go on to become Miss Georgia. Though that'd been five years ago, people never got tired of it, still proud though she didn't even place in Miss America. They kept up the billboard on the road that led out to the lake, a gigantic Diane Riggle looking down on us as we drove by, wearing her Miss Georgia crown, her face growing more and more bleached by the sun with each passing year.

"We grow 'em pretty in Worthy," the boys said that night, elbowing one another and gesturing from Diane to us on the sidelines, where we were holding our pom-poms and waiting patiently for Diane to get off the field so we could get back on it. We thought she looked like she'd gained weight.

After the game we had a party to get to, so we all went to Mary Claire's to get ready. Her mom was out with that weird girl, taking on a cause like Mary Claire's mom was always doing. "What can I say?" MC said, pulling the curling iron from her long hair to reveal a flawless blonde loop de loop. "She's already created the perfect daughter, so she needs a new project." MC rolled her eyes and laughed. "And this one is *definitely* a fixer-upper."

We laughed along with her, but we heard the note of hurt in her voice. Her mom had missed the game to take the strange girl—we called her the Runaway because of how Mary Claire's mom got mixed up with her—shopping in Macon.

Not one to dwell on depressing topics, Mary Claire cranked up "Style" by T. Swift and we all joined in, singing at the top of our lungs and laughing at Brynne's earnest attempt to sound like the singer. Brynne couldn't carry a tune in a bucket, but she thought she could. Though Keary went along with everything that night, she was kind of quiet, like she had something on her mind, something she wouldn't talk about no matter how much we tried to get it out of her. Her cheers had been flat in the second half, her jumps lacking any spring, her voice not nearly as peppy as it normally was. Whatever she had on her mind, we had a feeling it was good stuff. Stuff we planned to get out of her. But there was time for that, we believed.

We'd talked Keary into being DD, even though she only had her permit. "You'll be with two other licensed drivers," Mary Claire assured her. "It'll be fine." And because Keary was a sophomore and just honored to be part of the night—part of our group—of course she said sure, yeah, she'd do it. But Keary was nervous about it, and she wished Leah hadn't bailed on us to do whatever it was Brynne had put her up to. Leah would've made a better DD. She was so conscientious, so certain, so good. We all felt Leah's absence that night in one way or another, but when Brynne said she had something more important to do, we didn't argue.

And so we got ready for the party without Leah. We curled our hair and did one another's makeup and took ten times longer to do everything because we had to stop and dance, like, every five seconds. We danced to Luke Bryan and Taylor Swift and Beyoncé and once even Hank Williams Jr., and of course Mary Claire had to play "Can't Touch This" by MC Hammer because "MC Hammer" was her dad's nickname for her. When her dad heard it, he came busting in the room from wherever he'd been keeping himself and did some dance that we guessed was from the eighties. We laughed our asses off and MC about died of embarrassment. But we assured her that our dads were just as embarrassing. Her dad saw the beer cans but didn't say anything because MC promised him we had a DD and it would all be fine.

"I thought we were busted for sure," said Brynne after he left.

"My dad's cool about that stuff," said Mary Claire. "Now my mom, on the other hand . . ." She shook her head and buried the beer cans in a grocery sack to hide the evidence. "Let's just say we'd be locked in this room for the rest of the night."

Later, we would think back to that moment, to how things could've gone so differently, to how easily we could've been prevented from loading into Mary Claire's Civic with Keary behind the wheel and Adele on the radio. Sometimes we like to think we are still in that room, all of us happy, all of us young, all of us excited for the night ahead, anticipating what it would hold. Never once thinking it could hold tragedy. We imagine that night just keeps going on forever, and we guess that, in some ways, it does.

Ava

The day of the accident, a parent nearly hit Ava in the carpool line. She was doing her after-school duty—one she did not sign up for when she agreed to be Mrs. Dixon's sub, and one she was not trained for, which might've contributed to her near-tragedy in the fire lane. The sun was starting to descend, and according to the woman who nearly hit her, she'd been standing right in a sunspot that blinded the driver and rendered Ava invisible. She'd majored in English; she knew about metaphors.

Thankfully Ava had jumped out of the way just before the car drove into the very spot she'd been standing in seconds before. And though she was safe, that didn't mean she didn't feel breathless and out of sorts the rest of the day. She told Clay about it at the game that night, giving him a blow-by-blow of the incident. She told him about hearing the motor rev and knowing intuitively that it meant a car was headed toward her; how she leaped out of the way, jumping about as high as those cheerleaders were jumping on the sidelines. How afterward everyone looked sort of embarrassed for her, when it was the woman driving the car who should've been embarrassed.

Clay had stopped listening, staring intently at the field instead like he was actually interested in the game. Clay was not a sports kind of guy. Or at least he hadn't been before they moved to Worthy. Now he didn't miss a high school game, parading her and the kids around (she was ten years his junior—twenty-six to his thirty-six—and she never knew how much that meant to him till they moved to Worthy), politicking on behalf of the restaurant, glad-handing every man, complimenting every woman. Sometimes she didn't know him anymore.

When two-year-old Clayton said he wanted a drink, she jumped up and said she'd get it, mostly as an excuse to get away from Clay, who didn't seem to care that his wife had nearly been killed only hours before. So when she ran into *him*—the one she referred to as "Trouble" in her mind—it was natural to tell him the story, if only because she wanted someone to appreciate what had happened—or nearly happened—to her. She wanted someone to say how sorry he was to hear that, to ask if she was OK.

And he did. He looked at her intently and said the things she wanted to hear. He leaned in close, smelling of leather and laundry detergent. He smiled at her and flashed his dimples. He told her he wouldn't want a hair on her head to be harmed. Then he asked if he could give her a hug. She scanned the area to make sure no one was looking, but the game was nearing the half, and everyone was in his or her seat, riveted because it was a close one. He held out his arms, and she stepped into them, feeling the warmth of him as he wrapped her close. She squeezed her eyes shut, breathed in and out, tried to let the comfort he was offering be enough.

"Shit." She heard him exhale the word, and her heart picked up speed. She looked up in the direction of his gaze, both of them seeing that someone was watching. Both of them having forgotten for just a fraction too long that in Worthy, someone always was.

Marglyn

FRIDAY

Marglyn could hear Mary Claire's tires spitting rocks as she gunned the engine and sped away, anger making her foot heavy on the gas pedal, the bass thumping from her stereo so loudly they could hear the reverberations all the way inside the house. Marglyn went back to tidying up the dinner preparations, absently listening to the sound fading as Mary Claire got farther down their long driveway and turned onto the main drag that would take her straight through the middle of town to the high school. Deep down she was hoping her daughter would turn around and come back.

She heard Hale clear his throat from the kitchen doorway, waiting on her to stop fussing with the dishes, to stop moving and face him. At the table, their younger son, Robert, sat immobilized, no longer fiddling with his phone like he had been moments before Mary Claire walked in and World War III started.

She walked over to her son, ruffled his hair. "Let me talk to your dad," she said, freeing him.

Grateful, he nodded and all but ran from the room. She wished she could do the same. But Hale was waiting to talk to her, to ask the question she knew he wanted to ask.

He asked it, right on cue, swallowing hard before he did. "You sure you should still go?"

"It's one football game," she said, her answer at the ready. "I've sat through how many of them for her? Rain, cold, sleet, and hail. I've done it all. I can miss this one." She slapped the dish towel down on the counter for emphasis. They needed new countertops. She wanted granite ones. They were going to do it a year ago, but Mary Claire needed a car more.

She turned to face Hale, straightened her shoulders, feeling the invisible load on them as she did. "She barely speaks to me all week, then she picks a fight minutes before I'm supposed to leave."

Hale leaned against the doorframe, looking like the man she fell in love with, gone a bit blurry around the edges. He squinted at her, deciding, she knew, whether to push the issue, whether to voice his displeasure at her choice. She saw him decide: another fight wasn't worth it. "OK," he said, "whatever you think."

She crossed the room, gave him a kiss on the cheek, more relief than affection. She wasn't feeling affectionate toward anyone at that particular moment. The angry exchange with Mary Claire had soured her mood. And she'd been so looking forward to tonight. Doing something nice for someone else—someone who would appreciate it—always made her feel good. She hoped she could shake her spoiled mood before she and Ginny went out. She wanted to make the night special for the girl.

As if reading her thoughts, Hale asked, "Just curious—why this girl? Why tonight?"

Marglyn ignored the first question, because it was not one she could answer for herself, much less for him. She turned back to the kitchen, to the meal she'd made for her family even though she wouldn't be there to eat it. Dishes done, she busied herself with wiping down the counter even though it was already clean.

"Her job interview is tomorrow. She really needs the money. And she doesn't have proper clothes. You saw what she came over here in that time." Ginny favored skin-tight jeans or baggy sweatpants. And shirts that pulled across her boobs and had words on them. Nothing she could wear to a job interview and expect to be taken seriously.

"Mary Claire doesn't need me as much as Ginny does," she added, pointing out the obvious.

Marglyn looked over her shoulder at Hale, to see what his face was doing. He remained impassive, thinking over what she'd said. "Maybe," he said, after a time, "she does, but she just doesn't know how to say it."

She thought of Mary Claire's cruel words to her, her anger from out of nowhere. Something was behind it. Marglyn had simply tried to give her some instruction about the food she'd fixed, and before she knew it, Mary Claire had flown off the handle, gesticulating wildly and spouting off ridiculous platitudes, using words like *always* and *never*, exaggerating.

All Marglyn wanted was to take a young girl who had nothing to buy some nice things for a job interview. She wasn't asking to jet off to Vegas for a girls' weekend. More than anything, she wanted her daughter to tell her she was proud of her for thinking of others. Instead, Mary Claire had made it about herself, then she'd run out of the house, jumped into her car, and sped away, off to cheer at a game her mother would not be watching.

"Well, she sure has a funny way of showing it," she said matter-of-factly, as if that put the issue to rest when it did no such thing. She willed Hale to validate that going ahead with this evening was the right thing to do, that Mary Claire didn't always have to get what she wanted.

Hale obliged by coming over to give her a hug from behind, nuzzling her neck for a moment before he walked away, leaving her alone with her warring thoughts, torn between right and wrong. If only she could decide which was which.

Darcy

FRIDAY

With Halloween over, her neighbors were taking down their decorations right on schedule. Car keys in hand, Darcy paused on her sidewalk and watched as the couple across the street—new people who, thankfully, didn't know about last year—removed the orange lights from their bushes. Darcy's own house had stood naked all season save a lone cheap wreath she'd picked up at the Dollar General. Un-decorating had involved removing it from her door.

She used to live for Halloween decorations, putting up spiders and black cats and witches, hanging cobwebs. But last year she'd gone overboard. She knew that now and, looking back, felt a little embarrassed. She thought of the note in the mailbox from an anonymous neighbor: *I know you're upset, but terrifying children isn't the answer.*

In her own defense, Tommy had just left, and she wasn't in her right mind. She'd tried to soldier on, tried to keep things normal for Graham after Tommy left. Though Graham, fifteen at the time, probably didn't care, she told herself that routine mattered, that things should go on like they always had. So she'd pulled down the attic stairs and shimmied up the narrow ladder, trying to forget that this was a task Tommy had always done for her.

But as she was digging out the orange plastic Rubbermaid storage boxes, she'd seen it, packaged inconspicuously in a long white cardboard box, the words *Darcy Wedding Gown* written in black Sharpie down the side. In keeping with the time of year, she blamed an unseen hand, a dark force, that compelled her to go to the box, to break the seal and open it for the first time since she'd married Tommy eighteen years ago at the tender age of eighteen, fresh out of high school and fueled by romantic notions.

She'd lifted the lid, feeling the tickle of dust in the back of her throat, expecting to burst into tears at the sight of the dress, at the memory of the innocent girl who wore it. Instead she'd stared down at the dress and didn't feel sad at all. She glared at the white satin and seed pearls and lace and laughed the laugh of an evil villain driven mad by injustice. She saw scissors in her hand slicing through the fabric, snipping off the embellishments, destroying this dress just as surely as Tommy had destroyed their marriage.

She'd closed her eyes to erase the vision, took a few calming breaths (that was what her best friend, Faye, was always telling her to do), and replaced the lid. Then she turned back to the Halloween decorations. *Normality,* she told herself. *Routine. That is what will keep you on course.*

Do the next thing, her mother always advised. *It will get you through.*

Right. The next thing was decorating the house for Halloween. Maybe she and Graham would watch a scary movie that night to really usher in the season—any movie she wanted—and Tommy wouldn't be there to complain about her choice. She opened up the top box of decorations, just to see what was inside. Every year she forgot what she had.

Graham's costume from last year was right on top. He'd been a zombie from *The Walking Dead.* She'd helped him with the makeup, taken videos of him doing the zombie walk. Tommy had imitated him, and they'd all laughed, the guys on film and her behind the camera. Now she knew that Tommy had been seeing Angie Woodall even then. The happy image dissolved as her eyes fell on the bottle of fake blood they'd bought for the costume but never used.

She'd looked from the bottle of blood back to her wedding dress, thinking of Angie Woodall sleeping with her husband even as she made his dinner and picked up his dry cleaning and cared for his son. She thought of all the cliché things she'd wanted to do since Tommy announced that he was getting his own place—*taking time to sort things out*, as he put it. Like she was nothing more than his toolbox, his bank statement, his employees' schedule at the hardware store. Something he could pick through, rearrange to his liking. Or discard entirely.

She'd imagined slashing his tires, keying his car like the girl in that song "Before He Cheats." She'd thought of tossing all his shit out into the yard, making him gather it up in shame and humiliation as the neighbors watched. She'd thought of calling his precious mama and telling her just exactly what her son had done. But she'd talked herself out of all of it.

She'd walked back over to the *Darcy Wedding Gown* box, pulled off the lid again, and, before she could think better of it, tugged the dress from the box. She shook it out, studied it for a moment. She'd never wear it again. In eighteen years it had never even been out of the box. She didn't have a daughter who would ever wear it in her own wedding—and if she did, what bride would want to wear a dress tainted by divorce? She smiled to herself, already envisioning her plan. Of how awesome this revenge would be, how creative and unexpected. When Tommy came to pick up Graham for their weekly dinner, he would pull up the drive and see her handiwork. And he would know.

She'd taken the dress into the backyard, away from where the neighbors could see her. She hung it on a tree branch and held up that bottle of fake blood. She remembered Tommy at sixteen on the football field, a god worshipped by everyone in town. She remembered herself at sixteen, chosen by him, how glorious that made her feel. She remembered herself wearing this dress, walking toward Tommy, handsome in a tux at the end of the church aisle.

She thought of Tommy as a young father, Graham sleeping on his chest or, later, aloft on his shoulders. "Now I'm big like Daddy!" She thought of Tommy at her side when they found out another child wasn't possible, saying, "You and Graham are all I need." She thought of the night he got his promotion, the night they went to Atlanta for their fifteenth anniversary, the family vacations to Jekyll Island. All of it, every bit, rendered null and void by one woman, one stupid-ass decision.

She'd closed her eyes and depressed the nozzle, heard the liquid hit the fabric. She opened her eyes when she was done and saw the white fabric tainted with red. She felt a sadistic pleasure at the sight of it, this visual of what her husband had done to his bride.

When the dress was dry, she hung it up on the front porch, creating a macabre (albeit over-the-top) display to greet trick-or-treaters, the likes of which the neighborhood had never seen. Her mother had called, concerned, having heard all the way in Florida. Word also traveled to Faye, who showed up on her doorstep that night, bearing wine and a concerned expression. Graham had begged her to take it down. But she'd been uncompromising and kept the dress up until Halloween was over.

But come November 1, the dress was the first thing she'd taken down, almost as ready to have it gone as her neighbors were. She'd wadded it up into a ball and shoved it into the trash can, then stared down at the stained fabric, thinking that, though she'd closed her eyes when she aimed, she'd managed to get most of the blood in the heart area. Her aim, like Tommy's, was spot-on.

Now she saw that the new neighbors were looking at her standing immobile on her sidewalk, lost in memories. That was last year. She was better now. Not the same but better. She would never do something that drastic now. She was more resolved, less mercurial. Tommy couldn't rattle her anymore. He'd used all the tricks in his boring little playbook.

Across the street, her neighbor raised his hand in greeting, less a friendly wave and more an "Everything OK?" gesture. She gave him a thumbs-up just to assure him. Everything was OK.

Leah

Before the game, they held a parade for the Worthy Wildcats football players. Leah, Mary Claire, Keary, and Brynne all stood with the other cheerleaders lining the walkway shaking their pom-poms as the boys, dressed in suits and ties, looking so handsome and sure, sauntered toward the stadium. Some of the boys did little dances, some just waved, looking a little embarrassed at the attention. Some blew kisses to girls, who blew them back.

Earlier in the day, these same boys had shoved one of the JV cheerleaders into a locker and made her promise them sexual favors before they let her out. When she told on them, they said they were only kidding, that they certainly didn't expect what they'd asked of her, and couldn't she take a joke? The teachers and administration made a half-assed effort to get them to apologize to the girl, but she'd already called her mom to come and get her, she was so upset.

Everyone laughed it off, said it was boys being boys and they were just excited about the game and who could blame them. It was an important game, after all. The team was inching closer to the state finals. Leah could've told the girl that it was pointless to tattle on them. Those boys got away with everything.

By the time of the parade, all was forgotten. The students and parents held up homemade signs and #1 fingers and celebrated their hometown heroes. They hollered certain numbers, certain names. They whooped and yelled and raised a ruckus, and it was all allowed because it was for a good cause. The team was the one cause everyone in town agreed on. Religion, politics, business, personal—all were laid aside on nights when the Wildcats played.

Leah scanned the crowd. Some faces she knew from town, but some belonged to strangers from the neighboring towns that fed into the school. Excitement and anticipation reverberated inside her. Her muscles ached from holding up the pom-poms, but she didn't dare lower her hands. She spotted a sign someone had made: **HART OF STONE!!!** it said. Ian Stone and Webb Hart were the receiver and quarterback dynamic duo of the season. When they drove up the points on the board, like they would most certainly do at the game later, the crowd screamed, "Hart. Of. Stone." And on the sidelines, the squad formed a pyramid and threw Keary so high she flew.

Leah felt someone's eyes on her and looked over. Brynne tilted her head to indicate that Webb was approaching and gave her a little smile. Leah forced herself to smile back and shook her pom-poms harder, feeling the pain in her forearms and biceps increase as she did. She could sense Brynne still watching her, gauging whether her response was enough. Brynne was cheer captain, and Leah was, after all, just a lowly sophomore who was lucky to be cheering varsity. She knew the score. She was supposed to cheer loudest for Webb, for their quarterback, the one who was going to take them all the way to state this year. She was supposed to go the extra mile on his account.

Pushing through the burn, she lifted her arms higher, holding her pom-poms aloft as Webb passed by, giving her his sexy, smoldering grin as their eyes met for the briefest of moments. She saw his eyes quickly move to her chest, to the word *Worthy* written there. Then he strode on toward the stadium, toward victory, toward what mattered to everyone in town tonight.

The crowd followed the team as the cheerleaders formed a cluster and watched them go. Leah felt Brynne at her elbow, smelled that obnoxious watermelon gum she'd taken to chewing lately. Brynne blew a huge bubble and popped it in her ear. "You ready?" she asked. Leah turned to answer, but she was already gone, following the team, pulled in their wake like everyone else.

Marglyn

FRIDAY

The first time Hale called, Marglyn didn't answer. She didn't want to hear from home just yet. She and Ginny were having such a nice time, the tension from before all but evaporated. Ginny was smiling and talking in complete sentences, already communicating so much better with Marglyn's help, making the effort to cut out the "redneckisms," as Mary Claire called them, from her language. Marglyn had coached Ginny on removing the word *ain't* from her vocabulary and avoiding the use of double negatives; she was pointing out how to keep that deep drawl from her speech, too. Just because you're from the South, she told Ginny, doesn't mean you have to sound like a bumpkin.

And Ginny, God love her, was really trying hard to do all of it, which made Marglyn feel useful, valuable. She viewed her encounter with poor Ginny walking down the road, shoeless in the pouring rain, that day as a divine appointment, just like their pastor liked to talk about. Someone had helped her back when she was a girl like Ginny, and just look at the good it had done. She was paying it forward, is what she was doing.

At the mall, she'd bought Ginny some new clothes that didn't look like they'd come from the free bin up at the church. She'd even sent away for these swatches to determine Ginny's color classification to help them buy just the right colors. Ginny was, like her, a "soft," with dishwater-blonde hair and eyes that were not blue and not green but something in between. But Marglyn had learned to play up her assets, and she would teach Ginny to do the same. Teaching Ginny what colors to wear was just the beginning. Seeing the girl study those color swatches so intently—as if she would be quizzed later—just thrilled Marglyn to no end. Ginny was a work in progress, to be sure, but tonight had felt more like progress and less like work.

Exhausted from all the shopping (they'd closed down the mall!), they'd stopped for slices of cherry pie at a diner on the way home. It was the kind of night that demanded slices of pie, warm, with vanilla ice cream melting on top. Marglyn had had a cup of coffee with hers and tried to ignore the guilt she felt over not being at Mary Claire's game.

She'd watched MC cheer hundreds of times, and she'd watch her cheer hundreds more, seeing as how Mary Claire intended to cheer at UGA next year. She heard her daughter's voice in her head, shouting those ugly things at her before she left to pick up Ginny from that godforsaken trailer park she called home. She'd defended herself to Mary Claire, who was having none of her excuses about how Ginny's job interview was tomorrow, and she had nothing acceptable to wear.

"And I don't suppose you'd be willing to let her borrow something, would you?" she'd challenged MC, whose wardrobe was extensive—bordering on a kind of hoarding, Marglyn saw now, through poor Ginny's eyes.

Mary Claire had snorted in response. "Like her fat ass could fit in my clothes." Marglyn wanted to argue with her daughter, wanted to tell her how she would've never spoken to her mother that way even though her mother hadn't been half the mother to her that she was to Mary Claire.

She had let Mary Claire's "fat ass" comment ping around her brain for the rest of the evening. She and Ginny, she'd discovered as they were shopping, were the same size, a perfectly acceptable ten. Did her daughter think she was fat? She'd tried to be worthy of her child, to look the part of lovely Mary Claire Miner's mother. Mary Claire, the child who'd swam around in her and Hale's gene pools, selecting the very best of what they had to offer. On Mary Claire, Marglyn's dishwater-blonde hair became a vibrant, sunny yellow. Her hazel eyes became a stunning green. Their daughter had taken Hale's lean, willowy build, his perfectly shaped lips, and oval face.

Marglyn's phone rang for a second time, and she looked down at the screen to see who was bugging her. Hale. He probably wanted to make sure she knew MC's plans for the evening. The game would be over by now, and she and her friends would be cooking up some scheme. Hale would want to make sure Marglyn was OK with whatever he'd been wheedled into saying yes to. Sometimes she felt that she and Hale had five basic conversations going in circles at all times, like the rounds they sang in elementary school music class, voices overlapping and blending, different verses of the same song.

She snapped up the phone and shot Ginny an apologetic look. "Hale, we're on our way home," she said by way of a kinder greeting.

"Is this Marglyn Miner?" an unfamiliar voice asked. In the background, she could hear sirens and commotion. She felt the blood drain from her face as her stomach turned to stone. She instantly regretted the pie.

"Yes?" she squeaked out. Across from her, Ginny, oblivious, drew lines in what was left of her pie with the tines of her fork. Marglyn resisted the urge to reach across the table and still her hand. The girl had nearly no manners and at times seemed far younger than her fifteen years. There was still work to do with her; that was clear.

"Marglyn, it's Perry Congdon with the sheriff's department, and I'm here with Hale."

Her heart rate picked up. "Is he—is he OK?" She thought of all the things at once—heartattackcaraccidenthitandrunaneurysmstrokeseizure.

Guilt flooded her body. If he was alive, she promised herself, she would be a better wife. She would cook his favorite meals, thank him more often, and never refuse sex because she was too tired. She thought of his kind voice, trying to talk to her earlier, the way he'd hugged her goodbye even though he hadn't agreed with her decision to go, and they both knew it.

"There's been an accident," the voice on the line said, confirming her fears. She tried to remember the name the officer had given her, but it was already lost to her.

"Oh no," she gasped as her eyes filled with tears. Ginny stopped playing with her food and looked at her, her brow furrowed.

"We think you should come on home, ma'am. Drive as fast but as safely as possible. Is there someone with you who could drive you? Or I could send a deputy after you if you'll tell me where you are?"

She ignored his question, desperate to know just what she was facing when she did get home. "Just tell me," she said, hearing the hysteria in her voice. "Is my husband OK?"

"Ma'am," the sheriff said, "your husband is fine. It's your daughter I'm calling about."

Darcy

FRIDAY

Darcy paced in front of the picture window with a view of the street, alternately sipping a rapidly warming beer and murmuring to herself about her ex's latest stunt. And here she'd thought he'd exhausted all his tricks. Giving Graham that car was tantamount to giving the boy a loaded weapon.

And the way he had done it—without even letting her in on his plans, the two of them pulling up in that Charger at the game, Graham at the wheel and Tommy riding shotgun, sitting in the catbird's seat with that smug grin on his face. He'd had the nerve to be shocked when she dragged him aside and gave him an earful while Graham's friends descended on the car like flies on shit.

"Is that yours, man?" they all asked, incredulous and envious. She'd looked over at her son, who was beaming, and saw what Tommy had tried to do. He'd aimed to ease the pain of not making the football team, restore some of the cool Graham had lost in being cut. And maybe—just maybe—make it up to him that he'd walked out on them for that slut Angie Woodall. Darcy thought back to their high school days, to their (admittedly rather cruel) taunts of Angie.

"She'll take *all* the *wood* you can give her."

"She *would* do you *all*."

Angie Woodall had always had a thing for Tommy LaRue—who hadn't back then? Oh, how perfect life had been then: Darcy, the cheer captain, dating Tommy, the quarterback, as people like Angie Woodall looked on with envy. Sure, she and Tommy had been a walking cliché, but clichés became clichés because they work. Or at least, they usually worked.

Darcy had to hand it to her, Angie had carried a torch for Tommy as faithfully as the Worthy Wildcats fans stood by their team. In both cases it had paid off. Tommy'd left the game with Angie on his arm, his team winning and his son happier than he'd been in weeks. Tommy'd been proud as a peacock, and that car was his plumage. The image made Darcy see red all over again, or maybe it was just the lights from a police cruiser as it raced by the picture window with sirens blaring.

She half thought maybe Graham had already been busted for speeding. But no, not on his first night with the car. Life didn't work that way. Instead, life worked in such a way that she'd have to be the one who made Graham give the car back. She hoped Tommy'd gotten it from Conrad Hayes. She could force Conrad to take the car back. She and Conrad had been in church nursery together, rocked side by side as babes in arms. If he wouldn't listen, she'd get their mothers involved. First thing tomorrow. She wanted to kill Tommy LaRue. She wanted to wrap her fingers around his neck and squeeze until his eyes bulged out and his face turned purple.

Her hand tightened around the can, and she took a long, angry pull from the beer, draining the last of it. It had gone completely warm and tasted like piss. She swallowed it down and wandered into the kitchen for another. Graham was spending the night with Tommy (of course), and she was left to drink all the beer she wanted, then sleep it off tomorrow for as long as it took. And that was just what she intended to do. After Tommy's stunt tonight, she figured she was entitled.

Faye Starkey had invited her out after the game, and she'd said no as a reflex, without really considering her friend's offer. "Come with us to Chessman's," Faye'd said. "You never come out anymore."

Darcy had forced a smile and words from her lips. "I'm just busy is all," she'd said, even though that couldn't be further from the truth. With Graham in high school and Tommy . . . gone, she had all the time in the world. She just preferred to spend that time alone. It was easier than the pitying looks (much like the one that'd been on Faye's face as she invited her out) or answering the inevitable, prying question posed in the name of genuine concern: "What happened with you and Tommy?"

Angie Woodall happened was the short answer. But of course it was more than that. So much more than she had the energy or strength to go into.

She popped the top on her second beer and took a big gulp, the foam tickling her nose. Outside she heard more sirens and wondered idly what craziness was happening in the aftermath of tonight's victory. This town wasn't prone to what one would call gracious winning. They liked to revel in it. Usually the reveling involved a lot of beer, some whiskey, and more than a few fistfights.

She flipped on the TV and scrolled through the channels, mindlessly clicking past ads for pizzas and medicines and hamburgers and insurance. Based on what she saw, Americans were sick, scared, and hungry. That sounded about right. She found one of those true-crime shows and left it on, trying to catch up on just what had happened to the pretty girl who'd gotten killed. They flashed the same picture on the screen again and again of the dead girl when she was happy. The dead girl before some idiot (Darcy suspected it was her husband—it usually was) stole her life from her.

She thought of that girl's mama, wherever she was right now, and wondered if she was watching and how it felt for these TV people to splash her pain across the screen in high definition. She wondered if it made her a bad person for watching it. But she couldn't look away. Someone else's pain was strangely compelling. Americans were also, come to think of it, a bunch of voyeurs, and she ranked among them.

At the commercial break, she went to get another beer and heard the crunch of tires against asphalt outside. She thought of the murdered girl, how she'd been home alone when she got killed. Not that things like that happened in Worthy, Georgia. Nothing ever happened in their sleepy little town. But just for good measure, she pulled a knife from the block on the counter and wheeled around to find none other than Tommy LaRue at her back door trying—and failing—to use his key to get in. He looked up to see her standing there with that knife in her hand and nearly fell over backward from the shock.

She walked up close to the door so he could hear her with the glass between them. "I had those locks changed a long time ago, Tommy." She crossed her arms but held on to the knife. She was about to say something else—something about the car, maybe, or Angie Woodall. Maybe she'd tell him that Dan Lancaster had asked her out when they bumped into each other at the game tonight. Maybe make him jealous. Remind him that once upon a time she was just as appealing as Angie Woodall. More. Remind him that she used to be fun, the life of the party, even. But then she looked—really looked—at Tommy's face, and her words left her. She reached out and turned the lock so he could come in. He moved toward her, and she remembered the sirens from before, the police cars whizzing past the house.

Tommy took the knife from her hand and laid it on the table, moving in slow motion, the way one might do if cornered by a rabid dog. He gripped the chair in front of him, the very chair he used to sit in when they ate supper—Tommy and Darcy and Graham: the LaRues. On Fridays they had pizza from Tomasina's and on Saturdays they grilled steaks and on Sundays it was always Chinese takeout. But then the Chinese place closed down, and Tommy took up with Angie, and . . .

"Darcy?" She heard her name. "Did you hear me?"

She blinked at the man she'd loved since she was sixteen years old, the father of her son, the person who'd betrayed her, both tonight with the car and long before that. "Wh-what?" she asked. But she knew. Deep down inside she'd known when the first cop car went whizzing by. She'd told herself life didn't work that way, but it did. Lord help her, it did.

"There's been an accident. They've taken Graham to the hospital. I—I've just come from the scene, and . . . you need to know, Darcy, he hit a car with some girls in it. Some cheerleaders. I think they're all . . . Well, they might all be dead."

She glanced over at the knife he'd taken from her hands, then at the brand-new beer she'd opened, already starting to sweat on the counter. She'd heard Tommy say that the girls were probably dead, but that was not something she could address right now. She took that part of the story and put it in a box in her mind, a box with a lid that closed tight. The lid would stay closed until later, when she was ready to open it. She saw herself shove that box way back into the recesses of her mind. If those girls were dead, she couldn't help them right now.

"But Graham's . . ."

Tommy nodded. "He's alive, yes. He's in pretty bad shape. He's got some broken ribs, a collapsed lung, and they don't know what all else." He reached toward her, his hand trembling. "So we better go there now."

An image came to mind: Graham at age five, sitting up in bed after his tonsillectomy, wearing a little hospital gown, eating a Popsicle, still managing a smile for her. "Take me to him," she said.

Tommy nodded again, his dancing eyes from earlier gone flat in his head. "Let's get your coat and some shoes on your feet and we'll go." He began gathering things so they could get out the door. He was still moving with caution, speaking deliberately and slowly, and on some level she knew it was because he was expecting her to scream and yell about the car. But the fight had gone out of her the moment she heard Graham was hurt. Any fight she had in her would be for Graham now, for her boy.

Tommy slid her coat over her shoulders, let her balance using his forearm as she slid her feet into shoes she wasn't sure were even hers, then led her from the house and put her in the truck before getting in on his side. He slammed the door. When he spoke, he didn't look at her, keeping his face toward the windshield. "Before we get there, you need to know they think he was racing, not to mention driving with a provisional license. They think it was all his fault."

She turned toward him, seeing the older version of the boy she once loved, and said, "Well now, Tommy, what did you think was going to happen?" Then she buckled her seat belt and faced the window, not recognizing the reflection that looked back at her from the dark glass.

Ava

FRIDAY

The buzz of her phone against her hip roused her from the light sleep she'd fallen into. She woke, momentarily confused as to what had awakened her, picking up and checking the iPad that rested against her chest (she'd been pinning slow-cooker recipes on Pinterest) before she felt the phone go off again. For a moment she thought: *Clay!* Feeling the little thrill she always felt when he called, when he thought of her. She missed her husband, hated his long hours at the restaurant that took him away from his family, from her. Life in Worthy looked nothing like their life before. Clay didn't seem to mind, but she did, the loneliness gnawing at her until there was a hole inside.

But it wasn't Clay. She looked down at the screen only to see the number she didn't want to think about. Not after what had happened earlier. She could still picture the girl's eyes, wide and round and startlingly blue, the knowing look that had dawned on her face, whether or not what she knew was correct. Ava's cheeks burned at the memory. She swiped her thumb across the phone to read the text.

Him: Don't worry so much. It's fine.

She closed her eyes and held the phone to her chest, hoping the text meant he'd straightened things out. He'd said he would, so maybe he had. Maybe it would all blow over and this could just be a close call, something she'd one day laugh about. Just to herself, of course. She didn't intend for anyone to ever know.

She texted back:

Her: I hope so.

She waited a moment, watching as dots indicated he was responding. An emoji appeared: a winking smiley face. She tossed the phone back on the couch and huffed out her frustration. He didn't understand; he couldn't.

The dog, sleeping on the other end, raised his head at the interruption. He gave her the evil eye and lowered his head, asleep again in two seconds. She picked up the phone and checked to see if perhaps she'd missed a call while she was sleeping. She hadn't. Clay was still at the restaurant, yukking it up with all his old pals, in his element as the hometown folks reveled in tonight's victory. Chessman's always opened after the game, providing a place for the kids—and parents—to celebrate until the wee hours. Inevitably it turned into a rehashing of past football seasons, the old players recollecting their lost glory days, with a fair amount of embellishing for good measure, Ava imagined.

She wouldn't know. Someone had to be home with Clayton and Savannah at night. "Honey," Clay would say with that patronizing tone that had crept into his voice ever since they'd moved here, "it's my job." Then he'd touch the tip of her nose with his index finger like she was a child and add, "I have my job, and you have yours." He'd become so territorial, so possessive about his job since they came here, grabbing onto his new position with two tight fists. When he walked away, she'd looked down to find her hands fisted at her sides.

The phone buzzed again, and she frowned at it, already preparing her firm but gentle retort for her admirer. Yes, he was hot, as the girls she taught at the high school would say. Yes, he was charming. And yes, she was flattered. So flattered she'd let things get out of hand tonight at the game, and they'd been spotted. This town was too small, the gossip traveled too fast, the curiosity about her—the young Atlanta chick who'd snagged Clay Chessman—too intense for her to allow anything like this to happen. She had to be smarter, safer.

She answered the phone, grateful to hear Clay's voice on the other end instead. "Hey babe," she said, her voice still thick with the sleep that had claimed her earlier. She cleared her throat. "You on your way home?"

There was a long pause, and she felt fear grip her by the neck just as sure as a hand wrapped around it. *He knows.* The girl had told just as soon as she could find someone to tell, the news spreading like a grassfire. *Damn this town,* she thought, cursing for the hundredth time Clay's parents' decision to retire and put him in charge of the restaurant, luring him home, taking her and the kids with him.

He'd been out of a job at the time, and things had seemed dire, his manhood dinged pretty badly over the loss and the ensuing financial difficulties. He'd been forced to call his parents for help. Instead they'd offered him the job. But surely she and Clay could've made something else work. Something that didn't involve leaving behind a neighborhood of people they loved who loved them back. A community where she felt valued. A community where she belonged every bit as much as everyone else. The last time she'd gone back to visit, the people who'd bought their house had painted the shutters an electric blue so tacky she could barely speak. When she'd met the new owner—who everyone just loved, of course—Ava'd been downright rude to her, and for that she felt sorry. It wasn't the woman's fault she'd lost her home and been dragged here.

She looked out the window of the trailer his parents had set up on their land for them to live in till they "got on their feet." They had a direct view of "the big house," as she had come to think of it. For the first time since she'd awoken, she noticed that, in spite of the late hour, all the lights were on down there. "Clay, what's going on?" she asked.

She heard voices in the background, a noise that sounded like someone crying. "Is it your parents? Are you at their house? All the lights are on down there. Do you need me to go over?" She could rouse Savannah and Clayton, carry one in each arm the short distance to the big house.

"My parents are probably up because they heard the news. There's been an accident," Clay said. She heard the strain in his voice and felt awful for being relieved that this wasn't about her—that he wasn't calling to say they needed to talk when he got home, that he'd heard something. "I just wanted to let you know I doubt I'll be home before morning. I've kept the restaurant open so the rescue workers can come here, get coffee, something to eat."

He paused, exhaled, long and loud, into the phone. "Oh, honey, it's just awful," he continued. "Three girls at the high school—cheerleaders—were in a terrible car accident. Another student hit them. Rumor has it all the girls died, though I think there's hope one of them might make it. They think the boy who hit them was racing." She could hear the emotion in his voice, imagined the restaurant filling with Worthy citizens just looking for somewhere to gather after hearing the news.

"That's just . . ." She searched for the right words, tried to think of those parents, people who, hours ago, were at the same football game she was. "It's awful," she breathed. "Tragic." There'd been an accident at her high school that took the life of one of the football stars. It had altered the fabric of the community. For years, kids had tried to contact him through séances, acting as if he'd just moved away instead of ceased to exist.

"Yeah," he agreed. But he wasn't thinking the same as she was. Being ten years older than her, high school wasn't as fresh in his mind.

"Well, I'd better get going. I just thought you should know. Sorry if I woke you."

"No, it's OK," she assured him. And then her brain recalled something he'd said, the tragedy overshadowing the detail he'd touched on. "Wait—Clay." She stopped him before he could end the call.

"Yeah?" She detected the slight tone of impatience and imagined someone else needed him, probably that cute waitress who thought everything he said was hilarious, only too happy to stay late if he needed her.

"You said they were cheerleaders? The girls in the accident?"

"Yeah," he said. "Why?"

Her heart began hammering in her chest, and she hated herself for what she was thinking. But she couldn't stop now that her mind had latched onto this wild, fleeting idea. "Do you know who it was?" She willed her voice to sound merely idly curious. "I mean, I was just wondering if, maybe, you know, I had one of them in a class . . . or something. You know, when I've been subbing." She'd been unable to land a teaching job when they moved, but the school had hired her as a permanent substitute, which meant she floated all over the school, staying in some classes for longer than others. Currently it was English, the subject she was actually qualified to teach.

"Yeah, yeah," Clay said. "You probably did. At least one of them, if not all. At some point." He sighed again, and in the background she heard the clatter of silverware, the sound of ice hitting glass. "It was the Miner girl, the Ellison girl, and the Malone girl."

"Keary?" she asked, her heart so fully in her throat now she could scarcely talk around it. "Keary Malone?"

His voice sounded choked, too, but not, she knew, for the same reason that hers was. "Yeah, Keary. That's her name." There was a pause, and she knew someone was gesturing to him that he was needed. But he returned to the conversation, and she felt a thrill that he didn't rush off this time. It was the first blush of hope she'd felt all night.

On the other end, her husband talked about the boy who'd hit the girls, how Clay had known the boy's parents in high school, but they'd traveled in different social groups. How he couldn't believe someone his age had a high schooler when they had such young kids. She only half paid attention to the details of what he was saying. Instead she let the news he'd just delivered sink in: Keary Malone would never be able to tell what she'd seen, misinformation that could've ruined Ava's reputation in this town before she even got the chance to build one.

Leah

SATURDAY

When she couldn't get in touch with her friends, she went back to the football field because there was nowhere else to go. Everyone was long gone, so she walked right out to the fifty-yard line. She halfway thought someone would come along and tell her to leave, but no one did. They were all off celebrating the big win. She lined up her body with the chalk line and lay on top of it, imagining the white powder rubbing off on her clothes, making a line right down the center of her body, dividing her into two halves: before and after.

She lay on her back like that for a while, looking at the predawn sky and wishing she could go home, only she couldn't because she had lied to her parents and told them she was sleeping over at Keary's. But now Keary wasn't answering her phone, and she didn't know what to do. She wondered if Keary had been in on it and was purposely not responding. If that was the case—if they all knew what she'd been doing after the game—she didn't know if she could ever look the three of them in the eye again. In her jacket pocket, her phone buzzed and buzzed, but she refused to look at who was calling. What did it matter now? Shame slithered the length of her.

She felt dew from the grass wetting her clothes but tried to ignore it. *I am hollow now,* she told herself. *I feel nothing.* She concentrated so hard on not feeling anything that she dozed off, sleeping until the faintest bit of light creased the sky and a distant noise roused her. She opened her eyes to see people headed toward her, pairs of jean-clad legs and sneakered feet walking together, en masse. She thought one thing as she saw the group moving toward her: Brynne. Brynne had arranged this. Brynne had set her up. Leah'd been waiting for the final blow, and this was it.

She scrambled to her feet, prepared to run, expecting to be chased. They were the villagers hunting down the town pariah, the angry men from the Bible with stones in their hands. She braced herself for their taunts, their insults, which would feel the same as stones to her. When she'd come to this school, all she'd wanted to do was stay under the radar, to not stand out in any ways but good ones. Three months in and she'd already failed.

She had made it only to her knees when the first of them reached her. She froze, bowed her head so she didn't have to see their sneering faces, the hardness of their eyes. She'd known—of course—that they were capable of cruelty. She'd seen it firsthand in the halls and cafeteria. She'd heard the rumors of what happened in locker rooms and dark corners. She'd just never imagined it would be directed at her. And yet she'd put herself in this position, hadn't she? She'd let Brynne coerce her. Brynne with her megawatt smile and flawless skin, Brynne with her watermelon-gum breath whispering to her of duty and responsibility.

She could blame Brynne all she wanted, but it was her feet that had walked to Brynne's Jetta, her butt that had landed in that passenger seat, her cheerleading skirt riding up till her thighs were exposed, her tan faded to a pasty beige now that summer was over. Brynne was still tan thanks to regular visits to the booth in the back of the Cut and Curl. Leah's mom said that was pure vanity, a waste of money, and a cancer risk besides. Leah's mother also clucked her tongue and fretted about

Leah going to public school. "It's changing you," she said more and more. There, on her knees on that football field at dawn on a Saturday morning as the angry villagers found her, Leah had to admit that her mother was more right than she knew.

So no one was more surprised than she when the villagers—who turned out to be other students, no one she particularly knew, just familiar faces from the halls of Worthy High—also got down on their knees and bowed their heads. Afraid to lift her eyes, she scanned the ground, seeing bare knees and clad ones. She saw votive candles being placed haphazardly, the flames flickering uselessly against the lightening sky. Someone reached over and patted her shoulder. "So sorry," the hand's owner said. Another voice chimed in, "Yeah, sorry for your loss."

Loss? How could they possibly know what she'd lost? She thought for the second time: Brynne. But she consoled herself that at least they were being kind, empathetic. In English class last week, the sub had gone off on a long tangent about the difference between empathy and sympathy. Sympathy, the woman explained, meant you knew exactly what the other person was feeling because you'd felt it before.

"I always remember it like this," the sub had said. "*Sympathy* means *same*. Now empathy, on the other hand, means you have never experienced it, but you can imagine how it would feel." Leah guessed no one on that field had experienced the same thing she had earlier that night. So that meant that this show of support was empathy instead of sympathy. The substitute would be proud if she knew how fully Leah had grasped that concept.

Someone began to sing the first verse of "Amazing Grace," the voice coming out croaky at first but quickly clearing to reveal a sweet, rich sound that rose over them, seeming to hover like a cloud above their bowed heads. Other voices joined in, the combined effect causing a knot to form in Leah's throat. She opened her mouth to sing because she'd been raised to join in whenever a hymn was sung, even if it was being sung on a football field's fifty-yard line at dawn on a Saturday.

But her mouth wouldn't form the words. It was as if she'd forgotten them entirely.

She moved her mouth instead, lip-synching along in case someone was watching. Her father was a deacon at the church, after all. There were expectations. And in this town, someone was always watching. Her heart seized at the thought: So who was watching last night? Another thought piggybacked on that one: And why are they singing "Amazing Grace" now? Maybe they knew no one needed grace more than she did. She opened her eyes and surreptitiously glanced around. More bent knees had joined them. More candles. This couldn't be about her, and yet they'd gathered around her, offered condolences to her.

She thought of Keary not answering her phone all night, or Brynne or Mary Claire for that matter. They were supposed to meet up with her at the party but they'd stood her up. Or so she'd thought. This strange initiation Brynne had put her up to had involved the extra element of being left to wander afterward, abandoned by the first friends she'd made at this school. But what if that hadn't been it at all? What if something had happened?

Marglyn

FRIDAY–SATURDAY

The closer she got to the hospital, the more ill she became. The nausea that began in the tops of her thighs worked its way into her stomach, then crept up into her chest cavity, where it sat like a stone. Her hands shook, so she gripped the wheel tighter in an attempt to steady them. Ginny, to her credit, knew not to speak. She was glad of that, at least.

They spent the thirty-five-minute drive to the hospital in complete silence—none of the silly music she usually kept on the radio at all times, for the kids' sake, no idle chitchat just to keep the lines of communication open. There was nothing she wanted to communicate now, nothing left to say. All the things that used to be worth expressing had been stolen from her. She had gone as silent as her daughter now was.

She thought about what the cop had said before he hung up. That they'd taken Mary Claire to the hospital and were working on her. If they were working on her—Marglyn decided—that meant she wasn't dead. That meant she would have another chance to be a good mother to her daughter. In her head she heard MC's last words to her, resounding over and over. She glanced over at Ginny, silently blaming her for distracting her from the one thing she should've been doing all along.

As they rounded a curve a little too sharply, she could hear the shopping bags jostle against one another in the back seat. She couldn't get Ginny, or those damn clothes, out of her car and away from her fast enough. What had she been doing buying that child clothes for a job interview and missing Mary Claire's game? What business was it of hers whether that child had a job, whether she succeeded—or more likely failed—at life? She had a beautiful daughter who succeeded at everything she touched, but Marglyn had let herself get distracted by this girl who needed her when her daughter no longer seemed to.

The muscles in her lips cramped from being pursed for too long. She welcomed the pain, wanted it to register in a way that wasn't rooted deep inside her. She could deal with pain she could identify. She wanted to hurt in a tangible way, so she kept pursing her lips and tightly gripping the wheel all the way to the hospital parking lot, where she found a spot and, without looking directly at Ginny, said, "You're going to have to find your own way home."

Marglyn didn't wait for Ginny's response. It was not her responsibility to see the girl safely home. She was not Ginny's mother. She got out of the car and slammed the door behind her, leaving Ginny—*poor Ginny,* her conscience said—behind. She ran from the car, bolted into the hospital, falling inside the door. Arms caught her, familiar arms. She looked down at those arms, at the constellation of freckles she'd memorized back when she'd had time to linger within them.

"Hale," she said to her husband, her voice flooded with relief. "Where is she?" Hale righted her, attempted to smooth out her clothes. He gestured at the elevator, and she felt him moving her toward it somehow, as if she were floating. Together they floated into the elevator. Hale pulled her close as the elevator doors slid shut. The car rose, and she felt a disjointed, out-of-body feeling, as if they were still floating. She tried to anchor herself against Hale, to attach herself to his solidness. But when the doors quaked open, she slid from his grasp, going limp as he once again stopped her from falling. "Marglyn, honey?" he asked, but his question faded as he moved her out of the elevator and into the hallway.

She saw them all—the parents and grandparents and friends and, oh God, the clergymen—gathered in that hall. She saw the tear-streaked faces and red-rimmed eyes all blinking back at them, mouths round with horror. Someone in the crowd—in the state she was in, nothing was truly registering—began to wail loudly, a siren cry. Someone else—*one of the other mothers,* her brain told her, managing one healthy firing synapse—ran toward her and Hale saying, "They're gone! They're all gone. Our babies are gone!"

Marglyn and Hale were the last to arrive, so they were the last to know that not one of the girls survived the crash. Marglyn felt that fact sink like a stone inside her, pulling her down, down, down as the last flicker of hope died. This time Hale could not hold her up. No one was strong enough for that. She felt the floating feeling again, but this time it took her out of herself entirely, floating up, up, up toward the hospital ceiling, before she slammed into it and plummeted back down to the ground.

Darcy

Saturday

Darcy could hear the grief sounds coming from farther down the hall where the families of the girls were. She'd heard the term *keening* before but had never witnessed it until that night. She did not know who was making that mournful sound—one of the girls' mothers most likely—but it reached down inside her, touching the raw place where her son hovered between life and death.

The doctors had told them they could not predict when he would wake up, just that he should wake up. He should be OK. But there was something in their faces as they said it that told her they weren't sure at all. There was more that could go wrong, if that could be believed. The alarms could go off, feet could start running, and her son could slip away as she sat not ten feet from the door of his room. In a moment, she could become one of those grieving mothers. She tried not to think about it.

She and Tommy had been relegated to chairs strategically away from the family waiting area where they would "be more comfortable," as the nurse put it, her face a mix of pity and condemnation. They wanted Tommy and Darcy sequestered away from the girls' families because their son had caused the wreck. They were protecting the mourners from having to see them.

She could tell that no matter what story emerged later, it was this first story—the one that painted Graham as the villain—that would persist. She had lived in this town long enough to see the scenario play out again and again. In Worthy, truth lived right next door to perception, but they weren't exactly friendly neighbors. She tried not to think of what this meant for her, for Tommy, for Graham.

Instead she prayed, her prayers a babbling, stream-of-conscious litany that she trusted God would sort out for her. Her prayers waffled between *please let him be OK* to *please don't let him have caused this*. She could not say which request took priority in her mind, and for that she was ashamed. But the truth was, she was tired of being "Poor Darcy" in this town. As in, "Poor Darcy, you know Tommy just up and walked out on her for that slut Angie Woodall."

If Graham had caused the accident, they'd just add to it. She'd also become "Poor Darcy, you know her son's the one who killed those girls." She'd never been "poor" anything before, and she didn't like it. She saw herself on the sidelines at football games all those years ago, clapping and smiling as her beloved Tommy ran the ball and everyone in the stands approved and admired.

The keening erupted again down the hall, the sound making her turn reflexively toward Tommy, sitting still and silent beside her in the folding chair that nurse had gone and gotten for them out of some closet somewhere. The chair was far too small for Tommy; he was folded up in it, uncomfortable looking. But he didn't seem to notice.

She angled her knees toward him until they touched his, not because she was trying to touch him but because his knees stopped hers from going any farther. He'd always teased her about her knobby knees, and she half expected him to now, except of course it wasn't the time or place. And also, Tommy didn't tease her anymore. To tease someone you had to care about her—at least somewhat.

She cleared her throat to speak to him, but when she opened her mouth, nothing came out. He looked at her, sitting there with her mouth open but not saying a word. She closed it quickly, her teeth clacking together as she did, nipping at the edge of her tongue. Her eyes filled with tears as she tasted blood. She blinked the tears away and swallowed the iron taste.

"Did you . . ." Tommy's words seemed to leave him, too. "Did you need something?" He leaned forward, as if he were looking for a reason to spring up out of that chair. She didn't know how his bum knee was tolerating it. He got stiff and sore in church just sitting through the preaching. Of course Tommy didn't go to church anymore. Adulterers generally weren't welcome there. She'd all but stopped going, too—adulterers' rejected wives were plenty welcome, if they felt like being stared at and whispered about. But she got tired of that real quick.

At first she stayed home and watched a service that came on the TV. Gradually, she'd stopped even doing that, choosing to stay in bed long after it was appropriate, her mother scolding her when she got wind of it from Florida where she'd moved in with Darcy's aunt after Darcy's daddy had died. She'd entertained the thought of moving to Florida herself after Graham graduated. Mama and Aunt Lou had said she was welcome; they'd felt so bad about what Tommy did. She'd counted up the days until she could leave Worthy—something she'd never considered until Tommy left.

She thought of this again as she looked at Tommy: Could she leave them all behind and start somewhere new? The idea had a certain appeal. It would serve them all right, Tommy most of all. But to leave Worthy was to either take Graham from his father—which she could not do—or leave her only son behind, which she also could not do. The town had a hold on all of them, and its grip had never been tighter than right now, perched on a hard chair in the hospital hallway, listening to mourning sounds and avoiding piteous looks.

"You can get me a sweet tea," she said. She did not want a sweet tea. She just said it to give Tommy something to do. She knew him well enough to know he was desperate for an excuse to flee, if only for a little while. She started to fish in her pocketbook for some cash to give him, but he held up his hand to stop her.

"I got it," he said. She saw him bend his knee, working to relieve the pressure that had no doubt built up as he sat in that tiny chair. He gave her a little nod and ambled away, raising his phone to his ear as soon as he got out of earshot. He was, she knew, checking in with the other woman. Somewhere Angie Woodall was waiting for Tommy to come to her, to be free of Darcy so that he could. She watched him go, thinking that from behind he still looked the same as he had when they were in high school. She wondered how many times she'd watched his back as he walked away from her.

Ava

Sunday

On Sunday, they "fell back." At least that was the way Ava had always remembered it: "spring forward, fall back." This year the change seemed especially appropriate, the time change blamed for the overall gloom that had settled over the town in the wake of the accident.

Clayton and Savannah were sullen as they nibbled at their cereal before church, out of sorts over the time change, despondent over lost shoes and missing hair bows. She thought of skipping church altogether but knew that Clay wouldn't hear of it. That was another thing that had come with the move: church attendance—which had been sporadic at best in Atlanta—was now mandatory. "People expect it," he'd explained to her. "I'm a business owner, a leader in the community."

Your father is the business owner. You're just a glorified manager, she'd thought but didn't say. In Worthy she found herself liking this new version of her husband less and less. In their bedroom, she glared at him as he tied his tie and whistled a hymn she didn't know he even knew. It was all coming back to him, she could see—the rhythm and attitude that came with being a part of this town. And yet, it was completely foreign to her. She feared it always would be. She wondered if he remembered the things he used to say about the place when they first met, how he'd told her of his compulsion to leave and never come back. She'd believed him, and she guessed that was her mistake.

How can you settle in so . . . thoroughly? she silently, glaringly asked his back. She watched as he grew frustrated with the tie, ripped it out, and started all over.

He turned to look at her, their eyes meeting in the reflection of the mirror. He lifted his brows. "You OK?" he asked.

She nodded and glanced away so he couldn't see the lie in her eyes. Though whether he could even see that anymore, she didn't know. She'd told him enough little lies since moving here she suspected he'd stopped picking up on any of them. "I'm just out of sorts," she said. She was a coward, blaming the time change. She wanted to tell him just how miserable she was, how much she hated this new life of theirs. But telling him would mean she'd have to hear him say he didn't care that she was unhappy. Telling him the truth would mean she would know for sure that he didn't care.

"Well, you can have some time to yourself later today," he said. "I won't be here, and my parents'll take the kids after lunch." Lunch was always at the restaurant—a full Sunday spread that was delicious and perfect, just like Grandma would make. That part Ava didn't mind, even if Clay rarely sat with them the entire meal, always finding reasons to hop up and greet another diner or head into the kitchen to answer a question or address a problem, his father enjoying retirement from his chair, which he never rose from. When you were the senior Chessman, people came to you. Sometimes Ava looked at her own son, wondering if this would be his future, too.

"Why—why won't you be here?" She couldn't keep the defensiveness out of her voice, the challenge out of her words. In Atlanta, Sunday afternoons were "Mommy and Daddy time" behind closed doors, reading, napping, making love, talking quietly about plans for the week while the kids watched a movie. She needed an afternoon like that with Clay.

"I've got to get ready for all the stuff going on this week—there's staffing to see to, food orders to put in. We've got the visitations and funerals all starting tomorrow evening. We're likely to have more traffic in the restaurant because people will be busy with going to all the services and not cooking. And the church has got us making a full spread for the reception after Brynne Ellison's service. Keary Malone's, too."

At the mention of Keary Malone's name, a wave of residual terror shot through her before she remembered that there was no longer a need for it. Keary would never reveal what she saw. And as best Ava could tell, she never had.

"I should probably go to that service," Ava said, trying her voice as the adrenaline left her blood. "I mean, I taught her—I mean, briefly." She busied herself with fishing in the tiny closet for heels to match her dress. There was no casual dress for church in this town.

She thought of the pictures that had appeared on the town's website hours after the accident, the classic *Rest in Peace* scrawled underneath the three faces along with their names. Keary's, Brynne's, and Mary Claire's faces were all familiar, though she had had direct interaction with only Keary. She'd been in the English class Ava was currently subbing for, a class she'd have to walk into tomorrow morning and see Keary's desk sitting empty like a beacon of their collective loss. How different from what she could've faced: Keary sitting at that desk, eyes tracking her as she lectured in the front of the class, judging her, threatening her.

She would have to say something to the kids about that empty desk, and she wondered what it would be. A line from a favorite Emily Dickinson poem popped into her head: *Because I could not stop for Death, he kindly stopped for me.* She wondered if she still had that volume of poems. Maybe she'd look for it in all her free time this afternoon. She slipped on her heels, fastened her necklace. Finally satisfied with his tie, Clay sat on their bed to slip on his own shoes. As he did, she saw a dot of shaving cream just under his earlobe. She didn't tell him about it.

People lingered after the service, their faces serious and sad as they formed pockets to discuss what they knew, all the talk focused on the tragedy. Ava followed Clay, as she always did, standing just to his side as he greeted faces that were familiar even if she didn't know all their names. They hadn't tried to know hers, either.

"Heard Chessman's is providing the food for the Malone girl's funeral," one of the men, a portly, dour-faced man who owned the local Dollar General, said.

Clay nodded as Ava felt that little spark she felt when Keary's name was mentioned. She wondered when that would go away.

"Baptist?" the man asked.

Clay nodded again. They were Methodists. This distinction was important in Worthy.

The man chuckled. "Baptists sure do like to eat," he said. He clapped Clay on the back. "You be sure to make plenty."

Normally he would find this statement to be in poor taste, but Clay forced out an agreeable laugh. He was getting so good at politicking he might have an office in his future.

"You know what the difference is between a Baptist and a Methodist, don'tcha?" The man, whose name she could never remember, turned his attention to her. Everyone in the group began to smile and nod, already knowing the punch line.

She knew it, too—who didn't?—but she didn't say so. Instead she asked, "No, what?" thinking as she did of the time right after they moved here and she went to the liquor store to get some gin for gin and tonics. Clay had gotten a phone call at the restaurant from a good citizen who thought it would be best if he encouraged his wife to shop at the liquor store the next town over instead.

"A Methodist will speak to you in the liquor store." He guffawed, and the others laughed along with him, clearly feeling superior in their status as Methodists. And yet, she was fairly sure it was a fellow Methodist who'd called Clay that day. They could think themselves as better, but denomination didn't make much difference. The town of Worthy was what made the difference.

"Now, you teach at the high school, don't you?" the man's wife piped up. He slipped an arm around her proprietarily, and Ava wished—fleetingly—that Clay would do the same. But even as the man's arm was around his wife, his eyes were roaming Ava's body like she was a flavor of ice cream he'd like to sample.

"Oh, I'm just a substitute," she said. She felt compelled to explain that she wasn't a real teacher.

"She's what they call a permanent sub," Clay piped up. "She floats around to the different classes that need a teacher. Might be for a day, might be for a month. Right now she's subbing for the sophomore English teacher's maternity leave. But that's just till they have a position come open for her."

She turned to look at her husband's profile. The dot of shaving cream was still there, dried now.

Another woman—another familiar face whose name she hadn't learned yet—asked, "Did you teach any of the girls who . . ." She let her voice trail off, unable to bring herself to say the word *died.*

She thought of Keary, of the startled look on her face, the way their eyes had met.

"I knew Keary," she said. "She was in the English class I'm teaching right now."

She saw the women's eyes light up at the thrill of talking to someone who might know something, felt their bodies incline forward at the prospect of inside information. Ava cast about for something to tell them, something that would make her worthy of their excitement. "Actually," she said, "Keary and her friend Leah were both recruited as varsity cheerleaders this year. Even though they're sophomores. They're both quite good. They hung around all the time with the other two girls who were in the car—Brynne and Mary Claire, who were the two

Queen Bees of the school. They were just beautiful; did you see their pictures?"

"I know Mary Claire's mama," one of the women said.

"Keary looked up to Brynne and Mary Claire. She and Leah—to be honest I don't know why she wasn't with them that night, but she should be thanking the good Lord she wasn't—just followed them around like little puppies. You could tell that Brynne and Mary Claire ate it up. It was cute, seeing the four of them together, Keary and Leah like ducklings following Brynne and Mary Claire, trying so hard to be just like them.

"Once—" She looked around at her audience, making sure they were still interested. They were. "I was checking bathrooms after the bell rang, and I found them—all four of them—doing one another's hair like they were getting ready to go out on the town. And I said, 'Girls, it's third period, not prom.'" She laughed a little at the memory. She could see their faces so clearly, a mixture of defiance and fear. She felt a pang just then, one that had nothing to do with relief and everything to do with grief, with the realization of what their families, the school, the whole town had lost in one fell swoop. Those girls were special. You only had to look at them to know it.

"How do you think it's going to be tomorrow?" the wife of the Dollar General man asked.

Tomorrow. Tomorrow she would explain that they'd come too close, that people were already hurting, and they couldn't risk anything else. She would make him understand that she'd been lonely and let that cloud her judgment. They would go back to polite exchanges in passing. Tomorrow she would tell Leah she was glad she wasn't in that car and give her permission to go to the guidance counselor if she didn't want to sit next to Keary's empty desk, if Leah was even at school. Tomorrow she would talk to the class about loss. She would find that Emily Dickinson poem to read aloud to them. She would invite questions. They would throw out the lesson plan the teacher had left behind.

"I think it's going to be hard," she said.

They all shook their heads in unison. The Dollar General man patted her on the back much the same way he had Clay. "You have our prayers," he said. And they all nodded, giving her little pats and squeezes as they went to collect their respective loved ones and head off to lunch. It felt like an anointing, this attention, this acceptance.

Clay turned toward her and smiled his approval. "See?" he said. "They do like you." He looped his arm around her shoulder and kissed her cheek. She gave him a rueful grin. "Come on," he said. "Let's go eat. I'm starving."

He started to walk away, but she stopped him by pulling him back toward her. "You've just got something—" She licked her thumb and swiped at the dot of shaving cream, removing it. "You had something on your neck," she explained.

"Thanks, honey," he said. She kept hold of his hand all the way out to the parking lot.

Leah

Sunday

Talmadge Feathers was waiting for her when she got home from church, sitting on her back deck, playing his violin, the music mournful and haunting, matching her mood perfectly. She watched him play for a moment; his eyes were closed, his wiry body tense. His too-long chestnut hair fell across his brow. When he stopped playing and looked up, he had to shake the hair out of his gray eyes in order to see her. He waved at her in greeting, and she nodded and walked toward him, wondering how long they would be able to talk before her mother shooed him away.

Talmadge was homeschooled like she once was, but for the wrong reasons, her mother said. Talmadge's parents were "nothing more than hippies," who had moved to Worthy to live off the land and off the grid, eschewing school or church or any of the usual trappings of town life. They did not "participate in the community," to quote her mother again. And it had been the bane of her mother's existence that Leah and Talmadge had met and become friends through a homeschooling activity years ago. Homeschooling had been intended to "keep out the riffraff." But Talmadge had snuck in.

Talmadge had once been her best friend, but they'd been growing apart since she started at the high school. Leah knew that he was more than half the reason her mother had been OK with her quitting home-schooling to go to the dreaded public school. Though her mom liked to over-spiritualize the decision any chance she got. Just today at church someone had been talking to her about Keary and Brynne and MC and her mother had come up beside her—appearing out of nowhere—and said, "Well, that's why she's at that high school, you know. To be a light shining in the darkness. It's a mission field, is what it is." Her mother would die ten thousand deaths if she knew the truth about Leah's light, how quickly—and easily—it had been snuffed out.

"I like my music to have words," she said now, and gave Talmadge a smirk, attempting to lighten the mood, to ignore the real reason he was there: to check up on her.

He gave her a sly grin back. "Great music doesn't need words," he retorted.

She sat down beside him on the steps. A few beats of silence passed, but she didn't rush to fill it. They could be—and often were—quiet together. Talmadge took his time; he did not talk a lot; he preferred music. When he did speak, it was usually with very thoughtful words. She looked over at him, studying his patrician profile—the high cheek-bones; the thin, pronounced nose; the long eyelashes.

Once—before her mother really knew him—she'd called him beau-tiful, and Leah supposed that was as good a description for Talmadge as she could think of. He did not look like the other guys in town with their buzz cuts and ball caps and bulging biceps. He listened to classical instead of country; he craved sushi instead of steak; he knew the names of flowers instead of NASCAR drivers. Once she heard her father tell her mother they didn't have to worry about the two of them spending so much time together. "I think he's queer," her dad said.

But that wasn't true. Talmadge was not queer. He was in love with her. The night before she'd started school, he'd come over and told her

so, begged her not to go to school, showed her the tattoo he'd gotten—
her name on the inside of his left forearm so that when he held the
violin, he could see it. "I wrote you a song," he'd said, and he'd played
it for her. It had been a beautiful song, but she'd told him she preferred
her songs to have words, cutting him with her own words just because
she could.

Once, when she and Brynne and Keary and Mary Claire had been
sleeping over at Brynne's house, she'd told them all about it, the words
coming fast and easy in the complete darkness, her new friends listening
intently in the wee hours. She'd reveled in their interest, their questions.
She'd said more than she should've, gone further with making fun of
him than she intended. She'd kept talking despite her stomach aching
with guilt as she did.

And they'd laughed; they'd laughed and laughed over Talmadge's
unabashed adoration, how foolish he'd been marking up his body with
something permanent like that, his arm forever displaying the name
of a girl who didn't love him back. Later, when it was just the two of
them, Keary had confessed she felt bad for laughing. "I mean," Keary'd
said, "I think it would be kind of cool for someone to love me like
that." Leah had nodded, feeling guilty—no, it wasn't that, it was more.
Feeling *despicable* for using Talmadge's display of affection as a way of
fitting in with those girls.

She glanced at his arm, just to make sure her name was still there.
But he was wearing long sleeves. She thought of those three girls, now
all dead, how the way she'd hurt him had perhaps died with them,
absolving her. Some of her worst decisions had died with them. And
yet, she missed them. She didn't know who she would be at school
tomorrow without them.

"You OK?" His voice was surprisingly deep; it always shocked people the first time he spoke to them.

She felt tears prick her eyes in response to the simple question.
She saw their faces flash in her mind, thought of them trapped in that

burning car, as she had countless times since dawn the day before. She saw the hole in the passenger seat behind the driver, where she should've been.

"I guess," she said. She shrugged, and he put his hand on her knee, pulling her closer like he'd done so many times. But now that she knew his true feelings, she wondered if it was the best thing for her to sidle up to him and rest her head on his shoulder like she once would've.

She wanted—she needed—a friend. A good friend who wanted nothing more. It seemed that lately everyone wanted more from her— Talmadge wanted to be more than friends, her mother wanted more perfection, her father wanted more religion, Keary had wanted more time with her and Brynne and MC, Brynne had wanted more devotion to the cause. She squeezed her eyes shut, blocking out the images that played across her mind uninvited.

"I would've called before I came over, but . . . ," he said, trying, she knew, to talk about something different, lighter.

She grinned and finished his sentence, leaning into the familiar territory of their old joke. "You don't have a phone." Talmadge's parents didn't believe in cell phones, so no one in his big, crazy family had one. They both chuckled, feeling the mutual relief of shared laughter.

"You don't have to feel all weird about us . . . now," he said, his voice quivery and uncertain. "I'm just trying to be here for you. However . . ." He didn't finish the sentence.

She thought about meeting him when they were twelve. They'd gone to some Civil War reenactment, a nearby battle site made to look like it supposedly did back then. They'd both stood off to the side, refusing to participate in the mock battle, both seeing the futility—and utter foolishness—of re-creating something that was not exactly the crowning moment of a nation's history. Their cynicism had brought them together. Cynicism she understood. Smart-ass jokes and wry observations on life she could do. But love? With Talmadge? It was ridiculous.

"Thanks," she managed to answer. "I'm just not sure what to do or what to feel about it all . . . ya know? It's not just with you. It's with everyone."

He nodded and rearranged the violin on his lap. She reached over and plucked at a string, which aggravated him. She grinned at him. She didn't want to be serious, to talk about this with him or anyone. But from the look on his face, she knew he wanted to dig into all of it. He wanted to know what she thought, what she felt, what she'd heard. And she knew that, in talking about all of it, there would come a question she couldn't answer. The question he would eventually ask, the one that she'd already successfully dodged with other people by changing the subject. The question: *Why weren't you in that car?*

So she was grateful when her mom got wise to Talmadge's presence and came out on the deck to tell her she was needed inside the house. She made her apologies, working hard at looking disappointed instead of relieved, and scooted into the safety of her house, where everyone was mostly leaving her alone since the accident. Even her mom hadn't grilled her on where she'd been that night and why she hadn't been with the girls—she'd been too grateful that, no matter what the reason, Leah hadn't been in that car.

Leah wasn't sure she was as grateful as her mom. It seemed that one fantastic impact to end it all might've been the better way to go. Brynne and Keary and MC no longer had to worry about popularity or image, parents or teachers, boys or grades, secrets or lies. In death they had become perfect, wholesome, virtuous heroes. The football field was still filled with candles and mementoes, as was the scene of the crash. The town was just about going to shut down this week for their funerals.

From her upstairs bedroom window, she watched as Talmadge crossed the backyard and disappeared into the woods, the stand of pines swallowing him up as he took the shortcut home to his family's farm. She stared at the trees long after he was gone, watching as they swayed in the fall breeze, staying stubbornly green as the other trees around them gave in to the season.

Marglyn

They had to go right past the crash site to get to their house, a fact that was never going to change unless they moved, considering the accident occurred at the end of their driveway. They lived on the outskirts of town, just off the main drag that ran through town but far enough out to be considered "in the country." The land had been in Hale's family for years, and she'd never thought of leaving it until now, until it had also become the site of their personal tragedy.

Marglyn had taken to closing her eyes when they passed the spot going to and from the different places to make "the arrangements." But she'd seen enough to glimpse the memorial folks had constructed where the car had come to its final resting place, the earth scorched, the smell of smoke still lingering in the air. She'd seen the stuffed animals, the posters expressing condolences, the flowers from the floral department at Trout's, the little makeshift crosses adorned with the girls' names scrawled with a Sharpie marker. Someone had arranged three tiaras on the grass with a sign that said, **WORTHY'S PRINCESSES**.

People were trying to be respectful, to be comforting, but it all just felt so garish, like a carnival instead of a funeral. If it wasn't in completely poor taste, she'd walk out there and dispose of all the stuff.

She wondered when it would be appropriate to do so, if someone ever would or if the stuff would stay there forever, rotting as the seasons passed.

Hale drove her everywhere, the two of them moving like automatons, not speaking beyond the basic directions. Robert came and went without her knowledge of where he was or who he was with most of the time. She kept Mary Claire's room door closed, the sight and smell of the place too much for her to take in just yet, though she knew eventually she would have to go in there. They needed a dress for her to be buried in, for instance. And that was in her closet.

She knew just the dress—the one they'd picked out for homecoming, which was coming up in two weeks. Mary Claire had made homecoming court and was a front-runner for queen. One of the last conversations they'd had was about how she would react if she didn't win. Marglyn had thought to add, "But I'm sure you will." She was so glad she'd said that. She tried to focus on those good moments instead of that horrible last one.

Today Hale was driving them to the cemetery out near Lake Worth to meet the other parents to pick out plots. It had been decided (when exactly it had been decided she couldn't say—everything was a blur) that the girls would be buried together. Marglyn wasn't sure she liked this idea, but everyone seemed to think it was the right thing to do. So, not knowing the right thing to do, she went along with it, keeping her thoughts to herself.

She showered and dressed and applied a little makeup and got in the car beside Hale. She clasped her hands in her lap as they drove down their long drive, just like the girls had done that night, and turned left onto Main Street, just like the girls had done that night. But there was no oncoming traffic, and Hale was a more experienced driver than Keary Malone, so they were safe. They were safe and their daughter was dead and now they were going to pick out a plot to put her body in for all time. She could feel her mind staying just shy of this truth, circling it, alighting on it, then flitting away from it.

They drove through town on the main road, following a route they'd taken countless times, and turned onto the road that led out to the lake. Her eyes lifted as they passed under the billboard of Diane Riggle, gazing down upon them like the patron saint of beauty. She thought of the times she'd driven Mary Claire out to the lake, passing under this very billboard, recounting lake safety and sunscreen and all the things parents said and did to keep their children safe. Once she'd pointed up to that billboard as they drove by, wanting to say something encouraging to her daughter, something she would've wanted to hear from her own mother's mouth.

"You're every bit as pretty as she is," she'd said, though in truth Diane Riggle wasn't so pretty on that billboard anymore—her face had washed out so much from the sun's glare that it now looked like two large eyes peering out from beneath a disembodied crown. But she knew that MC knew what she meant. Diane Riggle's beauty was legendary in Worthy. "You could be Miss Georgia," she'd added. "If you wanted to."

They arrived and parked the car in the little gravel lot adjacent to the expanse of grave sites, the monuments flush in the ground instead of on top of it, bouquets dotting the landscape, with the lake sparkling just beyond and benches strategically placed around the property. The cemetery was beautiful, though not the place where she'd anticipated any of their family would be laid to rest. She'd assumed her people would be buried at the church like the rest of their ancestors. But if the girls—who all went to different churches—were to be buried together, this place became the only option. She got out of the car. And now, here they were.

The others were already gathered with the funeral director, who was playing the role of tour guide, selling the property as if it were a luxury vacation spot instead of a final resting place for three girls whose lives had been snuffed out far too soon. She felt the ground shift beneath her and reached for Hale's forearm to steady herself. They made their way over to the group with her gripping Hale's arm as if her life depended on it.

Together the little group made the rounds of the property, saying very little as the funeral director (what a job he had!) pointed out different areas that would accommodate three graves in a row. They discussed the benefits and detractions of having one joined monument spreading across the three graves, one that acknowledged that the girls were "taken together," as Brynne's mother, Cynthia, put it.

Marglyn had never liked Cynthia—she was one of those mothers who seemed to have it together all the time, never a hair out of place, never an extra pound to bemoan. Even today—in the wake of tragedy—she looked just gorgeous. She thought of poor Brynne, having to live up to that. It must've been hard. Marglyn wondered idly if Hale noticed the difference in gorgeous Cynthia and her, who looked like she was the one who died, in spite of her attempt at makeup. She and Keary's mother, Leslie, exchanged small, tight smiles. Leslie was acting more like Marglyn was—silent and scared and overwhelmingly sad.

Marglyn turned her face away from all of them, looking out over the lake. On this picture-perfect fall day, the water sparkled, undisturbed by boats or swimmers. She'd meant to take the kids out to the lake this summer, but first one thing and then another had kept her from doing so. Of course, MC would've probably said she had other plans. And if she miraculously didn't, she would've had her head in her phone the whole time, texting and taking selfies at a pace so rapid it made Marglyn nervous.

She spoke up, startling them all. "You said you had three spots near the lake?"

The funeral director looked over at her and nodded. "But it's going to be more expensive." She and Hale had discussed the costs already. They had the money. They'd been saving for college since their kids were born, and now they'd most likely donate MC's money to another kid—someone who wanted to go to college but couldn't afford it. When Hale mentioned the tax write-off that would bring, she'd had to restrain herself from smacking him. Good ole Hale, always the practical one. But an expensive grave site near the water, with a bench close to it so that she could come and be near her lost daughter? She could talk to MC, and for once MC couldn't walk away. That was a good investment.

"I think we should take those spots," she said. "There's money being raised if the cost is a problem for anyone." She looked around at the other mothers for confirmation. It was funny how quiet the fathers were. She wondered if they were normally talkative men or if grief had struck them mute. She used to think in passing about getting to know the families of the girls Mary Claire spent her days with, but there was never time. Now there was no need. They would have nothing more in common except this sudden, tragic loss. She wondered if they would run into one another at the cemetery like other people ran into one another at the grocery store.

Cynthia and Leslie both nodded. Marglyn fought off the urge to reach out and hug them, to say, "I'm sorry for your loss," as if she'd been untouched by this, as if she could keep herself from it somehow. But of course she could not. She offered Cynthia a small, weak smile. A smile that said, she hoped, *We will get through this.* A smile that said, *I'm with you.* Not because she wanted to be. Because she had no other choice. None of them did.

Darcy

SUNDAY

She was the only one with Graham when he finally woke up on Sunday evening, and it turned out that was for the best. He looked around confused and then, in a flash, pained. She reached instinctively for the call button, to let the nurses know he was awake. But she didn't press it. Instead she said, "I'm here, honey," which was stating the obvious. She rose from her seat and leaned toward him, then rested her hand on his arm, covered up by the thin white hospital blanket. "I'm here, honey," she said again.

He rubbed his lips together and whispered, "Water." She nodded and fumbled around on the bedside table, looking for the pitcher that had been set there hours ago. The nurse had filled it with ice chips and, for a while, Darcy had rubbed his lips with one, watching as the ice melted on his warm skin and dribbled down his chin. Eventually she'd given up and left the ice to melt. Now she poured the dregs of that ice into a Styrofoam cup and handed it to him. He winced as he sat up so he could drink.

"Slow and easy," she cautioned.

He sipped the water and handed her the cup, then leaned back against the pillows, winded by the effort it took to sip the drink. He forced a smile that was, she knew, for her benefit. "At least tell me I won," he said. He tried to also force a little laugh but began to cough, then grimace, as she sat frozen, looking at him as if she were seeing a stranger.

He stopped coughing as he registered the look on her face. "Sorry, it was a dumb joke," he said defensively. "I know you're going to be pissed that I crashed the car." He seemed to notice for the first time that Tommy wasn't there. "I bet Dad's not even speaking to me."

"You were racing," she said. This would be the first and last time she would say those three words together, out loud. The rumors were true. The eyewitnesses weren't just making stuff up to add to the drama. Her son had been racing when he hit that carload of girls. He'd killed them just as surely as if he'd picked up a gun and shot them all. She looked over her shoulder, just to be sure no one had heard him say that. So far the cops couldn't prove who was at fault. Tommy'd already talked to a lawyer who said there were ways around the racing claim. They could beat this rap; she just needed to set her son straight about what happened—and what was at stake.

He kept talking, his voice so weak it was barely audible. "I know, I know. It was stupid. I just—Whit Chambers was talking sh—I mean, he was talking junk, and he was saying stuff about Dad, and I just . . . I wanted to shut him up." He closed his eyes, taking a deep breath. "I guess I . . . lost control or . . ."

His eyes opened. "Wait a minute," he said, something like the truth, or close to it, beginning to dawn on him. "Was there another car? Did I—" He looked around the room. "Did I hit someone?"

She lowered her voice and leaned toward him, so close her nose nearly touched his. "You did hit someone. And you need to *never, ever again* admit you were racing that night. Your future depends on it. Do you understand?"

Sobered, he pushed his head deeper into the pillow as he nodded, his eyes wide with shock or horror or fear or remorse. She wasn't sure.

She didn't actually care at that moment. They were quiet for a few minutes as he seemed to notice the TV mounted on the wall, playing with no sound. *60 Minutes* was on. He stared at it with something that looked like interest before turning back to her.

"Did someone get hurt?" he asked.

She thought of that wail she'd heard coming from down the hall in the wee hours of Saturday morning. The girls' parents had all gone home, of course. Home to make funeral plans. Home to bury their dead children while she sat up in a hospital room and waited for her living one to wake up and begin the long process of healing. She'd been acutely aware that this was profoundly unfair, yet she wasn't electing to change places with any of them, even if she could. She wanted her hurt, guilty child instead of their dead, innocent ones.

Her eyes filled with tears, and she shook her head, willing him to understand that no, no one got hurt. Someone getting hurt would've been the best possible scenario. She didn't want to tell him the truth. She didn't want to level him with what he'd done. And yet, he had to know, and wouldn't it be best coming from her? She sat back but held his gaze, hoping the look in her eyes prepared him for the bad news she was about to deliver.

"Some girls were . . . killed."

He sucked in his breath sharply. She put her hand on his arm. She wanted to add, *But it's not your fault.* Only it was his fault, so she said nothing.

"What girls?" he asked.

"Girls from your school." She exhaled. "Three cheerleaders."

He drew in a ragged breath. "Who?" he asked, his voice quivering. Tears pooled in his eyes.

"Brynne Ellison, Keary Malone, and Mary Claire Miner," she said. The tears ran down his cheeks. She took a tissue from the container on the bedside table and offered it to him. He took it, blotting at his eyes and wincing when the tissue brushed against the bruises. "They were going to a party," she added, just to have something to say. "There's some thought that perhaps they pulled out in front of you onto Main Street. And, while you were undoubtedly going too fast, whether you were racing is another issue entirely. Another offense." She paused, swallowed. "So you cannot ever say you were racing."

"Whit Chambers hasn't said we were?"

She shook her head.

"It was him I was racing against. He knows the truth."

"Well, I doubt Whit Chambers is going to come forward to tell on himself, either. That makes him culpable for what happened to those girls, too. So as long as both of you keep your mouths shut, it's basically a few eyewitnesses saying they thought you were racing. And that's all they've got. In the meantime, Daddy's hired a lawyer who thinks we can make a case for it being the girls' fault."

Graham pulled back as if he'd been hit. "You'd blame it on them? Even though they're . . ." He whispered the next word as if it were too horrible to say aloud. "Dead?"

She reached over and pushed the nurse's button, ending the conversation. "We'll talk more later about the details. Right now I just want to get you better and get you home." She patted his arm and leaned toward him again. "I love you," she said, her voice stronger and surer than she actually felt, coming from a place within her she had never known was there.

◆ ◆ ◆

Tommy reappeared minutes after Graham fell back asleep, almost as if he'd timed it that way. Darcy could look at her ex-husband and see how uncomfortable he was. Duty bound, he hung around for the vigil, but sometimes she wondered if that mattered. Was his presence worthwhile if it was clear he didn't actually want to be there?

In some ways, it brought back the weeks before he finally dropped the other shoe and announced he was moving out, into an apartment, the only place he could find on short notice. She'd seen the place; it was an eyesore, far beneath the man Tommy should be. And yet, he'd stooped to it, and his temporary digs had become his de facto home. She wondered if he wanted to be there or if he'd just backed his fool self right into a corner that his pride wouldn't let him out of. Oh well, it was none of her concern anymore. Tommy wasn't her problem. Graham was.

"He woke up for a bit while you were gone," she said now, reporting just the facts, which was how they'd come to speak to each other.

A flicker of something—hope, she guessed it was—passed across his face. "Well, that's good, right?" he asked. She could feel his eyes on her, wanting her to reassure him, to make it all better, even now. In her mind's eye, she saw him with a young Graham, saying, "Let's ask Mommy. She'll know."

"Darce?" he asked, concerned by her silence. "He was OK, right? When he woke up?"

She thought of what Graham had admitted to. Should she share that with Tommy? A year ago she would've. But a year ago Graham was fifteen and just learning to drive a car.

"I . . . broke the news to him." She glanced over at Tommy. "About the girls."

Tommy shook his head, appropriately beleaguered. "How'd he take it?"

She looked at him, this time full in the face, her chin jutting at a defiant angle. "How do you think he took it? He cried. He's confused and heartbroken. Not to mention in a lot of pain. The nurse gave him some medicine, so he fell back to sleep." In the bed, Graham stirred, and she ducked her head, ashamed of herself for disturbing him with anger directed at his father. Shouldn't some of the anger be directed at

Graham himself? Something inside her answered immediately, reflexively. *Not yet, not yet.*

As if reading her mind, Tommy whispered, "It's my fault. I know that. I set all this in motion. Whether he was racing or not is beside the point." He paused, and she could hear him inhale and exhale, almost as if he was having trouble breathing. She cursed herself for caring.

"We need to be together on this," he said, the words *we* and *together* hitting their mark. His eyes searched hers, imploring her to agree with him, to lay down the weapons she usually brandished whenever he was near. Unable to do much else, she gave him a curt nod.

"No matter what, we support him. No matter what's happened between us in the past or what anyone else says in the days to come, he's our son, and we will do whatever it takes to save him. He can't have his life ruined over this." He paused, hoping, she knew, for more from her.

But she could not give him more. "OK," she said to the ground beneath her feet. "That's what we'll do."

Ava

SUNDAY

On Sunday night Ava left the kids with her in-laws and ventured over to Chessman's. She'd not done this in months—knowing after trying a few times when they first arrived that she'd just be the odd man out. But the scene at church that morning had infused her with hope. She was connected to this tragedy by her job at the high school, her knowledge of these girls. She could sit around with the locals and discuss the latest news. She could make Clay proud of her. She could belong.

But at Chessman's, Clay was busy and didn't seem thrilled to see her. "Where are the kids?" he asked, his face puzzled instead of happy.

"They're with your parents," she said, thinking the answer should be obvious. The next thing he said hurt worse than the puzzled look.

"But it's a school night."

She didn't hide the hurt look on her face. "The kids are two and four. They don't have school," she said.

"But you do," he said. He brushed past her cheek with something that was supposed to be a kiss, she supposed, but his lips didn't even make contact with her skin. He shooed her out of the way of the hostess stand, bustling past with excuses of being low on staff and overwhelmed with business. It seemed everyone wanted to be out, gathering to talk about the tragedy. She stood awkwardly off to the side, observing the tables of people but uncertain how—or who—to approach. She barely knew any of them.

Except. She looked across the room and spotted a familiar face. A familiar face that she should not respond to, with him sitting there next to Fig Newton, the football coach and town legend. And yet, that face broke into a wide, pleased grin at the sight of her. That face moved toward her rather than away from her. She told herself she didn't care that that face belonged to him. Any port in a storm. She forced her own face to look relaxed and casual as he walked over to speak to her.

She was aware that they were in a public place, but they'd been seen other times, talking in the very public high school halls and classrooms. And it didn't matter anyway. Nothing had happened. Keary's shocked face flitted through her mind like an uninvited guest. She forced it away, rationalizing the situation at hand. He was a male who was a friend. She'd had plenty of those back in Atlanta, and it had never mattered. Why did it have to be different here? She waved the thought away: because things were different here. This was different. And she knew it.

"Hey," he said.

"Hey," she said, feeling shy and not unlike a high school girl herself talking to him. He was handsome and charming, sure of himself in a way she envied. Perhaps it was the students rubbing off on her, making her develop crushes and keep secrets. Perhaps it was that she was increasingly aware of her youth beginning to slip away as she got closer to thirty. Perhaps it was just that her husband hadn't been happy to see her. Whatever it was, she knew this: she was glad to see him.

They both nervously scanned the restaurant to avoid each other's eyes. "Sure is crowded tonight," she observed.

"Yeah," he agreed. "People gabbing about what happened."

"It'll be hard, going back tomorrow," she said.

He sighed. "Yeah. Lotta girls'll be crying—that's for sure."

She nodded. She'd thought of what she'd say to the classes, especially the one Keary had been in. She'd heard there would be a special assembly. With any luck, it would fall during that period.

"Well, I was just getting ready to take off," he said, shuffling his feet and looking uncomfortable.

"Yeah, yeah, of course," she said. "I'm probably going to be leaving, too. I just came up here for some . . . business stuff. You know . . ." She gestured toward the hostess stand and tried to make her voice sound nonchalant. She waved at a woman she only sort of knew, just to look like she belonged. The woman waved back with a fake grin, then rejoined her conversation. Ava wondered if they would talk about her. If she even mattered enough to be talked about. When they looked at her with disdain, eyeing her warily, she knew what they were thinking: she was so much younger than Clay. Was she after the Chessman restaurant dynasty? If not that, what?

"I guess we could walk out together," he said.

"Yeah," she agreed, "we could." She couldn't repress the smile on her face. Seeing him had taken the sting out of Clay's brush-off. Walking out with him would be far better than walking out alone.

"Let me just get my coat," he said. He sauntered back over to the table full of people he'd been with to collect his coat and say his goodbyes. She saw him throw some money on the table. She moved strategically toward the door so as not to be too overt about leaving together. They would venture out to the parking lot and get into separate cars. There was nothing wrong with that. People did it every day. Except she was married, and she was attracted to him, wrong as that was.

She could hear her mother's voice in her head, saying the familiar phrase she used to use whenever Ava skirted too close to the edge of things. When she got caught skipping school, when she dated a boy who drove a motorcycle, when she failed a class, it was always the same refrain: "Better watch it, girl—you're playing with fire." But her mother's words fell on deaf ears, then and now. In the hazy bubble of suburbia and domesticity, Ava had forgotten how much she liked play-ing with fire, how instead of burning it merely warmed her skin.

At the door of the restaurant, she waved goodbye to Clay, who distractedly waved back from across the room. He held his thumb and pinkie up to his ear and mouth, the classic sign for "I'll call you." She turned away without acknowledging it, wondered if she would even answer when he did call. Let Clay feel a brush-off for a change.

She waited for him on the sidewalk by the door, trying to seem like she was looking for something in her purse in case someone saw. He sidled up to her and nudged her with his arm. "Thanks for waiting on me. I had to finish up a conversation."

"It's fine." She shrugged. "I've got nowhere else to be."

He grinned. "Well you should." They fell into step together, ventur-ing closer to their cars.

"It's . . . hard. Here." She looked up at him, noticing the way his eyes crinkled at the corners, the thoughtful way he studied her when she spoke. "It's not the easiest place if you're not from here."

He nodded soberly. "I can see that." He looked toward the restau-rant as if he were considering it from an outsider's perspective, then turned back to her. "But don't give up just yet. Give people a chance to like you." He stared at her until she met his gaze. "Like I do."

She could feel him leaning toward her as if he were going to kiss her. She took a step away to make that impossible. It was her turn to look back toward the restaurant, the sign blinking above it in red neon that bore her husband's—and her—last name.

Leah

On Monday she went back to school even though her mother told her she could miss if she was "too traumatized." The tragedy—and the unasked questions surrounding it—had thrown her mother into panic mode, confirming all her deepest fears about the dangers that lay "out there." Leah could feel her mother wanting to pull her in close. But if she stayed home, her mom just might finally ask those questions about the night of the accident.

She could almost see them inside her mother's mouth whenever she spoke, lurking just behind her teeth, waiting to be pushed out into the world with her quick-moving tongue. So far the "too traumatized" card had kept her mother at bay—but Leah knew that would last only so long. She had days, maybe weeks, if her mother was feeling especially generous, to dodge the inevitable truth.

She would be better off going back to school and getting grilled by the other kids about why she wasn't in that car. Her choice—even in light of all that had happened—was made. She would run the gauntlet at school and not think about anything else. As she dressed, she told herself: if she could get through the first day back, she would be OK.

She gave herself a pep talk: by the end of the week, the sharp memories would fade, the funerals would be over, and people would forget that she wasn't where she was supposed to be that night. Things would go back to normal—except for the fact that now she had to find three new best friends.

In first period English class, Keary, of course, wasn't there. Mrs. Chessman stood uncertainly at the front of the room, greeting everyone even as her eyes kept darting to the empty desk. Leah took her seat next to that desk and gave the sub a weak smile when their eyes met. The bell rang and class began. Instead of the normal chatter, no one said a word. The whole school seemed to have gone quiet except for the occasional sound of someone crying.

Leah was not going to cry in front of anyone. She'd made that promise to herself. Sometimes she pretended she had died that night, too, that she was as cold and still as Keary, Brynne, and MC were. It was not that hard to imagine.

"We suffered a terrible loss over the weekend," Mrs. Chessman said, stating the obvious. "And I want to make sure that anyone who needs to talk to someone"—her eyes darted over to Leah and quickly away again—"feels free to go to the guidance counselor's office anytime you need to." She glanced down at a piece of paper she was holding. Leah imagined it was a memo titled, "Helping Students Address Recent Tragedy." Mrs. Chessman kept talking.

"There are extra counselors and members of the clergy on hand all day to speak with anyone who might like prayer or just a listening ear." She tucked a piece of hair behind her ear. Mrs. Chessman was sort of pretty. Or she tried to be. She'd heard some of the boys talk about her, about what they wanted to do with her. There was a rumor that she and the assistant coach—Mr. Duffy—were having an affair, but Leah didn't believe it. She'd seen Mrs. Chessman at the games with her husband and their little kids. They seemed happy. Or as happy as most people are.

"There will be funerals held throughout the week, and anyone who chooses to attend will be excused from school to do so." Mrs. Chessman had resorted to reading straight from the paper. "There will also be no homework, since there will be many visitations held at night. Students are encouraged to attend as many of these events as they feel up to attending. The school wants to show its support to the families."

Sarah Chisholm, a fellow cheerleader, raised her hand. "I heard they were canceling the football game on Friday night. Is that true?" There was an edge to Sarah's voice, a challenge in it. It was one thing to let people out of school for funerals and such. It was another thing to call off an entire football game at the height of the season. Leah couldn't imagine cheering without Keary and Brynne and MC. Keary had been the flyer because she was the smallest. Who would fly now?

Mrs. Chessman nervously scanned the paper for the answer to Sarah's question. "Um, I don't see anything here about that. But perhaps that will be covered at a later time."

She put the paper down and plucked a book from the teacher's desk. "Now, seeing as how we go to the special assembly in a few minutes, I am not going to try to give a lesson." There was an exhale of relief from the class. "But I did want to read you this poem from Emily Dickinson, a famous American poet who is one of my favorites. Emily Dickinson was quite fascinated with death, and she talked about it a lot in her poetry. So I thought I would read one of those poems and then just have you guys write a short response in your journals. By then it will be time to go to the gym. OK?"

Mrs. Chessman asked "OK?" a lot—like she wasn't sure she was doing this right. Leah thought she did about as well as any other teacher here, even if she seemed more nervous, and far less angry, than they were. Leah couldn't help but like her. She was rooting for her probably because they were both new this year and, in their own way, both outsiders.

Mrs. Chessman began to read from a small volume that looked like one she owned—not one she'd gotten from the school library. This one was leather bound and had a ribbon marker, which danced under the book as she read. Leah watched it dance, thinking of nothing else but the words she was hearing. Not Gus Nyhan drawing a fake tattoo on his arm across from her. Not Andrea Hunt doodling her boyfriend's name inside a heart on her notebook on the other side of her. Not Keary's glaringly empty desk. Leah listened and had to keep her head from nodding along in agreement.

Emily Dickinson understood the inevitability of death. She wasn't afraid to look it in the eye. Like Emily, Leah knew that death was coming for her; it was coming for everyone. It had come for her friends and perhaps expected to find her in that burning car as well. She'd eluded (SAT word) it, but should she have? Was that night a cosmic mistake? And if it was, what did that mean for the rest of her life? Why did she get to have a rest of her life when her friends were having funerals?

When it came time to write the response, though, Leah wrote none of this. She wrote something stupid and inane, something that sounded like any other kid in this school instead of the person she was. She imagined she was Keary writing it instead. She had fun pretending to be Keary, imagining what Keary would've written about the death poem. She was enjoying herself—even smiling a bit, which she supposed looked strange considering what she was writing about—when Mrs. Chessman announced it was time to go to the assembly.

Everyone threw their pens and pencils down and leaped up, eager to go do something besides sit in class. But Leah didn't want to go to the assembly. She didn't want to hear the teachers memorialize her friends, didn't want to sit among her fellow students as everyone cried big, dramatic, attention-getting tears. Leah had cried once so far, in private late at night when she was sure everyone in her house was asleep. She liked being in charge of her tears, her emotions, her reactions. She liked being in charge of something in a world that had veered so very far off course.

Sarah Chisholm, who was a shoo-in for homecoming queen with Brynne and Mary Claire out of the way, saw her enter the gym and called out to her. "Leah! Sit here!" She pounded on an empty space beside her on the bleachers and gave Leah an imploring look. Sarah expected to be obeyed, especially now that she was, by default, the most popular girl in school. This tragedy had turned out well for her.

Panicked, Leah worked at keeping her face composed. Sarah would ask the questions, and she would ask them loudly, right within earshot of the football players sitting around her. (At Worthy High, the football players and the cheerleaders stuck together. Leah didn't know if this was true everywhere, but it was definitely true there.) Sarah began to wave demonstratively, her wispy blonde curls bouncing as she did. Leah thought Sarah looked like a fairy. She and Keary had given her the nickname "Tink" behind her back. Thinking of Keary in that way—just the normal, daily way—was what hurt most.

Sarah whined her name again. "Le-uhhh, come over here!"

She cast about for someone—anyone—familiar to her and saw a cluster of girls from her biology class sitting just behind Sarah. Leah made her face look sad and shook her head as she pointed to the girls, insinuating that she'd already promised to sit with them. "I'll see you after," she called back. Even though she had no intention of doing so.

She took a seat near the girls, who politely nodded and smiled at her before moving closer together and beginning to whisper to one another. If Talmadge were there she'd say to him, "Two guesses who they're talking about. And the first one doesn't count." But Talmadge wasn't there. And she'd run him off the other day when he tried to be there. But she couldn't worry about Talmadge. He was the least of her problems now.

The principal, Harold Query (a last name that drew all the expected jokes from students), approached the podium to start the assembly. They began with a slide show about the girls; someone had somehow found every photo ever taken of them at school, or so it seemed. With

Brynne and MC being seniors, there were lots more of them than of Keary. *As in life, so it is in death,* she thought.

Leah looked down at her hands in her lap, imagined them crossed over her stomach like they would be if she were in a casket. She wondered if the funeral home people would fix her chipped nails or leave them in the mess they were. They'd been painted green—the school color—for the game, but the polish had been chipped or chewed off in the ensuing days, with only little flecks of paint left clinging to each nail.

"Hey, there's you!" the girl next to her said, elbowing her. She looked up and saw her own face smiling back at her, right next to Keary, Brynne, and MC. She remembered the photo being taken at the first game. She remembered how surreal it had all felt that night, how blessed she'd felt to be there, with them, as part of them. She'd gone out for cheerleading on a whim, never dreaming she'd make it. Never dreaming she'd get moved up to varsity as a sophomore. She'd felt like the luckiest, happiest girl in the world. Looking at that picture, she could see that girl, frozen for all time in that moment, never dreaming she wouldn't—couldn't—stay just that way forever. That had been mere weeks ago, but it felt like a lifetime.

She felt tears prick her eyes and considered walking out. But that would only call attention to her. The last thing she wanted was all these pairs of eyes watching her leave. Especially certain eyes. She glanced down at the cluster of football players sitting near Sarah and the other cheerleaders. They were barely paying attention to the slide show. Instead, two of them were hunched over a cell phone, murmuring to each other and suppressing laughter. She turned away, disgusted. She'd heard they would be pallbearers at all three funerals this week. She focused on her hands again.

When the slide show ended, Mr. Query droned on about the loss the school had suffered and the collective pain they certainly all felt. He said more of what Mrs. Chessman had said about having counselors on-site and clergy (Leah's own pastor among them) available to pray. She tried to imagine going to the reverend Leland Bigham for prayer over her situation. She thought of the look on his face if she were honest with him about what she'd done that night and bit back a grin at the image that came to mind. Leland Bigham would turn red and sputter. He might even fall over dead of a heart attack right then and there. He was a big man, after all, and not in the best of health. Leah had seen him at Chessman's one time, stuffing his face full of fried chicken, grease shining on his chin.

After Mr. Query was done, Jill Dean, the cheerleading coach, made her way to the podium to talk about what an inspiration the girls were. A former head cheerleader turned hairstylist, "Miss Jill," as they called her, had volunteered to be the coach, which was actually good marketing for a stylist if you thought about it. She did just about all the cheerleaders' hair, and their mothers', too. Leah idly wondered whose appointments Jill'd had to cancel to make it to this assembly.

In her peripheral view, she saw a flurry of commotion where the football players sat. A teacher had walked over to where two of them were looking at something on a phone instead of paying attention. When the teacher tried to take the phone, they had put up a fight. Leah—and everyone else near them—watched with interest as the teacher prevailed and got the phone. Based on her expression when she saw what was on the phone, whatever it was was quite concerning. She stalked off with the phone in her hand, gesturing to some other teachers with her free one.

Moments later, the boys were ushered out, and the assembly was brought to a hasty close, leaving the students to stream out of the auditorium and back to class. But Leah stayed in her seat even after everyone left, until the only people still in the gym were her and the janitors. She watched as they dismantled the platform they'd used for the presentation, taking it apart piece by piece. She watched until all of it was gone.

Marglyn

TUESDAY

Mary Claire's funeral was first. Not because Marglyn wanted it that way, but because that was the way it worked out with the church and the funeral home coordinating everything. On Monday night they held the visitation, and on Tuesday they held the funeral. The church was packed, with people standing after the seats filled. They even stood outside on the church steps with the doors open trying to listen. Marglyn supposed it was good it wasn't raining.

She did not delude herself into thinking these people were here for her daughter. She knew that they were there out of curiosity, wanting to get as close to the tragedy as they could. She watched it all—the pomp and circumstance—as if from a distance, as if it were happening to someone else entirely. The funeral scene (for that is what it seemed to be—a scene like in a play) floated in front of her in a haze of color and motion, disembodied voices and faces looming in her field of vision, then disappearing. She'd taken a prescribed Valium just before the service and enjoyed the benefits, the emotional removal it allowed her. She would like to stay that way forever.

She'd known she would need the Valium after the dream she'd had early that morning. In the dream, she'd come into the church for the funeral, wearing one of Mary Claire's dresses. But she'd found the church completely empty. She'd glanced around, thinking maybe she'd come at the wrong time. Her eyes had fallen on Mary Claire sitting right up front, wearing one of Marglyn's dresses. Mary Claire had turned and patted the spot beside her, saying, "Mama, I saved you a seat."

Marglyn had run toward her daughter, so relieved to see her, whole and happy. It was her there: her voice, her smile, her bright, dancing eyes. She'd hugged her close, feeling her realness, glad that this was finally over, grateful for another chance to say something different from those final words that could never be taken back. She took the seat beside her daughter. Mary Claire turned to her, put her hands on Marglyn's knees. There was warmth coming from her eyes. "You're not going to believe it, Mama," she said. "It's so beautiful." And then Mary Claire disappeared, leaving Marglyn alone in the church.

"Wait!" she'd called, her voice absorbed by the tapestries of Jesus's miracles hanging around the sanctuary. She'd woken up with a start, her eyes trying to focus in the dark room as Hale breathed deeply beside her, his mouth open in sleep.

She'd spent the rest of the night trying to remember every detail in the dream, wanting to believe she really had just seen her daughter and that wherever she was, she was happy and whole and that heaven was beautiful, just as she'd said. And yet, Marglyn's arms ached from missing her. Her mind whirled with things she'd not had a chance to say before Mary Claire was gone from her again. When dawn flickered behind the closed curtains in her bedroom, she'd gotten up and gone in search of the vial of Valium their family doctor had pushed into her hand at the visitation.

Marglyn spied Ginny as they filed out ahead of everyone, Hale's hand cupping her elbow to guide her out, Robert at their heels, nearly clinging to Hale's coattails. They made a compact unit, the three of them, moving as one toward the limo that would carry them to the lakeside cemetery, their daughter's final resting place.

She glanced over to where Ginny was sitting, wondering how she'd gotten there and hoping that whatever ride she'd finagled would not be able to also take her to the graveside service. She did not want to see her there. She did not want to see her at all. Not now, and maybe not ever. The sight of Ginny's face brought back the night her daughter died in vivid recall—the angry words they'd exchanged, the evening spent with Ginny instead of Mary Claire, the horrible silent drive from Macon to the hospital with Ginny in the passenger seat.

She glanced over just before they exited the church, catching Ginny's eye. In that brief moment, a look of longing passed from Ginny to Marglyn, a look that asked one to forgive the other. But Marglyn quickly turned away, allowing herself to be moved down the church steps and across the sidewalk, to be ensconced in the safety of the limo with its doors that shut out the world, its windows that protected them from onlookers.

Thankfully Ginny was not at the grave site. Not many people made the trek out to the lake, which was a relief. When it was over—after one of the girls from Mary Claire's Sunday school class sang a song a cappella with a clear, beautiful voice and the preacher said a few final words and she and Hale and Robert laid white roses on the casket—everyone moved silently to their cars, the women's heels sinking into the ground as they walked. But Marglyn stayed.

Hale came over to her, to try to lead her away again. "I'm staying," she said, moving out of his reach. She didn't know why she was doing this. She did not want to see them lower the casket, to watch the men come and fill the hole. And yet she couldn't just leave her daughter. She thought of when Mary Claire was three and went through a clingy stage, always wanting to be right where Marglyn was. Sunday morning drop-offs at the church nursery were a nightmare. She saw that Mary Claire in her mind now—the little girl reaching for her with tiny hands, saying, "Don't leave me, Mommy!" The vision kept her rooted to the spot, standing sentry over the casket.

"Marglyn," Hale said, imploring. He stood as close to her as she would allow. "You're causing a scene here. The limo's waiting to take us home." He pointed to the parking area, as if she didn't know where the limo was. Hale hated a scene. Hale hated attention of any kind. On that they'd always agreed, marveling over how they'd managed to produce a daughter who soaked it right up.

She saw Mary Claire spinning around in her homecoming dress just a few weeks prior, singing a made-up song about how she was going to be the next homecoming queen, her chin jutting defiantly, as if she dared anyone to take that crown from its intended position on her head.

"Don't go getting too cocky," she'd said to her daughter. When what she should've said was, *No one deserves it more than you. I believe in you, my darling, darling girl.* Later she'd tried to ease the sharpness of her words in another conversation about homecoming—which she was glad for now—but even so, she hated that those words had ever come out of her mouth, despised her constant need to improve upon this child who was, in hindsight, already just fine.

Marglyn began to cry, her shoulders heaving, the emotion she'd been keeping at bay through sheer will and drugs breaking through to the inevitable surface. "I can't leave her," she gasped. Hale took a tentative step forward, uncertain what to say or do. She felt his hand come to rest lightly on her shoulder.

"I know," he said. She heard the warble in his voice, his own grief and uncertainty also very much on the surface. His grip on her tightened as he attempted to pull her to him. She allowed it, allowed him to encircle her in his arms, if for no other reason than that his chest gave her a good place to bury her face, away from those who'd stopped getting into their cars to gawk at her public breakdown.

Hale let her cry, heaving and sobbing until the tears eventually subsided, his white shirt streaked with mascara she'd naively applied that morning, hearing MC's voice as she did, instructing her on what kind of mascara to wear and how to apply it correctly, critiquing her even from beyond the grave. The grave. She looked up, her eyes taking in this place she knew she would return to often, if for no other reason than that it allowed her to hold on in some small way.

She looked toward the parking lot and was relieved to see that the onlookers had grown bored with watching her cry and left. She spied Robert sitting on the little bench nearby, kicking at the dirt, his eyes downcast. At the edge of the cemetery she saw the men with the back-hoe, waiting to do their jobs. She wondered if this happened often, if this type of delay was part of the routine.

She nodded to Hale that she was ready to go. But as they walked toward the waiting limo, she looked over her shoulder one more time, at the casket suspended over the hole, at the place she would leave her daughter one final time. But Marglyn wouldn't leave Mary Claire behind, and that was what both comforted and terrified her. Mary Claire was gone, but she was not.

As she stepped into the limo, she saw someone else there, lurking in a copse of trees between the grave site and the men waiting to fill it. Ginny. How she'd gotten all the way out there, Marglyn didn't know. They blinked at each other for the second time that day. And for the second time, Marglyn ignored her, communicating as best she could that their friendship, such as it was, was over. She hoped the girl would just quietly go away, but she feared that Ginny, too, would follow her home.

Darcy

Darcy went to Brynne Ellison's funeral because she'd grown up with Cynthia, Brynne's mother, and it seemed the right thing to do. She quickly discovered that right and wrong had switched places while Graham was unconscious. She'd exited his hospital room only to discover that the town of Worthy had turned upside down while she wasn't looking.

Suddenly the people who once loved her—or at least felt sorry for her—despised her, glaring at her for breathing the same air as them, saying things about her under their breath, just loud enough for her to sort of hear them but not be certain about what they were saying. One word she was always able to make out was *son*. People hated her for what her son had done, even though nothing had been proven yet. If it were up to her, nothing ever would be proven.

Cynthia's mother—Brynne's grandmother—at least owned up to her feelings directly. She walked right up to Darcy in the church vestibule just before the service was starting and pointed a crooked finger at her, her hand visibly shaking, though with old age or anger Darcy couldn't tell. "You have some nerve showing up here," she said, her voice a decibel above everyone else's. The other mourners stopped what they were doing to turn and watch. A woman who had been crying dramatically suddenly stopped for the show.

"If it weren't for your son," the old woman continued, "my granddaughter would be here today."

Darcy could feel her heart hammering so loudly she was sure others could hear it, too. She felt heat rise in her face—a combination of embarrassment, anger, and shame. This was a woman who had had them all over for a makeup demonstration when they were in the tenth grade. She'd taught them how to put on makeup tastefully, properly. She'd told them they were all lovely. She'd complimented Darcy on her cheekbones, showed her how to accentuate them with blush. Now she was the one causing the color to fill Darcy's cheeks, no blush necessary.

"We don't know that," Darcy said, summoning the fortitude she'd found inside her in the wake of Tommy's desertion. Her fists involuntarily clenched at her sides, the nails digging into her palms. "We don't know that Graham caused the accident. The girls—" She heard someone draw in a breath, sharp and shocked, and stopped speaking. She'd gone too far, blaming the dead girls at one of their own funerals.

She started to say something else, sputtered, and walked away instead. She saw Cynthia standing off to the side, waiting to be summoned into the church like she'd probably dreamed of doing as the mother of the bride someday. Now she was just the mother of the dead cheerleader. *I'm sorry,* Darcy mouthed to her, and scooted down the side hall that ran to the bathrooms and the rear exit by the church kitchen. She knew this church—and most all the churches in Worthy—by heart. It was part of growing up here. So much of the town's life revolved around churches. You were bound to be in all of them more than once.

She burst out of the building and stopped on the landing, gripping the railing as she caught her breath, and looked into the parking lot below. She gulped in the fresh air, swallowing it until her lungs could take in no more. She exhaled and bent her head as if in prayer, only she couldn't figure out what to pray for anymore. The truth, in this case, would not set her free. Angry tears pricked her eyes, and she blinked them away.

"Excuse me, ma'am," she heard someone say. She looked up to see a man holding a huge tray of food—biscuits and a roasted chicken and a large pan of baked beans. He gestured with his shoulder toward the door. "I need to get into the, um, kitchen."

"Oh sure, sorry," she said. She reached for the door to open it for him, and he disappeared inside it. She closed the door and started to scurry off to avoid any further encounters. The caterers were obviously arriving to bring food for after the service. There was no telling who she'd see if she hung around.

Her stomach grumbled in response to the smell of that chicken, and it occurred to her that she couldn't remember the last time she'd eaten. Tommy'd brought her a burger—cold and soggy—to the hospital, but that had been yesterday? The day before? She'd gotten so busy getting Graham home and set up she'd thought of little else but his comfort, his ability to get from the couch to the bathroom. It hurt her to see him move so slowly when just a few days ago, she'd had to holler at him for bounding through the house "like a herd of elephants."

"Darcy Stokes?" Just as she made it to the bottom of the stairs, she heard the man's voice calling from the top. She froze. From where she stood, she could see her car in the parking lot not too many steps away.

"Are you Darcy?" he asked. Slowly, she turned back to face the man for whom she'd held the door. The man who'd paired her first name with her maiden name instead of her married one, which was odd. She hadn't been called Darcy Stokes in a long, long time. She liked the sound of it, as though he were calling out who she used to be instead of who she'd become.

"Yes?" she said. He'd put the box of food down inside and now stood empty-handed.

He looked at his feet and shook his head, then looked up. Even from a distance, she could see that he was red-faced. "Sorry I ran after you like that. I just couldn't believe it was you. I—I'd heard you were still around, but I just haven't seen you." He touched his chest. "I'm Clay Chessman? We did that project together in eleventh grade? For French class?"

Darcy blinked up at him as she tried—and failed—to remember what he was talking about. She'd taken French because a foreign language was required for college, and she hadn't known at that point that she wouldn't make it to college. She'd taken French because she'd thought perhaps someday she'd go to Paris.

"I—I'm . . . not sure I—"

"We made coq au vin? At my family's restaurant? My parents let us use the kitchen after hours?" He chuckled. "It took us damn near all night." He stepped down two steps, coming toward her.

She took a few steps up just to seem friendly, agreeable. But she really wanted to turn and run to her car. Now there were just three steps between them. A memory returned to her, a wine bottle tilted toward her mouth, the smell of sautéed onions filling the air. "Yeah, I sorta remember that," she said. They'd planned to convince the Chessman's cook to do the work for them, but he'd bailed out when he heard they were making "fancy French stuff." They'd ended up drinking more wine than they put in the sauce, and neither of them had felt much like eating the food at "French Food Day" at school the next day. Funny how that memory had been right there—buried inside her head—just waiting for Clay Chessman to call it out.

"We drank all that wine," he said and laughed. He shook his head. "I don't know why I remember that so much. Except maybe it was the first time I'd ever had a real hangover."

She laughed as the details came flooding back. "Oh, and they served that chocolate mousse for dessert? And they'd done something wrong to it so it looked like shit instead?" She covered her mouth in horror when she realized she'd just cussed on the church steps.

He nodded and laughed harder. "Oh man, I'd forgotten about the chocolate mousse. That was awful. We both nearly threw up."

The laughter died out, and they stood there awkwardly, neither one knowing what else to say. She'd heard he'd come back to take over his parents' restaurant. She'd also heard he'd married some hot young chick. *Who knew Clay Chessman had it in him,* everyone said. The gossip mill had kicked into high gear upon his return, reaching even her.

She took a step down, one step closer to her car, and mustered up a smile that paled in comparison to the one he probably remembered from high school. But it was the best she could do.

He gestured to the door at the top of the stairs. "Rough one, huh?" he asked. He must've assumed she'd left the funeral because she was too upset to stay.

"Yeah," she said, letting him believe it.

"It's a real tragedy," he added.

"It is that," she agreed. She glanced over her shoulder at her car again, waiting for her there, her getaway vehicle. It would take her home to Graham. She should check in on him, though he was no doubt where she'd left him—playing video games on the sofa.

"I—I heard your son was involved," Clay said.

Not shocked that he knew but shocked that he would just come out and say it like that, she turned back to find him extending a cigarette to her. "It's not wine, but . . ." He shrugged. "It helps smooth out the edges." With his other hand, he held up a lighter and raised his eyebrows.

Darcy wondered what edges he needed to smooth out. She glanced around. No one was there, but . . . this was a church. In all her wildest days she'd never sat on the back porch of a church and smoked a cigarette! She started to shake her head, to tell him she couldn't possibly. But then she saw Cynthia's mother waving that trembling, accusing finger in her direction. She thought of her son at home and his daddy gone off to live with that slut. She thought of Graham's slow, painful progression to and from the bathroom, his world shrunk to an eight-foot pathway instead of an open highway. She thought of the secret she'd made him promise to keep. And then she took that cigarette, put it between her lips, and leaned forward like a girl receiving Communion. She heard the catch of the lighter, the fuel igniting the tiniest of flames. She focused on the end of the cigarette and watched as it began to glow.

Ava

WEDNESDAY

She never made it back to her class on Monday after the assembly. As she left the gym, Mr. Query was standing at the ready by the door, his eyes trained for a glimpse of her. "Mrs. Chessman," he intoned when he saw her. And something about the way he said her name told her that the secret she'd been hoping died with Keary had done anything but.

She'd known this on some level when she saw the boys removed from the assembly—but denial is a powerful thing. She'd clung to hope until the moment she felt Mr. Query's hand in the crook of her elbow, tugging her in the direction of his office. The rest of Monday had been a shit show, an exercise in horror and humiliation. No one believed her. And why should they? She looked guilty as hell. And, in some ways, she was guilty. Or, at least, culpable.

Mr. Query had looked at her like she was vile, rolled his distaste for her around in his mouth as he debated what to say. Instead he'd simply slid a phone—the boy's phone—across the desk. "This was discovered in the assembly today." He averted his eyes, as if he hadn't already seen it. As if it hadn't been passed around to quite a few faculty members while she waited on a hard chair outside the principal's office.

She nodded, her cheeks flaming. She recalled the day she'd let Ian Stone take her phone to Google something, something he'd said was true and she'd not believed, caught up in the moment, so happy to be liked by the students, to be one of the cool teachers whose classes were fun.

"Prove it," she'd said, and handed her phone to him, never thinking that he would do what he'd done: gone into her photos and found the ones she'd sent to Clay one night when he was working late and she was missing him: topless photos, meant for his eyes only.

Ian had sent them to himself from her phone. She knew that's what had happened. But by all appearances, it looked like she'd sent them to him herself. And then there were the texts between them to back up the allegations of an inappropriate relationship—something that had started innocently enough. She'd given her number out to all the students so they could text her in case they had any questions. Plenty of teachers did it.

He'd texted her with a question about homework. But then he'd kept texting. And she hadn't stopped it. She'd even responded. Because she was lonely and because he was nice to her and because she was stupid. In two weeks he would be eighteen, but he was seventeen now. And that made him a minor, and her, in the eyes of the law, guilty.

She thought of the texts, the double entendres he'd used:

Him: I'd like to have you tutor me.

Her: But you're not doing badly in English.

Him: It's not English that's hard.

Or:

Him: I'm getting a new car and when I do, I want to take you for a drive.

Her: Oh yeah? Where to?

Him: Anywhere you want. Maybe out to the lake.

Her: I've heard it's nice out there.

Him: I'll show you how nice it is.

When she'd read the texts, she saw herself trying to be kind, to not bruise his ego, yet to not engage. He was a kid, after all, and he was reaching out to her. She didn't want to outright reject him. That's what she'd told herself. But when she read the texts in light of the allegations, she knew it could appear—especially when put with the photos—that she'd encouraged their sexually charged banter. And maybe she had.

She'd spent all day Tuesday alone in an attorney's office over in Macon. Her attorney was a former prosecutor who'd decided to devote her life to defending women against abusers of the male species. Nancy, as she told Ava to call her, seemed to believe her and spent hours with her, trying to figure out how to get her out of the charges that would, inevitably, be brought against her: disseminating obscene material to persons underage and contributing to the delinquency of a minor, so far. There would be more if they could come up with more. When she cried, Nancy wordlessly passed her a box of tissues and waited for her to pull it together. She never once asked if anyone else would be joining Ava. She never asked how Ava would pay.

In the end, seeing no other options, Nancy had picked up the phone and made arrangements with the sheriff as Ava listened in and chewed on her fingernails, leaving them a bloody mess. When she hung up, it was settled. Ava was to turn herself in to the police tomorrow, voluntarily, and make a statement in her own defense. They might arrest her afterward.

Now she sat on the stoop outside the trailer and gazed off toward the big house, where Clay and the kids were. Clay was furious, of course. He'd left the restaurant Monday night and come home to confront her, having already heard all he needed from the townspeople, who'd been only too happy to fill him in. Her husband—the man who'd once promised to honor and protect her—had made up his mind without hearing the first word of her side.

"I don't know you anymore," he'd said, standing in the den of the trailer, their two bodies nearly filling the whole room. His mother had come and collected the children, Clay daring her to fight him on it. "I haven't really known you since we came here."

"*You* haven't known *me?*" she spat. "How about you're gone all the time now? How about I can't remember the last time we said more than two sentences to each other? How about *I* don't know *you* anymore?"

He'd looked at her with flat, dead eyes. "So I guess that's why you went after some kid? Some good-looking kid who showed you some attention? Because you were desperate for it?"

He stuck his hand in his pocket and jiggled his keys, a sign that he was thinking about leaving. A sign she had come to know well. She glanced at the door and thought of blocking it with her body, of making him stay there until they sorted this out. But it was not, she knew, something that could be sorted. Not that night. And maybe not ever.

Clay spoke again, and this time his voice was less angry and more sad. "My father warned me you were too young for me. He told me that the age difference was too great, that you'd have other interests, need different things." He gave a cynical laugh. "I just didn't think your interests and needs would be teenage boys." He thought about it for a moment. "Course, I guess he's no younger to you than you are to me. Right?"

"It's not like that, Clay!" she protested. "You've got it all wrong! Please! I need you of all people to believe me. I know the way it looks—I do—but if you'll give me time, I'll prove that I didn't do what they're saying."

Clay had sighed and let his shoulders fall, looking beleaguered and broken. When he walked to the door, she didn't bother to try to stop him. He turned back to look at her. For a moment his face betrayed his bravado. "He has naked pictures of you. There are texts between the two of you. I heard all about it."

She swallowed and, with all the resolve left in her, held his gaze and said, "Well, you heard wrong, and I'm going to prove it."

Clay smirked. "Good luck with that," he said. Then he was gone.

Now she watched the big house for signs of life, for signs of Clayton and Savannah. She'd been accused of harming children, so her husband had taken hers. But this boy was no child. He had a man's body and—thanks to the Internet—a man's knowledge. She'd thought she could trust him, so his betrayal hit hard. She saw now what she was to him. Not a friend but a conquest. He and his friends were lecherous predators. They had singled her out like a lion separates a weak antelope from the herd. She'd seen them eyeing her and whispering, bits of conversations floating in the air, words like *hot* and *young*, but she'd chosen to feel flattered, to brush it off as harmless. She'd cared about him, deceived herself into thinking she was helping him.

She turned her gaze away from the big house, looked off toward the rolling Georgia hills the town sat nestled in. "It's so beautiful there," Clay had said the night he'd pitched the idea of him taking over the restaurant. He'd been skillful about it, calculated—not unlike those boys, truth be told. Maybe it was men in general, a skill they were born with, along with the penis?

"You'll love it," he'd promised. Later, she'd told him she didn't love it. He'd been wrong. She wanted to go home. He'd crossed his arms over his chest and cocked his head, looking at her as though she were dim-witted. As though he had to tolerate her.

"You don't get it," he'd said. "There is no going home. There is no home to go to. This is it."

She'd let things go too far with Ian Stone. So far that she'd ended up here, sitting on the stoop of a trailer that was not hers, in the middle of a place she did not call home, waiting for the time to come that she would turn herself in for corrupting a minor when all she'd wanted was someone to talk to. She envisioned iron bars slamming shut, her own eyes blinking, confused, behind them. She could almost hear the sound of iron against iron, the reverb echoing across her heart.

Leah

THURSDAY

She did not admit that when she saw Talmadge standing outside the church before Keary's funeral, she felt her heart swell—literally swell—inside her chest. The sight of his tall, lanky frame slouching against the half wall surrounding the church property was as welcome as what a marathon runner must feel when they see someone holding out a water bottle. The feel of his arms wrapping her in a hello hug was as comforting as her mother's used to be when she was a very little girl. But she did not let herself lean into this hug.

She pulled away fast, blinked up at him, and thanked him for coming, keeping her voice controlled, cool. He nodded, looked like he wanted to say more, but stayed silent. There was something in her that wanted to ask him what he'd been about to say. But something else that told her it was better left alone. She looked toward the doors of the church yawning open.

Talmadge dug in his pocket and held up a dark object in the shape of a rectangle that fit perfectly in the palm of his hand. He grinned. "I got this for you."

She squinted at it, not understanding. "Talmadge, I have a phone. But thanks."

He shook his head and tucked the phone back into his pocket. "No, I mean I got a phone. For me. So you could get me anytime you need."

She looked away from his gaze, so intent on her, so filled with whatever it was that Talmadge possessed. Leah guessed it was the music, filling him up with something extra, something other people did not have. "Thanks," she mumbled, uncertain how to respond. "That was really nice of you."

"It wasn't that big a deal," he said. "I mean, I've been behind the times long enough." He shrugged as if it were nothing, but she knew that wasn't true. He'd probably had to save up a long time—Talmadge didn't have a job, so she had no idea where he'd gotten the money—and sneak behind his parents' backs to get the phone.

The church bells tolled somberly, and Talmadge tugged on her elbow, indicating with his head that they should get inside for the service. Looking at the church doors flung wide open, Leah imagined Keary walking into them on a Sunday morning, her face lit with a smile, maybe teasing the pastor about not going on too long so they could get to lunch on time or pulling a face behind her mother's back to make her little sister laugh.

Leah fell into step beside Talmadge. As they walked through the lobby, she saw Keary's mother and sister off to the side, waiting in the wings to be led in, on display for all the mourners to gape at. Keary's father stood away from his wife and surviving daughter, staring out the window with a stricken expression, the light from the sun causing his face to glow.

Keary's sister, Lauren, smiled when she saw Leah but quickly remembered herself, and the smile died on her face. Still, Leah gave her a little wave and a small smile back, to tell her it was OK to forget why they were all there, if only for a moment. She followed Talmadge to a pew in the back. The church, like all the other churches that week, was full. Talmadge stopped in the aisle, stepping aside so she could be seated before him. He had not been taught manners by his hippie parents. He hadn't needed to be.

Leah navigated past the knees of the other mourners, keeping her head down as she did, hearing the murmurs of the people around her. "That's the other girl. The fourth one. The friend." They did not say, *She should be dead, too.* They didn't need to. Leah understood that fact better than anyone in the room.

She sat down and adjusted her skirt, one that she'd fished out from the back of her closet, from her homeschooling days when she'd dressed for her mother, nondescript, modest, plain. The skirt she wore nearly reached the floor and fit loosely. It was solid black. Leah had paired it with a white T-shirt and a gray cardigan with black ballet flats on her feet. And pearls around her neck. The picture of virtue. She could act the part.

Her mother had told her how pretty she looked before she left, which meant, Leah knew, that she looked awful by teenage standards. Leah wanted to look awful. She wanted to look frumpy and out of it. She wanted to look as different from the way she'd looked Friday night as she could. Her reasons for this were numerous, and not something she wanted to talk about or think about. Instead, she thought of her own funeral, continuing something while she sat in Keary's funeral that she had begun during Brynne's and Mary Claire's.

She used their funerals as a springboard. Borrowing and discarding the elements from theirs to fit her own ideas and tastes like a bride preparing for a wedding. *I would have all white flowers,* she thought. *I would choose ones that smell nice, like gardenias, so the church would smell good. I would not have boys from school as the pallbearers. I would have my cousins and brothers. I would let Talmadge play one of his songs without words. I would not let stupid kids who claimed they knew me get up at the pulpit and make lame jokes to try to make the sad people happy. I'd have the minister say all there was to say. Which would be: she died, we're sad, but everyone dies, and she's gone to a better place.*

Did she believe in a better place after death? She thought of Keary and Brynne and Mary Claire. She could not picture them anywhere other than heaven. It made her believe in it more, now that she needed somewhere for them to be. It was better than their being buried in the ground, or trapped in that burning car, or just gone, absent from the world, from her life. Heaven made more sense.

She thought of them having fun without her for all eternity. If they were still around, they'd tease her about that, their eyes glinting like they did whenever they busted on one another, which was often. *We're going to heaven, and we're not inviting you. You have to stay in this lame-ass town forever.* She wasn't sure they were allowed to say *ass* in heaven even if it was in the Bible. She thought of the three of them without her, wondered if they missed her. If Brynne wished Leah'd been with them so they could all be together now. If she was sorry for what she'd asked of Leah that night. If she would take it all back if she could.

At the end of the funeral, Keary's sister got up and read the verses about there being a time for everything, her voice small and quivery. She had to stop in the middle of the passage, locking eyes with her mother for a moment before she mustered the strength to go on. The entire congregation seemed to hold their breath in anticipation. Leah wanted to stand up and argue with her: *There is not a time for what happened that night!*

If this were her funeral, she would not allow any verses to be read. She would insist that someone read an Emily Dickinson poem, one of the ones about death like Mrs. Chessman read on Monday morning before the assembly. After the assembly, Leah had gone back to the classroom to get her water bottle, which was one of those expensive kinds that kept the water cold or the coffee hot for hours. She knew better than to tell her mom she'd lost it, so she went back in search of it and saw Mrs. Chessman's Emily Dickinson book on the desk, the nice one that was obviously special to her. Mrs. Chessman was in some kind of trouble, something not good. Leah knew the boys involved and knew that, whatever it was, Mrs. Chessman probably wasn't to blame.

She'd picked up the book and tucked it into her backpack for safe-keeping. Maybe whenever she got the chance to give it back to her, she'd tell her what she knew about those boys. She'd tell her she knew what they were capable of. But Mrs. Chessman was gone from school. So in the meantime, Leah was reading Emily Dickinson's poetry, committing some of the lines to heart the way she once had memorized verses for prizes in Sunday school. She doubted her mother would be as proud of that, but she didn't care. She needed Emily Dickinson right now. She needed lines like, *Dying is a wild night and a new road.* That would be something she'd want read at her funeral.

When Keary's sister finished, the boys stood up to do their part in the service—the very same ones who'd been the pallbearers at the other two funerals, the ones who got Mrs. Chessman in trouble, the ones Leah never wanted to see again but would see in school for the rest of the year. And it was only fall. She studied her hands in her lap instead of watching them as they hoisted the casket from the stand in front and lugged it down the aisle.

Once they were past her, she looked up, her eyes focused on the empty pulpit where Keary's young sister had just stood so bravely and read words Leah no longer believed. She looked up just in time to see Keary's father, seated on the aisle, turn to watch the casket exit the room. With tears streaming down his face, he lifted his hand toward the casket as if he could call back his daughter, as if he were saying, *Don't go.*

Leah dabbed at her eyes discreetly with the tissue she'd kept balled in her fist, hoping no one noticed but knowing that Talmadge did no matter what. Talmadge noticed everything, which was either heartening or infuriating, depending on the day. He cast her a sympathetic glance, but she pretended not to see. She pretended not to see some things, not to know a lot of things, and not to feel anything at all.

Marglyn

Friday

It had been one week since the tragedy, and Marglyn was hopeful that today she would be left alone. The nice thing (though it sounded odd to say in light of the scope of the tragedy) was that with three girls being involved, the intentions of well-wishers weren't aimed solely at her. Once all the funerals were over, it seemed that everyone in town needed a break from mourning and, thus, the attention had tapered off. This was a welcome respite. She preferred being the one to offer help, not receive it.

Today was the first day Hale had gone to work since the accident, and a friend had taken Robert for a few days "to get his mind off things," which was wishful thinking, but Marglyn complied. She looked forward to having a few hours alone and hoped for no interruptions from the outside world. No concerned calls, no food deliveries, not even the mailman coming to deliver a condolence card.

She retrieved a pen from the desk to make a to-do list, a piece of normality from her old life. She held the pen over the paper for a moment, thinking of all the things she used to keep track of, all her balls in the air, as she called them. Now all the balls had fallen and rolled just out of her grasp. And no item on a to-do list would be the thing she most needed to do, which was to somehow get her daughter back. She took a deep breath, blinked away threatening tears, and forced herself to proceed.

She wrote the first item: *Call Sheila Brock.* Sheila Brock was a local Realtor. Sometime in the wee hours of the morning, she'd decided that continuing to pass the crash site every time they came or went was too much for all of them. She and Hale and Robert could not stay there. They had to sell the house.

She wasn't even going to ask Hale, who would argue, who would say she was making an emotional decision and to wait awhile before deciding. Marglyn didn't want to wait. The crash site wasn't going to go away. It was always going to be the place where her daughter, and two other girls besides, died. She did not need that reminder every day.

There was a knock on the door, the sound of knuckles on wood uninvited and invasive. Just one day alone. Just a few hours was all she'd wanted. She sighed as she stowed the pen and list in her purse, then crossed the house to answer the door, thinking as she did what a sight she must be. She'd not showered or brushed her teeth, and she was wearing old sweatpants and one of Mary Claire's T-shirts, something she'd taken to doing. This one was from a cheer camp MC had gone to last summer. She'd bought the T-shirt big, to sleep in. Which meant that Marglyn could wear it. It was even a bit big on her, seeing as how she'd barely eaten in the days since the accident. Mary Claire would be so proud.

The dog, Jinx (a birthday present for Mary Claire on her tenth birthday—a living, breathing, barking reminder of her that required care even though his master was no longer around), followed at her heels, barking a persistent warning. She looked down at him. "Hush, Jinx," she said. "It's probably just Delores."

Her mother-in-law had been by almost every day, under the pretense of "checking in," but she knew it was to talk about the crash—what could've happened, what she'd heard in town, how she was feeling, how Marglyn was feeling, and how everyone she knew was feeling, including the women in her Bible study, the choir director, and the man who cut her grass. This crash, and being at the center of it as the grandmother of one of the girls, was the biggest thing that had happened to Delores, possibly ever.

Marglyn tugged the door open, chastising herself as she did for thinking such cruel thoughts about her mother-in-law. She was a sweet woman, who, Marglyn worried, was ignoring her grief by focusing on the gossip. She didn't need to fret over what was going to happen to Darcy LaRue's son and whether or not he was racing at the time of the accident. She didn't need to discuss the results of the police investigation into the accident. She needed to face the fact that Mary Claire—their bright, amazing, sunshiny girl—was gone forever. When she did, Marglyn worried over what would happen. Delores had a bad heart, and Marglyn feared this loss would break it.

But it was not Delores standing on the doorstep. Standing there instead was a familiar face, but one that Marglyn couldn't place. She racked her brain as the two of them blinked at each other awkwardly and the young woman shifted on her feet, moving the manila folder she was carrying from one arm to the other. "Mrs. Miner?" she asked, her voice quivering slightly.

"Yes?" she asked, almost enjoying the worried look on the young woman's face. Marglyn tried to guess her age. It was so hard nowadays to tell how old someone was, what with all the fortysomethings trying to look like twentysomethings. As a result, Marglyn tended to divide people into three categories—no, four. Babies, children, teenagers, and adults. The person in front of her was no longer a teenager, but she hadn't been an adult long, Marglyn decided.

The visitor stuck out her hand. Marglyn took it in her own and shook it gently so as not to dislodge the folder she was holding. "I'm Holly Sparrow," the girl said matter-of-factly. Marglyn felt a panic rising—this was some sort of test she was going to fail.

"I'm sorry," she said. "I don't—your name—I don't." Her voice died on her lips, but the girl didn't jump in to explain. "I don't know who you are," she stated more bluntly.

"Oh!" the girl said. "I thought—I had so many conversations with Mary—" Her voice caught on the name. She swallowed and finished,

"Claire." Marglyn continued to stare at her, still not understanding. Holly Sparrow held up the folder as an explanation. "I have this for you. I was her guidance counselor at school? This is her file, and, well, I got the idea that maybe you'd like to see it. There're some essays and some interest forms she filled out, that kind of thing?" Her voice clearly indicated she wasn't sure about this, that she needed Marglyn to tell her she'd done the right thing. And yet, Marglyn couldn't bring herself to give her the approval she was looking for, couldn't show the gratitude that a better person might be capable of.

She knew this was a nice thing to do. She knew that this young woman didn't have to take the time to hand deliver this to her, this piece of her daughter she'd not realized existed until this moment. And yet, she couldn't help but see that innocuous manila file as something dangerous. She'd been terrified of finding something personal like this—a diary or a collection of unsent letters or . . . a file of her personal effects from her guidance counselor. A guidance counselor helped students with their futures, after all. And Mary Claire wasn't going to have a future now. She didn't want to see anything that her daughter might've been planning, didn't want to be confronted with what could've been even as she struggled to grapple with what was.

But her southern manners won out, and she motioned for Holly Sparrow to come inside. She offered her a seat and a glass of iced tea and, to her chagrin, her visitor accepted both. She watched the girl lay the manila folder on the coffee table in front of her. She eyed it as if it were likely to spontaneously burst into flames, already thinking of where she would hide it after Holly Sparrow was gone. One thing she knew for certain—she would not open it. She might just toss it in the garbage. And yet, that felt callous. And perhaps a bit presumptive. Maybe someday she'd grow strong enough to peek inside. Maybe someday she'd draw some strange comfort from seeing her daughter's handwriting on an application for a college she would never attend.

Darcy

They came for Graham one week after the accident. In truth, it took them longer than she thought it would. When the police cars pulled into the drive and onto the yard (which was disrespectful, and also, there were four of them, which was just excessive to arrest one boy) she hollered for Graham, who was in his normal position on the couch. "Stay where you are, son!" But of course Graham stood up from his spot on the couch and began to make his way toward her, to see what was going on.

Adrenaline coursed through her as she watched the uniformed men conferring with one another before heading toward the house. She knew some of them, of course. Traitors. Didn't they know her son was hurt in that accident? Though he was a little better, Graham was still moving slowly and in no shape to go to jail. "You go lay back down, son," Darcy said, patting him. "I'm calling Terrence Mangum. If they're going to arrest you, they're going to have to arrest me, too."

She locked the door and called the attorney Tommy had hired. To his credit, Tommy was sparing no expense in his fight to exonerate Graham. As she waited for his secretary to fetch Terrence, she thought of Graham's words to her. *At least tell me I won.* They were arresting him for what he'd done. They knew it, and she knew it. But it didn't seem right, or fair, for Graham to be punished for a foolish, reckless decision. She thought of Tommy buying him that car, and a fresh surge of adrenaline filled her veins. He should be the one being arrested. He should be held accountable. You didn't put a gun in a child's hand, then blame the child when he pulled the trigger.

Terrence's voice on the other end of the phone pulled her back to the scene at hand. "Darcy?" he asked. "What's going on?" Outside, a cluster of cops banged on the door.

"Did you know they were going to show up here and arrest him?" she asked. "Isn't there something you can do? He's ill. He was just released from the hospital after nearly dying. He can't be put in jail!"

"They won't put him in jail, Darcy. This is a formality. He has to be processed and go before the judge, then he'll be released on bond." Terrence's voice was resigned, controlled, which infuriated her more. She wanted him to get angry, too. She wanted him to come right over and put a stop to this. But from the sound of things, he was going to let it happen.

"But what if they don't?" she asked, her voice weak and small because her throat was closing up, filled with unshed tears, her fear choking her.

"They will, Darcy. I know how this works. There're a lot of people in this town who want something done. They want to see your son hauled into jail, made to account for his actions that night. Three girls were killed."

"I know that," she said. As if she needed reminding.

"Well, the sheriff's had a lot of pressure on him to do something about it. People don't really care what. They just want something done. It makes them feel like justice is being served. This is a way of shutting them up. Graham will be arraigned, and later he'll go to trial, and with the evidence I'm gathering—the doubt I can cast—he'll get off. No jury is going to convict a bright young man who had an accident. Ruining one more life won't bring those girls back."

Darcy could feel her blood beginning to cool as he talked. He was good at his job, and that mattered to her more than anything, considering he was the person who stood between her son and jail. "OK," she agreed weakly.

"Now open the door and let them take him. Caution them that he's still recovering, and I expect they'll be gentle with him. I'll wrap up some things here and head over there to make sure they expedite the process. I'll call you when you can come pick him up."

"OK," she said again. And, though it wasn't OK at all, she did what he said. She hung up the phone and unlocked the door. She gravely let the officers into her house and, through tears, watched as they carried out the arrest warrant for vehicular manslaughter and illegal racing. She looked away as they put the cuffs on her son but watched as they led him out of the house and into the waiting police car, standing guard as she'd done on those nights he had croup or those days on the playground when he was prone to jumping from high places. But this was a fall she couldn't save him from. She just stood by and watched from the front picture window until all four cars had disappeared from sight.

◆ ◆ ◆

The phone rang late that night, hours after Graham was back home (it had gone exactly as Terrence said it would, which increased her trust in him immensely) and Tommy had come to check on him and gone. (Blessedly her anger with him had abated by that time, and she was able to be cordial to him in front of Graham. He'd had enough stress that day without seeing his parents fight.)

She hadn't recognized the number, but she'd answered anyway, not knowing if it could be something about the arrest. The male voice on the other end wasn't a cop calling to wrap up some loose end. It was another, familiar voice, though she couldn't place it at first.

"Hey, Darcy? It's Clay. Chessman? Sorry for calling so late, but I just heard about Graham." There was a pause. "I, um, just wanted to make sure you were OK." He exhaled loudly into the phone. "I can't imagine what that was like. I have a son, and . . ."

She smiled reflexively at his words. It was nice to be thought of, to be checked on. "Thanks for calling, Clay," she said. "I'm OK. I mean, it wasn't the greatest day of my life, and I'm contemplating moving to Florida to live with my mother and maiden aunt, but . . ." She gave a little, fake laugh.

"I guess I just sort of . . . understand . . . ," he responded. "I mean, I'm probably the only other person in town who does."

He didn't need to explain what he meant. She'd heard bits and pieces about what had happened with his wife. But she didn't trust the Worthy gossip mill to be completely reliable now that she'd been at the center of it. "I'm sorry," she said. "About that."

"We're split up," he said, offering an explanation she hadn't asked for. "I'm living with the kids at my parents' for now."

"Do you really think she did what they're saying?" she asked. "I mean, are you sure those boys are telling the truth?" She knew of one teenage boy who was currently lying his ass off to save his own neck—after having been told to do so by his own mother. If her son were in those boys' position, would she do the same? Would she be willing to let a woman lose her career and her marriage to protect her son's reputation? She didn't like the answer. And it made her wonder about Clay's wife's story. What if she was telling the truth, and all of this had been a rush to judgment?

"I don't know all that went on—of course there're two sides of the story—but something did. She was . . ." He sighed again, long and loud. She could hear the fight going out of him. "She's—" He tried for words again. "Well, something's not right with her. It hasn't been right since we came here, really."

"I'm sorry," she said again, the words useless in her mouth. But like all the other people who tried to offer condolences in the wake of all this tragedy, she felt the need to say something.

"Well, I didn't call to talk about Ava. I called to check on you. I know this has got to be hard. Awful. How's your son?"

"He's exhausted. It was a long day, and he's still, you know, healing from the accident. He almost died himself." For a brief moment today, she'd had the thought—just a flicker, but still, it had been there—that maybe it would've been better if he had. What kind of mother thought such a thing? She'd added that guilt to the pile.

"Man, that's tough," Clay said. "Well, I mainly called to tell you that I'm keeping my ear out for the town gossip for you—just gauging how the talk is swaying." He chuckled. "I hear it all at the restaurant, as you can imagine."

"Yeah, I'm sure," she said. But she wasn't sure she wanted to hear whatever he was hearing. "Do I want to hear it, though?" She tried to add a laugh of her own, but it came out sounding choked.

"Yeah, I think you do. There're a lot of people who aren't against Graham. There's talk that those girls could've been at fault, that that young girl driving only had a learner's permit and had no business being the driver that night. That it was an accident, plain and simple."

He paused, as if to let her respond, but she didn't speak, so he continued. "I think it can be easy to feel like everyone's against you"—he gave a little, ironic laugh—"believe me, I know that feeling all too well. But not everyone is." He paused again. "I'm not."

She made herself laugh softly in response, to lighten the weight of his words, the meaning behind them. It was like he was offering something to her, but she couldn't see exactly what it was he was holding out. Clay Chessman was a man embroiled in a scandal of his own, not someone to form a bond with. And yet, he was right. He was the only other person in town who could truly understand what she was going through. "Well, thank you, Clay," she said.

"You're certainly welcome," he replied. "But there's one more thing," he added, as if he knew that she was going to end the call. The "but" in his sentence told her he hadn't saved the best for last.

"OK?" she asked. Her leg had gone to sleep, so she shifted her position, felt the tingling response shoot up her leg, like a warning.

"Well, I guess the real reason I called is some of the football players were in here tonight and . . . well, I got only bits and pieces of their conversation, but it sounds to me like they're not so forgiving. They're talking about revenge on Graham. Like they weren't happy that he got out of jail, and they're going to be looking for him. To take out their own form of justice. They think he killed their girls."

"Oh," she said.

"I just thought you'd want to know so you can maybe watch out for him."

"Well yes, yes, of course." She glanced around. Had she locked all the doors and windows? There was a time in this town she wouldn't even have thought of such, but that had all changed. "Thank you," she managed to add. She swallowed, her tongue turned to sandpaper. She got up to get a glass of water, padding silently through the house to reach the kitchen, looking over her shoulder as she went, suddenly feeling as though predators could be lurking right outside her windows. Predators who wore the town name on their chests.

Neither Clay nor Darcy spoke as she walked, and she supposed he listened as she retrieved a glass from the cabinet, filled it from the tap, and drank from it. The silence swelled between them. She was about to invent an excuse to get off the phone when one presented itself like a miracle. She heard a sound that was a cross between a trapped animal and a frightened child. It was coming from the den where Graham slept. It was her son, crying. Crying hard, like his heart was breaking. And perhaps it was. She knew this town and knew that whatever Clay had heard, chances were Graham had heard it, too. She knew he was probably terrified.

"Hey, Clay, I'd better go," she said, feeling her strength coming back to her, the strength that comes from being needed by someone else, by being able to help another person. She wondered if that was what this conversation was giving to Clay. If so, then she was happy to supply it.

"Sure, sure," he said. "Would you mind if I called you again? Just to, maybe, check on you?"

She knew the correct answer was no. A relationship between them right now wasn't the best idea. Was scandal ever a good basis for a friendship? Was heartache a good building block? But the idea of some-one else—someone who seemed to actually care, someone who hap-pened to also be a handsome man—checking on her felt like a good thing, a needed thing, in her life.

"I'd like that," she said. She said goodbye and ended the call, drop-ping the phone on the counter as she went to check on her son. Needing and being needed: as far as she could tell, it was the circle of life, an endless, dizzying loop.

Ava

Her father followed her into the trailer, glancing over his shoulder as if someone might sneak up and attack them from behind. But this town had already done all the harm it could do. For now. Her day in jail had stretched into nearly twenty-four hours as the police seemed to do everything they could to fumble the process, lengthening it beyond what seemed necessary. The boy who'd hit the girls had come and gone in the time she'd been there. At one point they'd waited in the same area, eyeing each other with a mixture of brokenness and fear but never speaking. She was thankful she'd never had him in a class.

She put down the paperwork that the attorney had handed her, the charges against her printed there in black and white, in the same alphabet she'd used all her life, only this time joined to form grotesque words that she could hardly believe were now connected to her. She felt as though they might as well have tattooed them to her forehead. That for the rest of her life, people would see those words whenever they looked at her.

The sight of those papers on her kitchen table—the same table that she, Clay, and the children sat at as a family and ate a proper meal—looked incongruous. She picked up the papers and slid them back into her purse instead. She'd figure out a more permanent place for them later.

Behind her, she heard her father's heavy steps cross the short distance to the refrigerator and cringed. There was nearly nothing inside, and she didn't want him to see that. It wasn't that she couldn't afford to buy food (Clay wasn't allowed to cut off her funds entirely, though she guessed he would if he could); it was that she couldn't face the possibility of running into other people at Trout's. She'd rather starve, and that was becoming more and more likely. She heard the suction on the door break as he tugged it open, probably for a water or Coke, or possibly even a beer. It had been a long day, after all. She heard him give a sigh of disappointment and shut the door. She turned to face him.

She'd hardly looked directly at him since he'd arrived to bring her bond money after Clay outright refused to pay it. She'd called Clay from the jail, her voice thick with tears, but he'd ignored her call, finally speaking to her through the attorney, who gravely told her he'd sought formal separation papers and would not be assisting her in her own legal process. She and her father had gone past the restaurant on the way home, and the place had seemed as busy as usual. She imagined the condolences Clay would receive, the way people would paint her—a pedophile, a whore. And he would agree, without even once asking her her side.

"I think you should come home and stay with us," her father said, not mentioning the empty refrigerator, his lips barely opening to utter the words. She knew he didn't really want to take her home with him, that this was an edict from her mother, who had fibromyalgia and was having one of her spells. He jerked his thumb back toward the big house. "He's clearly not going to let you see the kids."

She gestured toward the papers. "Dad, I'm not allowed to go anywhere. Not till my trial."

"I got the feeling that you were going to take a plea. That's what that lawyer said was best."

That had been her lawyer's advice, at least for now. "We're hopeful that more will come to light to back up your side of things, Mrs. Chessman," she'd said. "But if not, a plea bargain would expedite things. I'm afraid the hands of justice don't ever turn as fast as any of us would like." Which meant Ava was trapped in this town until the slow hands of justice wound their way around the clock.

"Tell Mom I'll come just as soon as I can," she said. She reached out for her father, who'd parted with a large chunk of his savings and driven more than a hundred miles to come and bail her out of jail for this shameful sin she'd been accused of. She had to make them understand. She had to figure out a way to clear her name. She inhaled the scent of her dad, the woodsy, Old Spiceness of him.

"I'm so sorry," she whispered. "I'm going to show you that I didn't do what they said." With her face buried in his shirt, she wasn't even sure he heard her. But then she felt him stiffen. He backed away and patted her shoulder, but he never once met her eyes.

"I'd better go," he said.

She nodded, her own eyes downcast, not looking up until he was out the door. "Drive safe," she called just as the door closed behind him. "Thank you," she added quietly, and began to cry, because she was sorry for everything, and because he didn't believe her. Her father—like everyone else—thought she was a pedophile.

Leah

She had one class with Graham LaRue, which meant "the street" in French. She'd never taken French—it had been cut from the budget at Worthy High—but she'd picked up things from reading. When she was homeschooling, her mother let her follow anything that struck her fancy, just so long as it was educational. She'd had a pretty long fascination with Paris and studied up on it.

She'd have been willing to bet that she knew more about that faraway city than anyone in town. Except maybe for Talmadge. She'd talked about it so much back then he'd probably picked up a lot of inadvertent information. She imagined them in Paris together, dancing to a song with no words under the Eiffel Tower at midnight, then banished the thought just as fast as it had popped into her head.

In math class the teacher, Mrs. Parry, announced that she needed someone to take Graham's assignments to him. She glanced nervously around the room, expecting pushback from the students. It was no secret that the football players had basically taken out a hit on Graham, swearing to beat him up as soon as they could get their hands on him, enacting their own warped sense of revenge for the deaths of Keary, Brynne, and Mary Claire. And in Worthy High, whatever the football players declared became the status quo. They were demigods in town, their influence spilling into all kinds of places it did not belong.

Leah thought of her secret and of how much she hated them. She hated them far more than she could ever hate Graham LaRue, a quiet boy who'd just wanted to be liked, the kind of kid who went along with things just because he thought it would help his status. He was Tommy LaRue's son, after all. Tommy LaRue still held some stupid record that he never let people forget, strutting around at football games letting everyone congratulate him on something he'd done decades ago. Graham was just trying to live up to the mantle he'd been handed. She could almost feel what he'd felt that night, driving that new car, everyone looking at him with jealous, coveting eyes. He'd felt powerful—maybe for the first time in his life. And maybe that power had settled in his foot as he pressed harder and harder on the gas. And maybe the accident had been his fault.

Or maybe Keary shouldn't have been driving MC's car. She was an anxious driver on the best of days, and this was at night, with Brynne and Mary Claire singing and laughing and probably headed toward a good drunk already, distracting her and making her more nervous. Leah had ridden in a car with Keary at the wheel, and she knew the accident could've been her fault. But to say that now, in the wake of the tragedy, was heresy.

Leah raised her hand. "I'll do it, Mrs. Parry," she said.

Mrs. Parry's eyes widened. "Are you—are you sure, Leah?"

Leah nodded even as she heard a rumble of disgust travel through the room. Behind her, a deep male voice blustered some protest, and other voices chimed in, but she didn't turn around. "He doesn't live far from school," she continued, making her voice sound strong and sure. "I can drop it by on my way home today."

"Well then, OK. I'll get everything together and have it for you at the end of the day. Thank you, Leah." Mrs. Parry smiled at her like she was a good girl, like she was doing something kind and selfless.

But what Mrs. Parry didn't know was that her offer was not that at all. Taking Graham LaRue his assignments was simply a small act of rebellion. It was a way to stand up after too many days of sitting down.

◆ ◆ ◆

Graham's house was dark and quiet, and his mother spoke in a whisper when she answered the door, almost as if she were afraid of being overheard. Leah tried to give her her brightest smile and exude sunshine, channeling someone deep inside her, the girl she used to be at ten years old, back when smiling came easy. That girl—the smiley pleaser—was long gone but not entirely dead. She could still be summoned if need be. Leah sensed this was a time when she was needed. Mrs. LaRue—Darcy, she said to call her, though Leah had been raised to address all adults by Mr. or Mrs. only—seemed frightened. Leah could guess of what. She wanted to put Mrs. LaRue at ease, to assure her she was friend not foe.

"What did you say your name was, honey?" Mrs. LaRue asked.

"Leah," she said. Then added, "Bennett."

Mrs. LaRue paused upon hearing her name, looking at her out of one side of her eyes. "Leah Bennett?" she asked.

Leah nodded and shifted the tote bag full of books she was carrying. She'd had to make Talmadge come pick her up from school. She usually walked home, but she had too much to carry, and Talmadge with his rusted-out beater car could always be counted on to give her a ride without asking fifty million questions, which was what her mother would do.

"Well, aren't you a friend of . . ." Mrs. LaRue's voice trailed off as if she couldn't bring herself to name the three dead girls.

"I was," Leah answered. She heard her voice warble a bit on the word *was* and hoped Graham's mother didn't.

She didn't seem to; she only gestured at the bag of books in Leah's grip—a bag that was growing heavier by the minute. "And you're . . . doing this for my son?" There was doubt all over her face, like maybe Leah was casing the joint, a scout for the boys who wanted to hurt her son.

Leah nodded. "Yes." She started to say more but noticed the woman wasn't paying attention. She was looking past Leah, out the open front door at Talmadge in his car in the driveway, scrutinizing him as if he might be plotting something.

"Oh, you don't know him," Leah hurried to explain. "He's homeschooled."

"Homeschooled?" Mrs. LaRue repeated, as if she'd never heard of the concept.

"Yeah, his family lives out in the country." She waved her arm behind her in the general direction of where the Feathers family lived, picturing in her mind the Feathers farm. Their house was little more than a shanty. Once Leah had seen a goat sleeping in the living room, right on the couch like a dog. Leah's dog wasn't allowed on the furniture in her house.

She waved at Talmadge, and he waved back, his face splitting into a smile. "He doesn't even know your son," Leah explained. "He just brought me here as a favor." She held out the bag of books. "I used to be homeschooled, too."

Mrs. LaRue accepted the bag. "Oh," she said, her face not looking so pinched and anxious anymore. "Well, thank you for bringing this. I guess I could've run over to the school and gotten it, but I don't like leaving Graham for too long. He's—" She paused. "Well, he's still quite weak. And . . ."

There was a moment of silence, and Leah knew they were both thinking of Graham still living while her friends were dead. She wanted to say, *I don't fault your son.* She wanted to tell Mrs. LaRue that one time Keary had spent fifteen minutes just trying to back out of a driveway and often ran up on curbs. She wanted to tell Mrs. LaRue that she hated those football players every bit as much as they hated Graham. But she couldn't say any of that, of course. Mostly because she didn't know this woman. But also because she couldn't say it to anyone at all.

"Would it be all right if I said hi?" she asked, surprising both herself and Graham's mother, who took a step back. The pinched look returned to her face. "I mean, if he's sleeping or something, I don't have to." She gave a little laugh. "The truth is we don't know each other well. Or at all." She waved her hand in the air, dismissing her own idea. "I'll just go."

She took a step back toward the door, which was still standing open. She heard her mother's voice in her head, as she did far too often. *Shut the door! Were you raised in a barn?* She and Talmadge used to laugh because he always said he could actually answer yes to that question. His family had built their barn first, and they'd lived there while they built the house, such as it was. In truth, his house was not much better than a barn.

"No, don't go," she heard Mrs. LaRue say. "I think Graham would like a visitor." She turned and began walking, expecting Leah to follow. Leah looked back at Talmadge, playing one of his songs without words on the car radio. When she got back in, she'd make him change the station.

She held up a finger to him, meaning, *I'll be back in a minute.* He would, she knew, wait for her. Then she closed the front door and followed.

Darcy

TUESDAY

The call came from Graham's boss down at the garage four days after he was arrested and ten minutes after Darcy'd found a printout of the girls' pictures from the town website stuck under Graham's mattress, a corner of the paper sticking out enough that she instinctively pulled it out to inspect it, then just as quickly shoved it back. But not before tears filled her eyes as her heart broke for her son and the weight he was carrying. She wanted to talk about what he was feeling, but he dodged her questions with a skill he could've inherited only from his father.

The tears had barely dried in her eyes when Rick Staley called to say that they were experiencing a downturn in business and wouldn't be needing Graham anymore. He sounded like a middle-school boy asking a girl out. He offered his apologies and hurried off the call, leaving Darcy holding the phone in shock, thankful that his classmate was there again to distract Graham so he wouldn't ask who it was. So she could work out how to deliver yet another blow. She heard laughter coming from the den—Graham's and Leah's. She tried to soak in the sound of her son's laughter, tried to recall how long it had been since she'd heard it.

When the phone rang again, she hoped it was Graham's boss calling back to tell her it was a mistake and he was sorry to have scared her needlessly. But of course it wasn't. Graham had lost his job because he was bad for business. No amount of time was going to change that, whether it was five minutes or five years.

She answered the call anyway and smiled when she heard Clay's voice. He'd been calling with some regularity, and their conversations had become a lifeline for her. He understood. He listened. And she listened to him. His wife had done something so despicable that she sometimes felt more sorry for him than she did for herself. They were quite a pair. A pair of pariahs.

"How are you?" he asked, as he always did. He usually called just before the dinner rush or late at night after everyone was gone. "What's going on today?" There was always something new for at least one of them. Some new legal development or rumor, some new hurt to process.

She lowered her voice and moved to the front room, away from the back den where Leah and Graham were. This was Leah's second day stopping by, and Darcy got the feeling her visits were going to be a regular thing. "Well, the girl is here again," she said.

"Leah?" he asked. The night before, he'd filled her in on what he knew of Leah. He knew Leah's dad, who was a bit stuffy but otherwise nice. He'd seen her around—she was the quiet type, he'd observed, pretty and sweet and a bit overwhelmed by the social strata of high school, yet desperate to figure it out. He'd seen her in the groups that gathered at the restaurant, taking it all in, learning how it worked. He said he recognized the look because he'd been much the same. Darcy admitted she'd never paid much attention.

"That's because you already had it figured out," he'd teased.

"Yeah, well, that didn't work out so well, did it?" she'd retorted, and they'd both laughed.

"Yes, Leah," she said now, and sighed. "She brought more assignments, and she's collecting the stuff he did today. I guess this is going to be a regular thing."

"Well, maybe it's good for them. They've both been through a lot. Maybe they're bonding over it."

"Mr. Chessman, did you just say *bonding*?" Darcy thought the word *bonding* was for Oprah and maternity books, not for middle-aged men who hailed from Worthy, Georgia.

"Hey," he said defensively, "I read."

She shook her head, though he couldn't see her. "Wonders never cease."

"Shut up," he said. And they both laughed, sounding not unlike the pair of teenagers in the other room.

"All I was trying to say was that maybe it's good for them to be able to talk about what happened, or to be together and not talk about it. She lost her best friends in that accident. And he's accused of causing it. There's a lot of . . . stuff there to wade through. I mean, *something* made her volunteer to do this."

"Yeah," she agreed, grateful she had him to talk to, to process things with. She and Tommy certainly couldn't talk about any of it. Lately all Tommy could focus on was wanting to show Graham how to shoot a gun in case anyone threatened him, which was just about the worst idea ever. If he wasn't prattling on about that, he was rehashing what the lawyer said. She felt Tommy moving further and further away from her, like that volleyball Tom Hanks lost at sea in *Cast Away*. Soon Tommy would be gone for good. In the meantime, Clay was the raft that kept her above the waves.

"Also I just now got a call from Rick Staley. He fired Graham," she said, tasting the words on her tongue, the reality of them settling in by saying them out loud.

"That sonofabitch," Clay breathed. "He was just in here at lunch. I shoulda punched him in the nose." He was quiet for a moment. "That son of a bitch," he repeated, this time drawing out each distinct word.

"Yeah," she agreed.

"Jeez, I'm sorry. Poor kid can't seem to catch a break, huh?"

"Yeah, and he's still got the entire football team talking about killing him. That's not going away, either." She felt herself begin to tremble. Sometimes it was too much. Sometimes she did think about heading to Florida, pointing her car southwest and driving as fast as she could, not unlike her son had done that night. But she'd be racing only herself.

"What if I gave him a job?" Clay asked, his voice jarring her thoughts from daydreaming about running away. "I mean," he added quickly, "when he's up to it, of course."

"You don't have to do that, Clay. Seriously. This is above and beyond the call of duty." She lay back and propped her feet on the wall, stared at her thighs, the slight stippling of the flesh where she'd gained weight. She lowered her legs.

"I can always use a busboy. It's not glamorous, but he'll make enough to put gas in his car." He caught himself referencing the car Graham no longer had. "Or whatever he needs money for," he quickly added.

"I'll run it by Graham," she said. She found herself smiling. A real smile, a reflex, not something she had to produce for someone else's sake. "That's really nice of you, Clay. I appreciate it."

She could almost hear him shrug. "It's no trouble at all. I'd actually like to have him around."

She started to say something about how nice it was having *him* around, but that might come across as flirty. Something the old Darcy would've said. Clay Chessman was very much a married man, with a mess on his hands. There was no place for flirtation or innuendo in whatever this was between them. There was simply this—one person helping another, someone willing to step in when everyone else had walked away.

Marglyn

Tuesday

From the kitchen window, she watched as Hale and Robert threw a baseball back and forth in the side yard, the white orb hurtling through the air again and again. She was ostensibly washing dishes, but what she was really doing was avoiding going out to join them. Lately she'd felt the pull of motherhood as it related to her surviving child. A better mother, she told herself, would not let this tragedy affect her relationship with her son.

But she was not a better mother. She was one who had to remind herself to smile at him, her lips exposing her teeth in a way that felt unnatural, wolfish. Today when she'd reached out to ruffle his hair, he'd pulled back in shock, leaving her to calculate the time since she'd last touched him. She had to do a better job.

She shut off the water and dried her hands, her feet moving toward the back door before her mind could tell them to stop. She walked outside and waved at them. "Can I play?" she asked, hoping her voice sounded as bright as she intended.

Both male heads swiveled around in shock. They looked from her to each other and back at her. "Mom." Robert spoke up first. "You don't have a glove." He waved his gloved hand in the air as if to clarify just what a glove was.

When she laughed, it was not on cue and it wasn't for Robert's benefit. Today was a beautiful fall day complete with mild temperatures, singing birds, and dappled light as the days ended earlier. She felt the tiniest bit of happiness bubble up inside, unforced and unexpected. Hale strolled over to her and handed her his glove. "Here, Mama," he said. As he pushed the glove onto her hand, he leaned forward and whispered, "Thank you."

He winked and hitched his thumb toward the kitchen, calling out to Robert, "Think I'll get a beer from the kitchen while you two have a go." She watched him leave, gauging whether his shoulders looked less slumped as he walked. Though he'd never said it, she knew her distance from Robert concerned him.

She turned back to Robert and held her now-gloved hand aloft. "OK, fire one in here!" she called, trying not to think of Mary Claire saying the very same thing not too long ago when she was the one throwing the ball with her little brother. Watching her oldest and youngest interact had always reassured her that, despite their differences and squabbles, they were a happy family. They were doing something right. And now she was doing something right, something healing. All it took was a borrowed glove and a few minutes of her time. She basked in Robert's laughter when she dropped the ball, called out taunts when she threw one and he missed, traded winks with Hale when he rejoined them.

"Time out!" Robert called. "I gotta go to the bathroom."

"Are you sure that's really why you're going inside? Or did I beat you down?" She could feel her blood pumping, her cheeks sore from smiling.

Robert laughed and shook his head, then walked inside, leaving Hale and her alone in the side yard. In front of them, she could see their long gravel driveway, Mary Claire's totaled car missing from its usual parking spot. Behind them, the swing set they'd bought for her fifth birthday sat empty, the swings moving as if a ghost child were playing. Their daughter would always be with them. But maybe that didn't have to be a bad thing.

"I know that wasn't easy for you," Hale said.

She shrugged. "I needed to do it."

Hale moved closer to her and put his arm around her shoulders. He planted a kiss on her head. "It was good for him. The normalcy."

She nodded. "For me, too."

They stood silently for a moment. She felt a breeze stir and inhaled the air, filling her lungs. Hale stared off at the driveway, and she knew he was thinking of Mary Claire, too.

"They were drinking that night," he said.

She nodded; she'd seen the bag of discarded beer cans poorly hidden in MC's room. She'd disposed of it as soon as possible, vowing to never mention it to anyone, lest it implicate the girls in the accident and taint their memories. Her daughter had expected to come home and bury the evidence in the big trash can outside. She'd expected to get away with it just like she always did. Life was hers for the taking, until life was taken from her.

The desire to scream, to wail, to thrash around, returned with a vengeance, and Marglyn exhaled all that fresh, clean air she'd taken in moments ago.

"I saw them," he said. "I was joking around with them that night, and I saw the beer cans. I saw them and I—" He broke off, and she watched as he closed his eyes to stave off tears. "I still let them go. I let them assure me Keary was the DD and it would be OK. I believed it would be because it always was."

She took a measured breath, trying to remember how it felt to laugh with Robert moments ago, to forget the grief she wore like an itchy burlap sack. She was too tired—emotionally and physically—to be angry with Hale over this confession, to blame him, because she'd already spent so much time blaming herself. She would not let this confession affect them, reduce them further. Because what did it matter? What did it change? To be angry with him now would not change his decisions in the past, nor hers. And so she said the only thing she could think to say. "Did you really think that?"

He looked away from the driveway for the first time, turning his gaze from the place their daughter disappeared down the last time and looking her full in the face with his red-rimmed eyes. "Did I really think what?"

"That everything was always OK?"

He smiled at her sadly and squeezed her shoulders. "Of course I did. Because it was."

"But she and I fought so much, and she was always running off with her friends and acting like she was too good for us. Like we were—" She caught herself. "Like *I was* an embarrassment to her." She wrapped her arms around herself and turned toward Hale, resting her head on his shoulder.

The back door opened and Robert emerged, pulling on his glove, a ready expression on his face. "Mom!" he called. "It's Dad's turn!"

She gave a little ironic laugh at Robert's choice of words. It was Dad's turn to look for someone to blame for what happened and decide that that someone was him. She pulled off the glove, smelling the leather and sweat and dirt. Hale took it and pulled it onto his own hand.

"I wasn't worthy of her," she said.

He gave her a sad smile. "None of us was," he said. "She was too good for this world."

"Is that how you see it?" she asked, surprised.

"It's the only way I can." He indicated their waiting son with a nod of his head, and, with an apologetic look, left her staring at the driveway, her eyes searching the horizon for a car that was never going to return.

The doorbell rang while Hale and Robert were still outside, soaking up the last bit of sunlight. Marglyn went to answer it with trepidation. She wasn't in the mood for company, not after the tumult of the afternoon. She hoped it wasn't her mother-in-law come to commiserate. She tugged the door open to reveal a familiar face, but not the one she'd expected. Ginny.

The two of them blinked at each other like people who'd once shared something intimate but were now embarrassed about it. She took in Ginny's attire—the too-tight jeans, the plain white tank top that had been washed so much it was nearly gray instead of white—and an unfortunate new haircut. She'd warned the girl about letting her older sister (who was literally a beauty-school dropout, like the song said) near her head with a pair of scissors. But Ginny was eager to please and therefore easily persuaded to go along with things she should not do. Without Marglyn in her life to help her, who knew what would happen?

Marglyn pressed her fingernails into her palm, the pain a jolt to her senses. She could not get sucked back into this girl's world. It was not her job to save her. That mentality had gotten them to right where they stood now: with Ginny on the other side of her front door, shifting awkwardly, a shopping bag dangling from her fingers, the nails painted an opalescent color that caught the sunlight and refracted it onto Marglyn's cardigan when she lifted the bag.

"I brought you these," she said. The bag dangled between them for a few seconds as Marglyn registered the store name printed on the side, remembering the cashier folding the clothes and slipping them inside it as Ginny waited for her to pay and accepted the bag, her body literally vibrating with excitement over the purchases. Marglyn was willing to bet the clothes had not been touched again since that night.

"Ginny, I bought you those," she said. "You don't—" She stopped. "You don't have to give them back," she finished.

"I don't want them," Ginny said. She looked down at the ground, suddenly absorbed in the pattern of bricks in the stoop. "You can probably take them back still. Get your money back," she said, drawing a line with the toe of her flip-flops. They were the plain, cheap kind that they sold for three dollars at the Dollar General, the same kind Marglyn had worn at that age. She could still remember the blisters they rubbed between her toes. It was too cold for such shoes.

Ginny looked up. "I got plenty of clothes," she said. There was a defiance in her voice, a pride. Next thing out of her mouth would be, *I don't need no charity.* And Marglyn would have to refrain from correcting her double negative. All things she never had to teach her own daughter.

She dug her nails into her palms again. But this time the pain only brought back a memory: Ginny walking in the cold rain along the very road her daughter was killed on, Marglyn pulling alongside her and asking, "Do you need a ride?" when it was obvious that of course she did. No one in her right mind wanted to be walking in that weather. That had been the beginning. And the night of the accident had been the end.

Behind them, a car horn sounded, and they both looked up, startled. Marglyn had been so taken by Ginny's presence that she'd not noticed the old, faded truck. She locked eyes with the driver, a sullen-looking young man with hair as greasy as Marglyn's, a lock falling down over his eyes so that it made him look more shifty. He took a long drag from a cigarette and flung it out the open window, the same defiant look on his face as she'd just seen on Ginny's. She watched the smoke from the butt float up into the air from its resting place on her driveway. *Oh, Ginny, not this boy.*

Marglyn knew this boy; she'd known many like him before she graduated high school. And she'd avoided his millstone around her neck, landing herself here in this house, with this life, instead of the one Ginny was headed toward as fast as she could. She could see it all so clearly, Ginny with a couple of dirty kids in clothes that never quite fit, living in a trailer with never enough money, repeating the same life in an endless cycle of desperate humanity. Marglyn had meant to change that, to stop what she guessed now was the inevitable, the circle of redneck life.

"You're such a do-gooder, Mom," Mary Claire had said just days before she died. But Mary Claire hadn't meant it as a compliment. That was after the disastrous dinner. Had it all been hopeless from the outset, and Marglyn was just the last one to see it? Even Ginny knew it.

"I gotta go," Ginny said, hitching her free thumb over her shoulder to indicate the boy waiting for her. She did not say who he was, but she didn't have to. She shook the bag a little for emphasis. "Here."

"I don't—I don't have any need for those," Marglyn said help-lessly. The thought of going back to that store and answering the bored cashier's series of questions: *Reason for return? Well, my daughter was killed the same night I bought these—she might've been hit at the exact moment you swiped my card, actually—and the girl I was with decided she didn't want them, after all, for obvious reasons.* Polite smile. Wait for the bank to acknowledge the transaction so she could flee. No, if Ginny didn't want the clothes, she'd just donate them to the church. Surely there was some mission that could put them to good use.

"I wish you'd keep them," she said. "I mean it. It was—"

Ginny put up her hand. "I know, Mrs. Miner. It was your gift to me. You did a nice thing. But I just . . . I can't wear them. They're pretty things and all. It's just—" Her voice broke. "We both know you shouldn't have been with me that night. You should have been with her. And maybe if you were, she—" She looked up at Marglyn's face with desperation in her own. She dropped the bag at Marglyn's feet. "She might still be here," she finished. "I'm sorry."

She turned on her heel and fled, her feet kicking up gravel as she flung herself into the truck that was neither tan nor gold, though at some point it must've been some color. Everything was something lovely once, something to behold. It was only after the world got to it that it became too worn to appreciate anymore.

The boy pulled forward and turned the car around violently, spinning gravel in an arc behind the tires, leaving a little rut. Later she would have Robert cover up the marks with the shovel, erasing the evidence that they'd ever been there, as if it were that easy. She pulled her cardigan tighter around herself even though it was not really cold.

She watched the car disappear, making the same perilous turn the girls had made that night. But there was no screeching of brakes, no sound of impact. Only the sound of a motor revving as it strained to go fast, faster, fastest. Marglyn reached down for the bag Ginny had left behind, carrying it into her daughter's room. She left it on Mary Claire's bed like an offering.

Leah

In the halls at school, she could tell things were going back to normal. Not that people were forgetting about Brynne, Mary Claire, and Keary, exactly. (They would never be forgotten. The girls were legends now, made immortal by being mortal.) The students were just resuming life, thinking about test grades and college applications and crushes instead of death and tragedy and scandal.

Which was fine by Leah. She wanted to go back to normal, or find a new normal. Her life had turned upside down so much that night—to degrees no one could fathom—that in the aftermath she found herself at school but not in school, there but apart. For the first time in a long time, she found herself considering homeschooling again. At least at home she didn't feel like she didn't fit. Except that wasn't exactly true, either. She thought of her mother that morning, her searching eyes looking for the truth about that night but still resisting asking. She could feel her building up to it and, in that regard, school was her escape.

At lunch, instead of sidling up to the other table of cheerleaders as she was expected to do, she found an empty table in the back, near the trash cans, and buried her nose in her book of Emily Dickinson poems, the book distracting her from the smell of rotting food and sour milk that wafted in her direction. That book had become her constant companion, her talisman designed to keep inquiring classmates at bay.

If she ever saw Mrs. Chessman again, she intended to thank her and offer to pay her something for it. She couldn't possibly give it back now. She'd taken to scribbling in it, little notes about the lines she liked best, the human truths she found buried in the stanzas. The book had become as personal as a diary.

She had looked it up online: a replacement copy cost about thirty dollars. She had enough money saved up for when the time came. But sometimes she wondered if the time would ever come—if Mrs. Chessman would ever come back, would ever even think of the book of poems she'd left behind on what was probably the worst day of her life. Leah knew about worst days of your life. She knew that things once held dear could easily be discarded.

She felt Webb Hart approaching more than she saw or heard him. The air around him changed—that had always been the case, even before the night of the accident. But now the atmosphere seemed charged whenever he got within ten feet of her. She could almost see the waves shimmying through the air, a current of truth and lies intermixing and undulating, stealing the breath from her lungs until she could regain composure. She held on to the fact that eventually it would get easier. Hadn't she heard that from countless well-meaning people in regards to the loss of her friends? It had to apply to other kinds of losses as well.

She smelled his cologne as he ambled past, carrying his trash to the trash cans, a demigod reduced to human mundanity. She did not raise her eyes. She did not dare risk eye contact. Though once he'd tried to catch her eye, at one of the funerals, wearing a sympathetic mask, as though he were a real, feeling person with an actual soul. She'd felt his eyes imploring her to look in his direction, but she'd turned and walked away. Beside him, Ian and Seth had elbowed him and jeered. "She blew you off, man." Hatred for all three of them surged through her, molten lava replacing her blood.

She looked up once he'd passed her and it was safe to take her nose out of the book. She glanced at the huge clock that hung on the opposite wall, ticking away the lunch hour. She had a few more minutes to read before she would throw her trash away and head to apparel class, which her mom said was just the same as the sewing class she'd once taken, only with a fancier name. Leah had no illusions of being a seamstress—she sucked at it, in fact—she just had to have an elective, and the thought of making something she could touch sounded better than yearbook, where she would've spent her time creating a book extolling the virtues of a school that was increasingly holding less and less appeal for her.

She glanced back down at her book when something caught her eye: Webb Hart cornered by a girl, a freshman she recognized from the JV squad tryouts. Leah had planned to be a JV cheerleader before Brynne and Mary Claire plucked her and Keary from the squad and moved them up to varsity. Being designated varsity cheerleader while still a sophomore, she would later learn, was every bit as momentous as Diane Riggle being crowned Miss Georgia. Back then she'd felt lucky, singled out, blessed. She'd felt worthy. But that invisible crown Brynne and MC had placed on her head had somehow become a target.

Leah watched the exchange between the girl and Webb with a mixture of curiosity and horror, wondering if anyone else was seeing what she was seeing. It seemed the girl had chosen a place toward the back, away from other eyes, a moment to get him alone when his entourage of admirers and henchmen didn't surround him. And then she'd struck. She watched as the girl pinged between tears and anger, one minute wagging her finger, the next wiping her eyes. Webb seemed to shrink a little more with each minute, looking around for someone to come along and rescue him, but no one did. For that reason, Leah was enjoying the scene.

Finally, of course, Ian Stone swaggered along, putting his arm around the girl and leading her away from Webb as Seth Bishop leaned over to Webb and whispered something in his ear. Something they both laughed hard at. But in the middle of the laughter, Seth glanced over and saw Leah watching them. The laughter died on his lips, and he waved at Webb to follow him out of the cafeteria.

Empowered, she shut the book and dropped it into her backpack, then quickly gathered her trash and tossed it. Then she followed the path Ian had taken when he led the girl away, out the door and onto the sidewalk outside that connected one building to another. Sure enough, she saw them together, standing farther away and out of the path of other students. Ian was leaning over the girl, a giant compared with her, his stature imposing. Leah stepped back into the shadows and waited until he patted the girl's shoulder "good little girl" style and walked away. She searched the archives of her mind for the girl's name, then stepped forward tentatively. When she called out, her voice was hoarse with something she could only guess was fear. She was getting involved, something she hadn't intended to do.

The bell rang. The girl didn't hear her; she started walking away, head down. "Sidney," Leah called again, her voice stronger this time.

Sidney Riggle—who was Diane Riggle's cousin and just as pretty in her own way—turned to search for who had called to her. Leah took in the strawberry-blonde hair, straight and thick, hanging like curtains on both sides of her flawless face. Her china-blue eyes were red rimmed and swollen, the tears pulling ahead of the anger in the emotional race she'd just finished. And yet, as she blinked curiously at Leah, she was still stunning.

In a few years she would be of Brynne and Mary Claire's status. Waves of students would part when she walked the halls. People would make concessions for her with a single raise of one eyebrow. But she did not know that yet. Webb Hart must've known, though, a talent scout for the underrated but promising underclassmen, with a knack for getting to them before anyone else.

Leah waved her arm, indicating for Sidney to come over to where she stood, in the spot where she'd taken refuge, out of the way of the thundering hordes of students hustling to class, out of the way of any administrator's sight. But she could probably get away with being late, or just not going, to class right now. The loss of her friends was her get-out-of-jail-free card, and she intended to play it for the rest of the year.

She watched as Sidney looked in the direction she should be heading if she were going to make it to class. Then, with a sigh, she tossed one panel of hair over her shoulder and walked to Leah, looking like she was marching to the gallows. *She must think I'm going to take up for Webb,* Leah thought. *How sad that she's coming over here anyway.* Sidney wanted to be popular, which meant Sidney had already learned the rules. Being summoned by an upperclassman with even a modicum of popularity trumped being on time for class.

Though Leah was only a grade ahead of Sidney, she was a varsity cheerleader, and in this town that meant something. It meant when you waved someone over, he or she came. Even if you'd spent the last several weeks avoiding any and all social contact and spent your lunchtime reading poetry. Even when every afternoon you went to the home of the boy everyone in school hated, and you stayed a little longer with each visit. Even when the year before, no one in the school had known you'd existed. Brynne and Mary Claire had changed everything for her with just a nod from their perfectly coiffed heads.

She remembered the first time they'd ever spoken to her. It had been the summer before, late one afternoon at the town pool. She'd gone with Keary after cheerleading practice, anxious to cool off from the heat, to sit with her newfound friend and talk about the other girls, the hottest styles, the best music, whatever it was that kids her age talked about. She was learning. She'd blown off Talmadge, lying to him that her mom wouldn't let her go out after practice. But he'd driven by the pool, idling outside just long enough for her to see him see her there.

Just after he'd left, Mary Claire and Brynne had approached, materializing out of nowhere, like fairy godmothers. Neither Keary nor Leah had seen them enter the pool, which was odd. Because people noticed when they came or went from anywhere. Yet there they were, in the tiniest bikinis Leah had ever seen. They had switched tops and bottoms so that they looked like two halves of a whole, which was the way that she would always see them.

"Sure is hot today," one of them—later Keary said it was Brynne, Leah insisted it was Mary Claire, both agreed it really didn't matter—said.

"Yeah," Keary and Leah replied dumbly, nodding like a couple of bobbleheads. Leah could feel the sun beating down on her shoulders, beginning to sear the skin; she'd neglected to put on any sunscreen. As soon as they walked away, she told herself, she'd go put it on. But they never walked away.

They stood and talked, as if she and Keary were interesting, as if they were funny, as if they mattered. And Leah, afraid to break the spell if she moved, continued to stand there. Eventually they found a table, and Keary bought them all sodas from the drink machine. And they drank and talked, and something that felt like friendship—the kind she'd only dreamed of having when she dreamed of attending high school—began to happen. Brynne and Mary Claire both wore mirrored sunglasses, and Leah studied her reflection in their lenses, seeing nothing special there, wondering what they could possibly see in her. Before they knew it, Keary's mom arrived to pick them up.

As they got up to leave, Brynne reached out to touch her, and Leah startled. But Brynne meant only to touch her shoulder, the burned skin whitening under the pressure of her finger, then quickly returning to a shocking pink color. "Ouch," Brynne said, then wiggled her fingers goodbye. Leah wondered if they'd ever speak to her again.

Later, she knew, she would be lectured for being irresponsible. She would shiver from the burn in spite of the heat, wince as the shower water hit her tender skin, pop ibuprofen just to make it through practice. Her mother sermonized on the dangers of skin cancer, but Leah hardly listened. Skin cancer was one of those someday things. And didn't she know no one was guaranteed a someday?

Maybe she would grow up, be an old lady, and get a melanoma removed from her back, one that started on a day at the pool when she was fifteen years old and she let herself get burned in order to become popular. Or maybe something else would kill her, just like it had killed the other three girls who had sat with her at the table that day, drinking Dr Peppers without a care in the world, thinking they had their whole lives ahead of them.

Now, months out from that fateful summer day, she moved farther into a copse of trees. There was a picnic table where some of the stoners sometimes sat and ate lunch, when they bothered to stay around for lunch. "Yes?" Sidney asked when she got close to Leah. Her voice shook a little. She cleared her throat, and Leah couldn't determine if it was leftover nerves from her encounter with Webb and Ian or if Leah's summons was making her nervous. "Did you need something?"

Sidney toed a clump of grass with her red cowboy boot, rumored to have been bought in actual Texas. If things were different—if Leah hadn't made varsity—then maybe she and Sidney would've become friends. Maybe they'd be hanging out after school today, talking about who they had a crush on and trading clothes. Maybe Leah would know just where those boots came from. Maybe she'd even borrow them to wear from time to time.

She came close to making up something else to say to Sidney, something less confrontational. She didn't have to do this. She could ask her where she got those boots, ask her to help with a project, ask her if she wanted to hang out sometime. Anything but what she'd called her over to ask. Then she remembered something she'd read at lunch, the words of Emily Dickinson: *If I can stop one heart from breaking I shall not live in vain.* Her friends were gone, wiped off the face of the earth in one explosive instant. She had remained behind, living in their stead. That had to mean something, she decided. Though she had planned her own funeral, she was very much alive.

"I saw you with Webb Hart just now," she said.

Sidney took a step back, shock crossing her face. "I'm sorry," she said, a reflex. Apologize first; then figure out what you did later. "Is he your . . . boyfriend?" Leah could see Sidney trying to puzzle out what her endgame was. Was she friend or foe? Had Sidney crossed some line she hadn't known existed? There were as many lines in this school as a sheet of graph paper. The whole place should've been drawn on a grid.

"No," Leah said. She gave a little scoffing laugh. "Not even close."

The two girls blinked at each other. For a moment, Leah thought of brushing things aside. She could say something light but meaningful. Something like, *Just be careful with that one.* Then she could amble away, leaving Sidney to chew on what she'd said and make of it whatever she would.

"I have a feeling I know what you were talking to him about." She made her spine straight, pretended she was made of iron when she felt like spaghetti. She was suddenly very, very tired. She would call her mom after this, ask to go home early. But then she thought of Graham, waiting on his couch for her. Graham, who always had a smile for her even though she knew it still hurt him to smile. Graham was her friend, which made no sense considering what had happened. But he was. Other than Talmadge, he was the best friend she had.

"You don't know anything," Sidney said, mustering up whatever had been inside her when she confronted Webb. Calling it back to the surface like a tired athlete who was just hoping for some time on the bench.

"I think I do," Leah replied. She tried to make her face look kind. Brynne once told her she had a resting bitch face and that she should smile more. But smiling in this instance did not seem appropriate. She thought of one word as she looked at Sidney, poor little Sidney who just wanted to belong.

She tried to think of the one thing Sidney needed most. The one thing she herself needed. Leah held on to the word as she looked at Sidney; she tried to emanate it, to feel it shining out of her skin like rays of light. She hoped Sidney felt it. She hoped there was love all around her and that Sidney could feel it just as sure as the November breeze that had picked up, crisp and cold as it ruffled Sidney's lovely hair.

"I know about Webb's plan, and I have a feeling you were a part of it." She reached out, intending to rest her hand on Sidney's forearm as a comforting gesture, but Sidney dodged it like Leah had thrust a knife in her direction.

"I have no idea what you're talking about," Sidney said. She glanced around to see if anyone was watching. "I was upset about something that I heard Webb said about one of my friends, and I was taking up for her." She forced a laugh. "You know how they're always saying mean stuff about people."

Leah scrutinized her, as if she could determine whether Sidney was telling the truth just by looking at her. She decided she couldn't—that this girl could be telling the truth about Webb and Leah could've read too much into what she saw. Because she wanted to.

"Sorry," she managed to say. "Guess it was my mistake." She leaned down to pick up her backpack from where she'd laid it on the picnic table. She hoped Sidney would just turn and walk away.

"It's none of your business anyway," Sidney added, still standing there even though she was free to go.

Leah nodded, feeling stupid for getting involved. She shouldn't have stuck her neck out. She needed to learn her lesson. What business was it of hers to worry about Sidney Riggle's broken heart when she had one of her own? What did Emily Dickinson know anyway? "Sorry," she apologized again.

But Sidney wasn't through. She crossed her arms over her chest. "You know, everyone's talking about you. How you've gone a little crazy since the accident. I said they were being hard on you, but now I'm not so sure." The stronger Sidney got, the weaker Leah felt. She leaned back on the picnic table, right on the spot where some clever idiot had carved, WORTHY GIRLS = NOT WORTH IT.

"Maybe I have," she mumbled. She stared down at the carvings marring the table's surface, studying them as if there'd be a test later. She thought perhaps she was missing a test right then. She struggled to recall when the teacher had said it was exactly. Her mind was filled with too many other things.

"Well you'd better not go spreading your crazy talk about me to anyone else, you hear? My stuff with Webb? It's my stuff. Mine." Sidney jabbed herself in the chest, hard. Her face jutted forward, her neck muscles strained against her skin like they wanted to come out of her throat. Her creamy, perfect skin had changed to a mottled red. Leah imagined this was what Webb had seen when Sidney confronted him.

"I'd better not hear about me getting mixed up with any crazy ideas you have in that head of yours." Sidney blinked a few times, swallowed. As soon as she left, Leah decided, she was going to walk to Graham's house. Or call Talmadge to come get her. She would not stay on school property one second longer.

She nodded again, anxious to get Sidney away from her. "OK, Sidney," she said. "I was wrong."

Sidney tugged on her own backpack, cinching it up needlessly. "You're damn straight you were wrong." Her voice broke on the word *wrong*. She looked away, but Leah saw her swipe at a tear. "You were wrong about everything," she said. She looked back at Leah. There was something . . . familiar in her face. The two girls stared at each other for less than a second before Sidney broke the gaze and stalked away. Leah stood for a long time after she left, trying to place who Sidney had just reminded her of. It took her several minutes to realize who it was. The girl she'd seen in the mirror that morning. The one with frightened eyes desperate to hide the truth.

Darcy

THURSDAY

.

She heard the noise like in a horror movie: a twig snapping, then footsteps, heavy, coming closer and closer to her window. She sat up in bed, moving around blindly for her phone on her nightstand, feeling alone and exposed without a man in bed next to her. When Tommy left she'd never been scared to be alone in the house, just lonely. Worthy, after all, was a safe place—or it had been before. Something had shifted the night of the accident. Something unknowable yet permanent, as if they'd opened the door of the town and invited the devil right on in.

She shuddered and hit the last number dialed. He answered on the first ring, though it was beyond the middle of the night, much later than their usual late-night talks. "Darcy?" he asked. "What is it?"

In spite of herself, she thrilled at his concern. And yet, as she started to give voice to her fear, she felt stupid, silly. She listened for a moment, to see if there were more noises outside her window before answering. "Darcy?" he asked again. "You there?"

"Yeah, sorry. I guess I had some sort of dream that freaked me out, then I woke up and thought I heard noises and . . . with everything going on with Graham and the football players' threats, I got spooked.

I'm sorry." She laughed a little to lighten the mood. But outside, the darkness seemed pervasive, seeping into the cracks and filling the house.

"Do you need me to come over there?" he asked. She heard him moving around, as if he were already up, putting on pants, maybe running a comb through his hair. She liked the way he wore it a little longer than most of the men in town, who tended toward buzz cuts. His hair was a symbol, a lingering reminder that he'd gotten out, been other places, been shaped by a place beyond Worthy. Sometimes she had to refrain from reaching out and running her hands through it.

"No," she said. But at the same time, she thought she heard the noise again, her voice not quite drowning it out. "Wait a minute," she added, trying to listen.

"I'm on my way," he said, and ended the call. She crawled out from under her covers, putting her feet on the cold floor. She was sleeping in a T-shirt and nothing else, so she quietly pulled a running bra from her drawer, a pair of sweatpants. She tiptoed around without turning on any lights, hoping that she wouldn't let whoever was out there—if there was anyone out there at all—know that she was awake and aware. Once dressed, she brushed her teeth by the glow of the night-light she kept on in the bathroom, ran a brush through her hair. Then she went to check on Graham.

She found him sitting up on the couch, hunched over his phone, his fingers moving across the tiny keyboard, texting with God knew who at this time of night. He looked up when she entered the room. "I heard a noise, Mom," he said. He pointed to the large sliding glass door in the den. "There was someone on the deck." Though his voice was deeper, and he was working hard to keep the fear at bay, she heard what was underneath it—the small, scared voice of her little boy. She went over and sat down beside him. She patted his leg. She was about to tell him she'd called someone when he piped up. "I texted Dad, and he was up. He said he's on his way."

She blinked at her son in the darkness, his eyes so like her own in shape and size. People used to say how pretty he was as a baby, which always made Tommy mad. "My son's not pretty," he'd say, which irrationally hurt her feelings, as if that meant she was not pretty, either.

"You called your dad?" she asked, slow to take in what Graham had said. "And he's . . . coming here? Now?"

Graham nodded. "He was worried, Mom. He said these guys mean business. He said we're not safe. I was just about to come get you, but now that you're up . . ." He shrugged. "I guess we can wait for him together." She said nothing in response, merely nodded, patted his leg, and leaned back on the couch to wait for Tommy and Clay to come to her rescue, in the wee hours of the morning, most likely arriving at the exact same time.

◆　◆　◆

Clay arrived first, which Darcy tried not to interpret as symbolic. He parked his car and walked the perimeter of the yard before approaching the house. She saw his white T-shirt prowling the backyard, and her breath caught in her throat. "Is that . . . Dad?" Graham, still beside her, asked.

"No," she said. "It's Clay."

"That dude who said I could work at Chessman's when I got better?" he asked.

How like a teenager to filter information through how it fit in his world, forgetting altogether that there were other ways people fit, other meanings they held in other lives. "Yes, that dude," she answered, a little smile crossing her face for a moment. "I called him when I heard the noise from my room."

Graham looked at her as though she had betrayed him. "You heard it, too?" he asked. "You didn't tell me that." Beside her, his leg started to jiggle. She reached out and stilled it.

"I didn't want to alarm you further."

"You know what that means, don't you?" he asked. Beneath her hand, she could feel involuntary movement, the muscles inside his leg still trembling even though he'd tried to still them, tried to master his fear.

"It's OK," she said. "We're safe in here. Clay's here, and Dad's coming. Whoever it was—or wasn't," she quickly added, "has certainly run off by now."

He mumbled something she couldn't understand in response.

"What, honey?" she asked.

He shook his head. "Nothing."

She stood up and moved toward the sliding glass door, intending to open it and call out to Clay across the yard. "No, honey, what did you say?"

Graham paused but then answered. "I said, 'But they'll be back.'"

Instead of tugging the door open as intended, she let go of the handle and moved instinctively toward her son, her mouth forming words of argument, of protection, promises of safety. But at that moment she heard behind her a deep voice yelling, another deep voice responding, and the unmistakable sound of gunfire.

She turned back, forgetting that she hadn't actually opened the door, and ran smack into the glass, her body making impact, then ricocheting back. Graham flew off the couch as if he'd not been sidelined by an injury. The sight of him coming to her aid was oddly comforting, her stunned brain stuttering out the thought—*just look at him move.* He grabbed onto her. "Mom? Mom? Are you OK?"

With no time to spare, she shrugged him off and went back to the door, this time tugging on the handle to open it so she could get out. She felt blood trickle down the side of her face and reached out to wipe it away. Her head throbbing from the impact with the glass, she crossed the deck, calling the two men's names: "Clay! Tommy! Clay! Tommy!"

Her heart pounded in her ears as she walked down the steps to the yard, willing her eyes to adjust to the darkness quickly so she could see.

"Over here," one of them said.

Movement caught her eye, two figures in white on the edge of the yard, near the wooded part of their property. One seemed to be kneeling, the other still standing. She strained her eyes to see more clearly as she drew closer, looking for a dark splotch of blood on the white T-shirts they both wore. But she could see nothing.

On the deck, Graham called out, "Mom? Dad? Are you guys OK?"

Tommy didn't answer him, so she did. She wiped away another trickle of blood. Then wiped her hand on her sweatpants. In the darkness, the blood appeared black against the gray. She hoped it came out. They were her most comfortable sweatpants, the ones she'd worn for years and hoped they'd never wear out. They'd once been Tommy's, fitting her loose and comfortable, like a hug from an item of clothing.

"Go back inside, Graham," she called out. "Everything's fine." Though she didn't know if it was fine.

She came upon the two men, both huffing and puffing, still posturing, holding fast to their manhood, their self-held images of tough guys, of rescuers. They'd both come running. But had they both come running for her? Clay, yes. But Tommy? He was likely there for Graham.

"Everything's fine," Clay said. He was the one standing.

"Easy for you to say," Tommy replied. He was the one kneeling, but as Darcy arrived on the scene, he began the process of standing up. It was not an easy maneuver for him, with both knees badly damaged from years of football. She heard the popping noises of protest as he endeavored to get to his feet. He looked at her and pointed at Clay. "He shot at me." He looked every bit like a hurt little boy on the playground telling on another child. She had to stifle a laugh.

Clay held his hand up, which was, incidentally, still holding the gun. "You ran at me without telling me who you were. I was here looking for an intruder."

Tommy puffed up—she watched him do it, like one of those lizards Graham used to be fascinated by. He widened his stance and stared Clay down. "I'd like to know why you were at *my* house looking for anything." He turned to Darcy like he'd caught her in the act. But the act of what? He'd moved out more than a year ago. He'd shacked up with Angie Woodall. His house? He had some nerve.

"I asked him to," she said, enjoying it. Let Tommy think there was something between them; let him think Clay had been in her bed when the noise occurred. He deserved the torment, if it would torment him at all.

"She called me." Clay filled in the gap a bit too quickly. She'd planned to let Tommy stew. "When she heard the noise."

"Well, *our son* called me," Tommy shot back.

"It's nice you both came," she said. She felt the blood again and raised her hand to wipe it away. Seeing it, Clay reached out to her, forgetting the gun was still in his hand.

Tommy stepped forward. "Easy there, fella," he said, pushing away Clay's hand. Chastised, Clay stepped back, his hand held up like a man surrendering. Then Tommy stepped in.

"What happened, darlin'?" he asked. She knew this man, could measure the sincerity of his words by the arch of an eyebrow, the inhalation of a breath. And that word, *darlin'*. He'd called her that early in their relationship, when he'd held her very life in his hands but she'd not known yet that he could close his hands and snuff that life right out. The word took her back, back to love and wanting and trust and innocence, to all the good things they once were.

"I . . . hit my head," she said. She waved her hand in the air as if it were nothing. "It's just a scratch." But she knew scratches didn't bleed like that. She could feel the air hitting the opening where the skin just over her eye had split when it encountered the glass. She had butterfly bandages in the house. In raising a boy, she had learned how to bind up wounds like a pro, though it was likely this would leave a scar. She welcomed it.

From behind them came Clay's voice. "We should go inside and see how bad it is." She nodded and began to walk. The two men followed her, and she registered how odd all this was.

"I'm glad no one got shot," she said, making polite conversation as they walked. "I thought for sure I was going to find someone laid out and bleeding."

The two of them laughed a little in response, the nervous laughter of people who find themselves in an awkward situation and want to get the hell out of it just as fast as they could. Later she would look in the mirror and press a cotton ball soaked in peroxide to her wound as she opened the butterfly bandage with her teeth, thinking all the while that the only one who was bleeding was her.

Marglyn

Thursday

She hung up the phone and looked out the window, noting that the weather matched her mood perfectly—cold and rainy, which inevitably, unwittingly, reminded her of Ginny. The first time she saw her, the girl was walking down Main Street—the very same street her daughter would be killed on months later—in the freezing-cold rain, wearing baggy sweatpants, a tank top, and no shoes. Her hair was matted to her head by the rain, obscuring her face, and she was sort of shuffling along, hugging the edge of the road as if it were a high-wire and she had to keep her balance lest she fall off. She never did get to the bottom of why the girl wasn't wearing shoes.

Marglyn had been driving home from somewhere, fiddling with the radio dial; she'd looked up and seen someone walking there in the nick of time, barely avoiding hitting her. Now she wondered: Did that one act—avoiding killing that teenage girl—lead to the death of her daughter somehow? It was the butterfly effect, the kind of round and round thinking that could make you crazy. And yet, she couldn't help but think that somehow all of this was tied to Ginny. That their lives had been inexorably changed the day she pulled over onto the shoulder, rolled her window down in the icy rain, and asked one simple question: Do you need a ride?

Ginny had peered into the car skeptically, her eyes darting around as if someone might be hiding there, ready to harm her, as if this were some sort of trap. She had the haunted, hunted look of someone who, at best, is used to being forgotten, and, at worst, is used to being a victim. Marglyn recognized that look all too well; she knew that the two of them were "of a pair"; Marglyn in the past, Ginny in the present. In that instant, she was certain she would help this girl. She just didn't know how yet.

When Ginny saw she was just a middle-aged mom in an otherwise empty car, she'd visibly relaxed, a look of relief filling her face as she nodded yes, she would very much like a ride. She got into the car, dripping cold water all over the seat. She mumbled an apology, her eyes studying her feet, her lips barely parting to speak. She hugged herself, and that was familiar to Marglyn, too, hugging yourself when no one else would. She wished for a towel, a blanket, something to hand this cold, wet girl in her front seat.

"Is there somewhere I can take you?" she asked instead. She reached for the button to crank up the heat, though she was plenty warm already. Warm air filled the car, making her feel slightly nauseated, but she saw the way the girl leaned forward, lapping up the heat like a dog at a water bowl. The girl shrugged and would not meet her eyes.

"I'm locked out of my house," she said. Marglyn had to strain to hear her. Another car drove by, blaring its horn at her for being on the shoulder, though she'd pulled far enough off the road; she was hardly obstructing traffic flow. Some people were so impatient, so angry all the time for no good reason. Marglyn had thought of her father then, his blowups; his tirades; his red, red face. She'd been out in the cold herself back then—many times—with nowhere to go. Until she met Hale, she'd never really had anywhere she considered home.

"Then why don't I take you home?" she'd asked, the offer an impulse that, at the time, had felt like the only thing to do. "To my house," she added. This girl had no shoes; she was soaking wet. She couldn't exactly drop her at the little public library in town, couldn't take her to a restaurant for a hot meal, couldn't just leave her at the convenience store. What if she were picked up by one of those sex traffickers? Marglyn had seen a story about that just this morning. It was a national epidemic, the reporter had said.

No, the best thing to do was take this girl home; find her some warm, dry clothes; let her have a shower; feed her something; let her use the phone to find someone to let her into her house. She would do the right thing, then she would feel good about it like she always did when she did a good deed. She'd even involve the children when they got home from school, which would be soon. Maybe Mary Claire would be in a good mood, would offer to braid the girl's hair, invite her to hang out in her room. Maybe the girl would stay for dinner, and the five of them would talk around the table, and the girl would get a glimpse that life could be this way, instead of the way she'd always known.

But of course none of that happened. Robert had outright asked, "Who's *she*?" so rudely that Marglyn took his phone away for one week. (At his age, he shouldn't even have a phone, but Hale was indulgent.) Mary Claire had come home angry over some fight with her boyfriend, Ian. She'd locked herself in her room and refused to even say hello to poor Ginny, who was visibly uncomfortable, sitting perched on the edge of the couch wearing Marglyn's sweatpants and a hoodie, her feet encased in a pair of slipper socks one of the kids had once given her for a gift. Marglyn had never seen any of those clothes again, and sometimes, idly, she'd wondered where they were, wondered if Ginny had kept them or tossed them out.

In the end, she'd driven Ginny home to a run-down trailer as darkness set in, making dinner late and her family even grumpier. The dreamy scenario hadn't played out the way she'd envisioned when she'd rescued Ginny from the rain, the cold, the lurking sex traffickers. Marglyn had been—was—a dreamer, a romantic idealist whose inner spring of hope sprang eternal. Even now, with her daughter dead, her family shattered, and the town in turmoil, she could feel it there—that little light of hope, hardly more than a dying ember but still there. In the days following Ginny's visit to return the clothes, she turned it all over and over in her mind, trying to make sense of all that had happened, not so much wondering what could've gone differently but just what she was supposed to do now.

◆　◆　◆

For a moment when she awoke, she thought that Mary Claire had really been there talking to her. She looked around to find her same old bedroom with the wedding quilt her grandmother had made covering the bed, the rocking chair she rocked her babies in in the corner, her husband sleeping next to her. But down the hall, she knew, she would not find her daughter. It had been only a dream.

She was having one every few days now, and she couldn't help but think that it really was MC, visiting her in the only way she had left—through the last portal available, Marglyn's own subconscious.

Though it went against everything she'd ever learned in church about the afterlife, she couldn't help but hope it was true. She would take a visit with her daughter any way she could get it. There were, after all, things she still wanted to say. And each time she had one of her dreams, she hoped that she could finally say them. But Mary Claire in death was a lot like Mary Claire in life, flitting about, never staying anyplace long.

Marglyn glanced over at Hale to see if he was sleeping. As if in answer, he snuffled and rolled over, entering a whole new state of REM, reminding her just how separate they were—his sleeping, oblivious, her wide awake and disturbed. She slipped out of the bed and ventured down the hall, leaving behind the warm comfort of that quilt, the one her grandmother had promised would bring her a lifetime of happiness.

The light was on in Mary Claire's room. But she hadn't left it on. This also happened with some regularity. The next morning she would ask Hale and Robert if they'd been in there, and they'd look at her strangely, answer no like it was the last place they'd go. She shivered a little and wished she'd grabbed her robe. Winter was coming on, leaving fall behind. She pushed open the door, her eyes landing on the little sign mounted there that had adorned their front yard when MC was born, fastened to a great, big, absurd-looking stork.

IT'S A GIRL!
MARY CLAIRE MINER
5-18-99
8 LBS. 3 OZ.
19 ½"

She was always surprised that MC hadn't taken it down as she got older, but there it was, heralding her arrival forever. And now over by the lake there was a tombstone marking her departure forever, bookends of a life cut short. She thought of that grave site and the phone call she'd received earlier. The other mothers, as she'd begun to think of them, had all but demanded that she come to a meeting in two days.

She hadn't seen them since the funerals, but they'd apparently been in communication in the ensuing days. They were threatening a lawsuit against Graham LaRue's family. "If the law isn't going to do right by us, then we'll get justice for ourselves," Cynthia Ellison had said.

Marglyn had heard her take a long pull from a drink as she waited for Marglyn to jump on board their vengeful bandwagon. But all she could think to say was, "It was an accident," her voice weak and uncertain, like she was a kid in school not sure she was giving the right answer.

She'd told no one about the beer cans, of Hale's tearful confession that he'd seen the girls drinking, had let them placate him with the promise that Keary was driving, that it would all be OK. Though they'd agreed not to taint the girls' names by revealing that detail, Marglyn couldn't help but think that perhaps the girls had somehow contributed to what happened that night. It niggled at her like a hangnail, waiting to be pulled, with pain sure to follow.

She'd declined the invitation, felt Cynthia seething on the other end of the phone when she did. "I just don't think a lawsuit is going to do anything but make a bad situation worse," she'd tried to politely explain. "I mean, we know Darcy and Tommy. They were our—" She stopped talking when she realized there was no one there. Cynthia had hung up on her.

Now she stood in her dead daughter's empty room and wished with all her might that she would find her there waiting for her, sitting on the bed reading some book for class or agonizing over a math problem. She wished she could scold her for texting when she was supposed to be studying, could ask her to come help her set the table for dinner and listen to her excuses about why she could not. But it was the middle of the night, and her only chance to speak to Mary Claire had disappeared when her eyes opened.

In this dream, she recalled with surprising clarity, she'd come into the room to find Mary Claire tossing clothes out of her closet, willy-nilly, the items flying over her shoulder and landing in piles on the floor all around her. Mary Claire just kept pulling clothes out and tossing them, never turning to see where they landed. Marglyn had stood in the doorway and watched the back of her daughter's head, her long, blonde hair curling perfectly, the result of hours of patience with a curling iron.

Mary Claire's hair was straight as a stick. But she coaxed it into the loops and sprayed them into submission each day. Marglyn used to watch them bounce on her shoulders as she walked out of the house. She couldn't say when it became normal for her to see more of the back of Mary Claire's head than her face. But it had. That girl, always walking away, determined to leave her behind.

Mary Claire had turned and regarded her, blinking those green eyes slowly once, twice, three times before turning back to what she was doing. She lofted a blue sweater over her shoulder. Marglyn remembered buying it, remembered taking it to the dry cleaner because she didn't want to risk ruining it in the wash.

"Hey!" she'd called out. "That's a nice sweater! I paid a lot of money for that!"

Mary Claire froze, turned, and looked at her again, her face emotionless. She studied her mother as if she were determining something. But what, Marglyn couldn't guess. She never could. Mary Claire spoke, and her voice was so familiar that even in the dream Marglyn started to cry. "So give it to Leah," Mary Claire said. Then she turned back to the closet, and Marglyn was back to staring at those loops of blonde hair. Once she'd fit her finger through one, looping it around and around until Mary Claire wrenched away.

"What do you mean?" she'd asked Mary Claire's back. A white shirt flew through the air, then a T-shirt from church camp, and MC didn't respond. "Mary Claire!" she'd called louder. And though she was dreaming, she'd looked around as if she might wake someone. She'd lowered her voice and asked again. "What do you mean, give it to Leah?"

Mary Claire had turned so that she could see only her profile, the cute little upturned nose, the long lashes resting on her cheeks, her pouty little lips. So much about her daughter had not changed since she was a little girl. "Give the clothes to Leah," Mary Claire had answered her, her voice sounding not sad but not happy, either. Resolved. Resolute. "She needs them."

Marglyn had stood frozen in the doorway, sensing that this was her daughter's way of saying goodbye, of making some odd sort of amends. Why had she chosen Leah? She thought of the girl Mary Claire and Brynne had inexplicably befriended in the summer before school started. Leah and Keary had been their little pets; they'd taught them how to dress and act, and in return for their efforts, Leah and Keary had followed Brynne and MC around like footmen, panting alongside them, desperate to keep up.

Marglyn had felt nearly sorry for them, but for whatever reason, the girls had thought her daughter and her best friend worthy of following. Keary had followed them so close she'd let them talk her into driving that night. Anything to please them. But Leah had not been there. There'd been speculation as to why she wasn't in the car, which had quickly turned to talk of her great fortune, how "it just wasn't her time."

Those words made Marglyn want to tear her hair out. As if it had been her beautiful daughter's time, as if her daughter's life had been lived out fully while Leah had more living to do. As if it were just that simple. When she saw the girl at the funeral, it had been hard to look at her ducking around, sorrowful and lost. She'd felt vaguely angry with her. As if she would've felt better if there were a fourth funeral.

"Why Leah?" she'd pressed. Mary Claire had stopped throwing clothes. And, though she didn't look back at her this time, she'd answered in a quiet, small voice.

"Because we left her behind," Mary Claire said. "We left her all alone."

Marglyn had woken up before she could ask her the other question, the one that burned inside her still: *But don't you have anything for me?*

Ava

Friday

Because she was accused of a sexual crime against a minor, they said Clay was within his rights to keep the children away from her "for their protection," as if she'd morphed overnight into a hideous human capable of atrocities against her own children. Her attorney said she could have supervised visits with Savannah and Clayton, but Clay and his parents kept them holed up in the big house, coming and going at odd hours so she wouldn't see them. So she couldn't see them. Now you see them, now you don't. The Chessmans were magicians, something she hadn't known about them.

She wanted recourse but couldn't find any. In a larger town she would have allies, people who didn't immediately get in line to throw stones, but here everyone was against her. She longed to simply take the kids with her to Trout's—a normal activity just weeks ago, one she even complained about. The last time she'd gone had been an exercise in public shaming, the stares obvious, the words spoken about her just loud enough to be heard but not understood. It was not an experience she ever wanted to repeat.

The one place she went now with any regularity—the place that had been her first indicator that things were different here—was the liquor store. She no longer cared if other people saw her in there because once she was inside, she was with others who'd stopped caring what the rest of this town thought. It had become her oasis: to slip inside its doors and feel welcome somewhere.

She'd taken to stocking up on the hard brown stuff, which she drank neat, like a man. She wandered up and down the aisles with a freedom she once used to enjoy in any store. Reading the labels, taking her time selecting because she had nowhere to go and no one to see. She admired the funky shapes of the bottles, the colors of some of the alcohol like liquid jewels. But in the end she came home with bourbon or Scotch every time, something that burned going down, reminding her of the bitterness of life with each sip.

Tonight she'd guzzled a glass for liquid courage, eyeing the big house from a strategic point in the trailer as she did so, watching Mrs. Chessman's puffy hair as she moved about in the kitchen, preparing dinner. Her stomach rumbled. It was Mrs. Chessman's cooking that had launched the family into the restaurant business decades ago. Ava had never eaten a bad meal at their house. Now she lived on peanut butter crackers and bananas gone spotty with age, things she picked up at the gas station on the edge of town, another place where she was not hassled or even noticed.

She finished the glass and left it on the coffee table where it would most likely sit for days—until she ran out of glasses and had to grab the closest one and rinse the fine brown film from it, wash the lipstick print from the rim. Her housekeeping standards had declined considerably since she no longer had a family to keep house for. She had a hard time recalling the woman she'd been in Atlanta: a person who cared about preschool teachers' gifts packaged in cute baskets with tulle wrapping and fancy bows, who pinned recipes on Pinterest like she was being graded for how many she accumulated, who could spend hours planning a child's birthday party with *themes* and *favors*. And for what? It all had gone away without a backward glance on the part of her husband, as if she were superfluous.

She sucked in a breath and held it for a few seconds before exhaling deeply. She'd read somewhere that deep breathing was supposed to empower her, but it just left her feeling deflated. She glanced nervously out the window again, watching the big house like it might turn into the hotel from *The Shining* or the house from *The Amityville Horror* or . . . something terrible.

Instead it just looked the same as always, a large brick house sitting on several acres of land, horses grazing in the pasture off to the side, her in-laws' dog, Chopper, weaving in and out of their legs, risking getting kicked. She sympathized with the dog. She was risking getting kicked tonight. But she had to see her kids, had to hold them in her arms, look into their eyes (they'd both gotten Clay's blue eyes, and for that she was thankful), and inhale that scent that was uniquely theirs. She wanted to hear them say, "Mommy."

She crossed the distance between the trailer and the house in no time and found herself on the side porch, her arm raised to knock, when the back door opened to reveal her mother-in-law, looking dour and disapproving. Ava recalled meeting Elaine Chessman for the first time. They'd gotten on like a house on fire, her new mother-in-law had relayed to someone later in front of Ava, startling her with the statement. She'd thought Clay's mother had only been pretending to like her. Tonight she wasn't pretending.

"Ava, I don't think you should be here," Elaine said. "Clay's not here, as I'm sure you know." She glanced over her shoulder to make sure the kids weren't around and pushed the door closed a bit more, so that only half her thin frame showed through the gap. Ava could see only one disapproving eye now.

"I came to see my kids," she said, feigning a bravery she had not possessed. Any liquid courage she'd gained from the drink had drained out the bottom of her feet with the sight of impervious Elaine answering the door. She swallowed. "I have the right to at least say hi to them." She swallowed again. "You can supervise."

Elaine rested her head against the door like it was simply too hard to hold it open of her own accord. "I will tell Clay you stopped by and that you wish to see the children. I'm sure he will accommodate you as soon as he possibly can." She started to shut the door, but Ava stuck her foot into the shrinking space. She saw her chance, elbowed the door open, and lunged forward, plowing past a startled Elaine, who jumped out of the way before she could be knocked down.

Ava began to holler, "Clayton! Savannah! Clayton! Savannah!" In response, she heard running feet coming reflexively to the sound of her voice. She felt something fill her—not air but something else entirely—something primal. Something she needed to live, she realized, as much as air. Her babies. To be without them was to be half-alive.

Savannah rounded the corner, a grin filling her face. Behind her Ava could hear Elaine calling for Clay's father, Donald, who must've been in the barn. Her time was limited. She knew they'd call Clay, and he'd come home, angry and all but snorting like a bull. She held out her arms for Savannah, and she rushed into them. "Mommy," her daughter said, and they both began to cry. She crushed Savannah to her, feeling her daughter's tears wetting her midsection. "I missed you," came the muffled words from Savannah, her face buried in Ava's shirt.

She bent over and kissed the top of Savannah's head, her own tears wetting the child's hair. "I missed you, too." She looked up, glanced around. "Where's Clayton?"

Savannah popped her thumb in her mouth, a habit they'd broken her of months ago. A habit that had returned in Ava's absence. Around the thumb she said, "He's with Grandpa." Savannah tightened her grip as though she'd never let go. "I wanna go home, Mommy," the little girl said.

"I know, honey," Ava said. "I'm working on it, trust me." Behind her she could hear her in-laws coming closer to her. They weren't going to let her visit; this wasn't turning out like she'd hoped.

"I'm going to fix this," she said, less to Savannah and more to herself. "So we can be together again." She held out her pinkie, like Savannah used to insist on when she said she'd pay her a dollar to help her with a chore or she'd promised a trip to the ice-cream shop. Simple childhood promises that should've been all she ever had to make. But they were past that now. She crooked her little finger and wiggled it at Savannah. "Pinkie promise," she said.

Savannah turned as Donald came into the room. Elaine was not with him, and she guessed she was hiding somewhere with Clayton, keeping him away. "Ava," Donald said, his tone menacing. "I think it's best you leave now."

She didn't budge, staying focused on her daughter. She wiggled her finger at Savannah a second time. "Pinkie promise?" she asked again.

Savannah nodded, extended her own little pinkie, linking it with Ava's. She pulled her daughter close one last time and planted one last kiss on her head, holding in her tears with a resolve she didn't know she had, a resolve she could draw on later. And with that, she turned and left a house that used to feel like her second home to return to a trailer that had become her lonely prison.

◆ ◆ ◆

She drove to the restaurant in a fugue state, no longer noticing the song on the radio, the landscape outside the car window. She drove fast, then faster, not caring about the repercussions if she got pulled over. Not caring if they put her in jail. She was already imprisoned. The actual bars would only be a formality. She thought of Clay, and her eyes burned. She pressed harder on the gas pedal, her car aimed for Chessman's as if it could get there without her assistance.

At the last minute, she pulled over at a convenience store, parked the car, and went in. She plunked a ten-dollar bill on the counter and pointed at a package of Marlboro Lights, then plucked a lighter from a display by the register and threw that down, too. She knew Clay smoked secretly, and right now that sounded like a good idea.

She paid, got back into her car, and fiddled with the wrapping on the package, the cellophane making a crinkly noise as she peeled it away and extracted a cigarette, trying to remember the last time she'd had one. She put it to her lips and heard the catch of the lighter as the fluid and the flint worked together to make fire. She lit the cigarette and filled her lungs with smoke. It felt like a victory, like the smoke was at work within her, making her someone else, someone closer to who she used to be, that girl who wasn't afraid to wear what she wanted or say what she thought. That girl who'd jumped on a table and danced the night she met Clay. It was how he had noticed her. Then he'd done his best to change her so no one would ever notice her again.

By the time she reached the restaurant, the place was empty of customers; just the waitstaff remained, cleaning up and cashing out. She left the car, noting the nip in the air as fall started giving way to winter. She let the crisp air blow away the smoke, lifted her chin, and inhaled deeply, as if the fresh air could erase the cigarette smoke. Her eyes lit on a shadowy form against a car a few feet away. She looked closer as her eyes adjusted to the dark and realized it was actually two shadowy forms standing very, very close together. A sensation passed through her that at first she thought was fear. Later she would understand that what she felt was something altogether different. It was knowing. Knowing on a level that outpaced her eyes and her mind. Knowing that had everything to do with her heart.

She called his name, and sure enough, he stepped away from whomever he'd been holding so close, so that the one shadowy figure became a distinct two. He turned toward her voice and craned his neck forward as though that might bring her into focus in the blackness. "Who's there?" he called. He didn't recognize the sound of her voice anymore.

"It's me. Ava," she said. She began walking toward him.

He began walking toward her, leaving whomever it was standing by the car. "Ava?" Clay shouted. "What are you doing here?"

She refrained from saying, *I could ask you the same thing.* She said instead, "I was looking for you." They met in the middle. She looked past him, at whomever it was, but the person stayed in the shadows. He moved his head to block her view.

"You're not going to tell me who that is?" she asked, then gave him a little smirk.

He glanced over his shoulder, and she felt a little pop of something in the air between them. "We're still married, you know."

He chuckled and turned back to face her. "It's not like that." He shook his head. "And it don't seem to me you took our marriage into account a coupla weeks ago. So who're you to talk?" He spat on the ground between them. The Clay she knew before didn't use double negatives, didn't have such a pronounced drawl to his voice, didn't spit on the ground for no good reason except to punctuate his point.

"What are you doing here anyway?" he asked again, folding his arms across his chest.

"I was—I went—"

"My parents already told me you went to the house. They said you scared Savannah real good. I can't believe you did that."

Behind him, whoever it was got into the car, and, when the interior light came on, they both looked. Illuminated, it was easy to see just who it was. Someone Ava had felt a strange kinship with recently. The one person who might understand how it felt to be in her shoes, the other most hated woman in town: Darcy LaRue. Odd that Ava's husband would be comforting Darcy.

She stopped talking, realizing that she shouldn't—couldn't—trust Clay. She couldn't trust anyone. She'd driven here to ask him to come with her, to a place she probably shouldn't go alone, to witness what she hoped was her redemption. But her pleas would fall on deaf ears. She hugged herself. The longer she stood outside, the colder it got.

"I'll let you get back to . . . Darcy," she said.

She looked at Darcy, tried to catch her eye, but the interior light had gone out, and she was cast in blackness again. "It's not what you think," she heard Clay's voice saying. "She's just a friend."

She gave him a wry smile. "Said every man ever caught in a situation like this one."

She walked back to her car, ignoring his voice calling her name. She waited to see if he would come after her, but as she got into her car and shut the door, she saw him head in the opposite direction, away from her, back toward Darcy, choosing another person's shame over her own. She squeezed the steering wheel hard, until her hands throbbed. Then she drove away knowing only one thing—only she could heal her shame.

Leah

Graham wasn't there when she got to his house after school. His mother met her at the door. She looked tired and drawn, her face devoid of makeup, her hair in need of washing. She usually looked so pretty. Not because she tried, but because she just was. Today she didn't look especially pretty. She looked worn out. She said that someone had been prowling around their house, leaving a smear of red paint (meant to look like blood, *real* original) across their front door, something they hadn't seen until the next morning when it was light outside.

Leah had tried not to look at the door as they stood there talking. The red paint, still there, looked like one of those inkblot tests she'd learned about when she was into psychology, thinking she'd grow up to be a profiler, probably like most kids who'd ever watched *CSI* or *Criminal Minds*. But she knew more now than she did then, and she didn't want to get any further inside people's depraved minds than she'd already gone. These days she had no idea what she'd be when she grew up. These days growing up looked like less and less fun than it had when she was younger.

A man arrived to paint over the door while she was standing there, and they moved inside so he could get to work. Graham's mother glanced over her shoulder with a worried look, her eyes landing on Talmadge waiting in the car before darting back to Leah. "Don't you need to get to the game? Isn't it away tonight?"

It was funny how, even with everything happening, Graham's mother still knew the football schedule, still expected everyone in town to live by it, just like before.

"I'm, um, taking a break from cheerleading. They said I could."

"Oh well, yes. That makes sense."

Leah shifted the papers she was holding, not knowing what to do with them with Graham no longer there. "So, he, like, moved out?" she asked, sounding stupid but also feeling confused.

Mrs. LaRue—she just couldn't call her Darcy—nodded. "His father thought it was best for everyone if he moved in with him for a while. Just until this blows over. There've been . . . threats. People at school who're angry with him. And with just us here, I guess they felt like we were unprotected, so they could just do whatever they wanted." Graham's mom started to cry and covered her mouth as if that would stop it. "I'm sorry," she apologized. "I just feel like it will never blow over. Like, for the rest of my life I'm going to be 'the mother of that boy who killed those girls.'"

Leah nodded, uncertain of what to say. "I'm sorry," she whispered.

She glanced over at the doorway that led into the small den where Graham always sat, propped up on the brown leather couch watching movies or playing video games. Every time she visited, she came closer and closer to saying to him what she'd wanted to say when she raised her hand in class and said she'd bring his work to him—the thing she thought of at least fifty times a day since it happened: *I wish you'd killed me, too.*

"No, I'm the one who should be sorry." Mrs. LaRue wiped at her eyes with the heel of her hand. "Talking about this with you—when you lost your friends." She reached out her hands, and at first, Leah panicked, feared she was reaching out to hug her. Then she realized she was just reaching for the papers. "I guess they'll just have to make other arrangements for him to get his work," she said.

"Yeah," Leah said. "Well, tell him I said hello and that I, um, hope he feels better and . . ." Graham's mother looked like she was about to start crying again. She needed to get out of there. She started backing up. "I'll just see him around, I guess."

She gave a little wave and turned for the door, completely forgetting in her hasty retreat about the man painting on the other side. Thankfully he saw her coming and stepped out of the way. He gave her a grin that looked more like a leer. "Wouldn't want to get this paint all over you, now," he said. It occurred to her as she walked toward Talmadge's car that some people could make almost anything sound sexual.

She was almost to the car when she heard her name being called. She turned back to find Graham's mother standing on the porch. The man had resumed his painting, and Graham's mother stood on the steps, now leaning forward, wrapping her jacket tighter around herself. Leah signaled to Talmadge to wait a moment longer and met the woman on the sidewalk. Sometimes when she felt sorry for herself, she thought of other people in town who had it bad, too. Mrs. LaRue. Mrs. Chessman. The parents of Keary, Mary Claire, and Brynne. Then she felt oddly comforted, knowing she wasn't alone in her misery.

"Sorry," Graham's mother apologized. She gestured to Talmadge. "Is that your boyfriend?"

Leah laughed. She shook her head. "No, he's just my ride." She felt a small squeeze in her heart as she said it, and she couldn't decide whether it was her conscience because that wasn't exactly true or her guilt because she knew it would hurt Talmadge if he heard her say it. Talmadge was good to her—far better than anyone else in this lousy world. She wondered if he *should* be her boyfriend. If maybe that made about as much sense as anything else.

She looked over her shoulder at his car, idling there, at his profile as he waited without complaint. She could hear his music playing—jazz, something so opposite of what any other boy in town would be playing. Talmadge was not any other boy. And that was why she liked being around him. And with Keary, Brynne, and MC gone, she was free to be around him again without social repercussions. No one cared anymore who she spent time with, how she dressed, or where she went. She was a horrible person for feeling relief at the thought. She was a horrible person for living when they were dead.

"Leah?" Graham's mother was looking at her, waiting for the answer to a question she hadn't heard. The sun was nearly down. Her mother would wonder where she was. She would worry, and say so. But Leah didn't care about that so much anymore. Because no matter what happened from here on out, her mother would not be able to stop something terrible from happening to her. All her rules and sermons could not protect her anymore. They never could; she knew this now. The thought filled her with two opposite emotions at the same time—fear and exhilaration.

"Sorry," Leah said. She shook her head as though that would clear it. She had in mind something to ask Talmadge when she got back into his car—something she thought he might be able to do. Something he'd hinted at in the past. But she'd never been interested before. "What were you saying?" she asked Graham's mother, and smiled at her.

"I was wondering if maybe I could come by your house from now on? I could get his assignments from you and then just run them over to him." She gave a little shrug and a smile of her own. "That way I'd have a reason to still see him every day."

"If he's not far from me, I could just take them," she offered, wanting to be as helpful as she could. She liked Graham, liked his mother. She wondered how Keary and Brynne and Mary Claire would feel about that. Was it a betrayal for her to befriend the boy who was driving the car that plowed into them?

"No—I want to. I . . . miss him." She gestured to the house, the man standing on the porch covering up the red paint with big wide swaths of black, the dark, empty windows with no lights on inside. "I don't like being here alone."

"OK," Leah said, feeling sorry for this woman, feeling once again that she wasn't the only one suffering in this town. She wasn't the only one who saw the sun go down and dreaded another night of strange shadows and bad dreams. But not tonight, not if she had her way. She nodded. "That'll be good."

Graham's mother brightened. "So, I guess I'll see you later!" she said. She leaned forward and in a mock whisper said, "That guy in the car? The one who's not your boyfriend?"

Leah nodded, grateful it was nearly dark to cover the blush she felt creeping up her cheeks.

"He's cute. And he has excellent taste in music." She was pretty sure Graham's mother winked before she turned and disappeared inside her house.

◆ ◆ ◆

Talmadge got back into the car carrying a bag, which was a good sign. "Did you get it?" Leah asked.

He grinned and nodded, resting the bag on the seat between them. Leah already had a beer, one he'd snuck out of his father's cooler. In an act of chivalry, he'd let her have it to sip on while he went into his uncle's trailer to get a real supply for them—this was what he'd hinted at in the past, back when he'd tried to lure her away from her new friends with claims of his own coolness, with promises of what he could be. But she hadn't wanted him to be anything but what he was. That was the part he didn't understand.

He leaned over and plucked the can from between her legs, raising it to his lips. They'd been meant to share it, but she'd taken more than her share when he was inside the trailer. He swallowed and made a face. "You drank almost all of it!" he said. "And it's warm."

"Well you took too long!" she retorted. They were flirting, and for once she didn't mind; she didn't feel afraid. She reached into the bag and withdrew a cold new beer. She popped the tab and took a long pull, then gave him a smile.

"I can't believe we're doing this," he said, and took another polite sip. He was, she noticed, finishing her warm beer. She said nothing of it and took another sip of her cold one.

"We are so doing this," she said. "Where do you want to go?"

He turned the beer can up and drank the rest, crushing the can. "I've got a place we could hang out and finish these," he said, tossing the crushed can into the air and catching it again. "Then I thought we'd go to Stooges and shoot pool?"

She eyed him. "*You?* Go to Stooges?" Stooges was a dive on the outskirts of town, a place only the bravest and most brazen of high school students attempted to get into. It wasn't that Stooges carded or even had a bouncer. It was that Zig, the owner, was likely to beat the shit out of you if he caught you drinking underage in his establishment. Then dare you to tell anyone who beat you up. And threaten worse if you ever tried it again.

Talmadge gave her a grin that told her perhaps she didn't know everything there was to know about him. Maybe Talmadge had been doing some changing of his own while she was blowing him off. "Zig's a friend," he said. "A patron of the arts, I guess you could say." He turned toward the windshield, leaving her to study his profile and wonder.

◆　◆　◆

She clung to the sleeve of Talmadge's coat as they entered Stooges—partly because she wasn't steady on her feet after the beers and partly because she was terrified to be there. She wasn't sure they should be doing this, yet Talmadge sauntered in, carrying his violin case out in front of him like a passkey. Several people glanced over, then turned back to the bar or their pool cues, clearly nonplussed. She relaxed a little until she heard the bartender call out to them, "Hey!"

Talmadge glanced over, and from her vantage point behind him, she wished she could see his face, feel his heartbeat to know if he was afraid, so she would know if she should be. "Yeah?" Talmadge's voice was nearly a sneer. She'd never seen this side of him, this tougher, harder side. He tossed his head a little bit, and his hair, soft and the slightest bit wavy, resettled itself on his collar. She noticed a bald man watching with naked envy.

"You looking for Zig?" the bartender asked.

"Yeah," Talmadge said, lifting his violin.

"He's in the back," the bartender said. "He said to send you on when you got here." Talmadge nodded and walked on, weaving his way through the crowd like he knew where he was going, like he'd done this before, possibly numbers of times. She gripped his coat tighter and tried to keep up.

For a split second she forgot that Keary, Brynne, and MC could not be there, and she wished they were. She wanted them to see just how badass Talmadge was. She imagined what they would say if they were there, asking a million rapid-fire questions she couldn't answer, fearing they'd be molested by the men, fearing they'd be tossed out, excited to be doing something unusual, something so outside their normal existence they could scarcely breathe. This was living, she told herself—being afraid and excited all at once, buzzing from the beer, not knowing what was next. She was alive.

They walked down a dark hallway into the recesses of the building, ending up at a shut door. Talmadge knocked, and a muffled, "Come in," came from the other side.

Talmadge turned to her. "Just be cool. Don't say much." He narrowed his eyes at her. "And don't worry." He flashed a grin, and she heard Graham's mother's voice in her head. Had Talmadge always been good-looking, or had he become good-looking while she was busy with other people? She followed him inside, keeping her eyes trained on the floor.

"Well, well, if it isn't my virtuoso," a deep, booming voice said. She raised her eyes long enough to take in a large man sitting in a desk chair with wheels, his hair buzzed in a military style, his belly spilling over his waistband. He looked at her, and she dropped her gaze back to the floor.

"Who do we have here?" he asked, and in the question was the same bit of innuendo she'd heard in the painter's voice earlier. "You didn't tell me you got a little girlfriend." He stood and clapped Talmadge on the back approvingly.

Talmadge nudged her, and she looked up again. "This is my friend, Leah," he said. "Leah, this is Zig." She reached out her hand to shake his hand even though she wasn't sure she wanted to touch him.

Zig chuckled and took her hand in his own, pumping it up and down just once before dropping it. He winked at Leah. "Good home training; you can tell your parents I said so." He laughed. "Though I'm betting you won't be telling them you met me." He looked from her to Talmadge and back again a few times, laughed, and shook his head. "Your friend, my ass," he said. He sat back down and gestured at a folding chair across from him, instructing her to sit. He pointed at Talmadge. "Let's hear it."

As she took her seat, Talmadge extracted the violin from the case. He ran the bow across the strings a few times, warming up. His sleeve lifted, and she saw the curl of a letter. She'd forgotten about his tattoo. Talmadge began to play, and Zig closed his eyes. After a few minutes, he lifted his chin so his face was pointing toward the ceiling. The violin's mournful song filled the room, and she listened and watched, her heart clinching with a kind of pain that wasn't pain.

Her emotions scaled the range as he moved the bow, slow, then fast, across the strings. She looked from Zig's face to Talmadge's, both of them with eyes closed, both of them seeming to have mentally left the room. Where they'd gone she didn't know, but it was a place no one could follow. She knew that kind of leaving; she'd done it herself, but not in a good way.

By the time Talmadge was finished, tears were leaking from her eyes, and she knew that she would tell him the truth about the night of the accident. That he was the only one she could tell.

Talmadge lowered the violin, and Zig wiped his eyes, then shook his head and laughed, embarrassed. "Gets me every time," he said. He pointed at Leah. "Talented boy you've got here." He rose and reached to shake Talmadge's hand, and she did not argue that Talmadge wasn't hers.

Talmadge tucked the violin under his arm and shook the hand extended to him. "Thank you, sir," he said.

"Sir!" Zig threw back his head and laughed. "I'm no sir." He pointed at the door. "Go on and get out of here," he said.

He picked up a roll of bills on the desk, peeled some off, and thrust them at Talmadge, who pocketed them swiftly with an embarrassed "Thank you."

"Grab something at the bar and play a few rounds of pool on me." Zig waved his arms in a "go on" motion. They started to walk out, but Zig called after them. "You'll come back, won't you?" he asked, sounding much smaller than he was and far less tough. Later she would ask Talmadge how he met Zig and just what this arrangement they had was. Later she would say a lot of things.

Talmadge flashed that grin that he seemed to have acquired when she wasn't looking. "You bet," he said. He opened the door for her, and together they walked down the hall, the violin case swinging from one of his hands. With the other, he reached out and took hers.

Darcy

FRIDAY

After the girl left and the painter left and darkness completely took over, fear crept in. Though the red paint had been covered, she could still feel it there, fingers forever tapping on her front door saying, *Let me in.* The sanctity of her home, the peace of her life, whatever she'd managed to cling to before, was gone. She paced in front of the window again, though this Friday night there were no sirens whizzing by. Instead the road remained untraveled. She began to feel like the last person on earth.

Eventually she got in her car and, though she told herself she was just going for a drive, she headed straight to Chessman's. She sat at a corner table out of the way and ordered a piece of chocolate pie and a cup of coffee. What she really wanted was a beer. In one of their many late-night conversations, she'd told Clay he should start serving alcohol.

"Not while my parents are alive," he'd said. "They won't hear of it. Said Chessman's is a family establishment."

"Oh well, I was thinking someone should give Stooges a run for its money." They'd laughed about that—Stooges and Chessman's were two entirely different establishments with very little in common. Case in point: her ex and his hussy girlfriend hung out at Stooges. She had reason to believe their affair had started there.

Clay dropped into the chair across from her and, startled, she looked up from her pie. He pointed at it. "Can I have a bite?"

She smiled and started to cut into her pie with her fork. He held up his hand. "No, I was just kidding."

She looked up, the forkful of pie frozen in midair. "I'll share," she offered.

He smiled. "I'm sure you would." He made a motion with his hand for her to put the fork down. "I'm good, though."

She ate the bite of pie as he watched, feeling embarrassed to be watched while eating. Especially while eating pie, a total indulgence. She'd spent most of her life eschewing desserts, leaving food on her plate, and claiming she wasn't hungry when she was. But after Tommy left, she'd said screw that. Sitting there with Clay watching her, those old thought patterns started back up. She swallowed and put down her fork.

"Hey—you're not finished!" he said.

"You're weirding me out, watching me," she replied playfully.

He reached forward and slid her plate toward himself. Another of the many differences between men and women: men did not seem to struggle with eating what they wanted, when they wanted, no matter whether someone watched or not. She thought of Tommy, biting into a chicken leg he'd pulled out of the refrigerator while wearing his boxer shorts and sporting a serious case of bedhead. When she'd said, "You look like a caveman," he'd merely shrugged and kept eating. She would have never in a thousand years.

Clay finished the last bites of her pie and dropped the fork to the plate with a clatter. A server scurried over to collect it from him and asked Darcy if she needed anything else. She shook her head, and the girl walked away, glancing back at Clay and Darcy as she did. She was sure they were the talk among the staff. The very married boss consorting with the very unmarried scorned woman. Let them talk. Let the whole damn town talk.

"So," Clay said, leaning forward. "You OK?"

Just the question brought the prick of threatening tears to her eyes. She blinked rapidly and nodded. "Just needed to get out of the house. So quiet." She'd told Clay earlier in the day about the paint they'd found, about Tommy's decision to move Graham over to his house.

"It's for your protection as much as his," Tommy had said when he showed up to get him. "Soon as people hear he's with me, this'll stop. They know it's just him and you in that house. They wouldn't try that shit with me there." She knew it was true—that he was probably right—but she didn't understand why she had to lose one more person in her life as a result, why in the end everything that had happened had just left her more and more alone.

"Come to Florida," her mother had said again that afternoon on the phone. "Sit by the ocean, play cards with Aunt Lou and me, eat seafood. It would do you good. You could stay as long as you wanted." But she couldn't leave Graham with the charges against him still pending. Though right now she hated Worthy as a whole, she couldn't imagine leaving it.

She looked at Clay across the table from her and admitted something else. She couldn't leave him, either, with all he was facing. They'd become a support system to each other. He was the one real friend she had, the only person who understood. Even her friends who'd stuck by her after the divorce had drifted away after Graham's accident, distancing themselves lest some of her tarnish rub off on them. She didn't exactly blame them; she probably would've felt the same if the tables were turned.

Clay stood. "Well, I best get busy closing up."

"Oh sure," she said, reaching for her wallet to hand him her credit card.

He waved his arms. "Put that away." He smiled at her like she was a cute puppy in the window begging for a home. "The pie was my treat."

Her smile in response was a mere upward lift of half her mouth. She dropped her wallet into her purse, took a last sip of coffee, and stood as well. Clay held out his arms, and she stepped into them, feeling him grip her tightly but quickly. He also knew they were being watched, scrutinized, discussed. In her ear he whispered, "Wait for me outside?" before he released her.

She stepped back, looked into his eyes, nodded.

He winked and walked away. She left the restaurant and got into her car, cranked it but did not drive away. She turned on the radio. A love song came on, and for the first time in months, she did not change the station.

They were only hugging when his ex-wife showed up. Granted, it was a full-body hug with nary a space between them, but it was just a hug. Though she had been thinking about kissing him, even as the headlights from another car swept across them. She was pretty sure he'd been thinking about kissing her as well, but the headlights had distracted them, turned their gazes toward the car and away from each other.

Wrong as it was, something had shifted that night. Clay was her friend, her confidant, her ally. But he was also a handsome man whose marriage was basically over. A man who'd come to her rescue without a second thought. A man who smelled like spice and fire and looked at her like he thought she'd invented beauty. He was a man who winked at her and asked her how she was. And all of it—every bit—had led to the moment his wife pulled up to see.

"Is that . . . ?" she asked, watching him take in the car, squint to see the driver.

He nodded, his mouth a grim line.

Later she'd wonder what would've happened if Ava hadn't shown up when she did. Later she'd wish Ava hadn't shown up when she did.

Later she'd curse Ava, who seemed to be excellent at messing things up for other people. But in that moment all she felt was the need to flee. Clay took a step away from her, his face illuminated in the headlights. She saw the creases beside his eyes, the way they had deepened with—concern? Fear? Guilt? She didn't know him well enough to discern exactly what Ava's appearance had produced in him.

"I should go talk to her," he said apologetically.

"Of course," she said. "I'll just go." It was what she wanted to do, and she wanted him to give her permission to do so.

Instead he said, "No, don't go. Just—" He held up his hand. "Wait."

He trotted across the parking lot toward the woman who was still his wife, a woman she had judged and despised based on what she'd heard. Kind of like what people in this town had done to her, and then to her son. She shivered and slid inside her car. She turned the key in the ignition and turned up the temperature to make warm air blast from the vents. Then she focused on the radio again, fiddling with the dial so as not to stare at the scene transpiring in front of her. What was Clay saying to Ava? It's over? I don't love you? You're despicable and I'm ashamed of you? These were things he had said to her about Ava, but would he be brave enough to say them directly to her?

She looked up once, and her eyes met Ava's. Though it was from a distance, she felt something, and what she felt was not adversarial. It was not *You don't deserve him. You're a horrible person.* It was simply *Look at us. Here. In this great mess. Not sure what we did to get here. Or how we will get out of it. But we will. I have to believe we will.* Darcy broke eye contact first.

Movement caught her attention. She looked up to see Clay walking back to her car. He opened the car door, and the cold whooshed in. He sat down in the passenger seat and closed the door. Ava's headlights swept across them once more as she drove away. "Sorry about that," he said.

"You don't need to apologize," she replied. She kept her eyes trained on the radio, the readout telling her each new song as it played even though she'd turned the sound down. "Last night was my night for crazy; tonight's yours."

He chuckled, and she could feel him relax. "We both have our share," he agreed. He reached over and poked her thigh playfully. "Makes us a good pair."

She smiled at him, feeling cared for, accepted. "You made a rhyme," she said.

He blinked a few times, and she could feel whatever had been happening between them before Ava showed up begin to flicker and spark in the air again. "Just in time," he answered, his words laden with meaning. He slid over and took her in his arms, confirming what she'd suspected as he put his mouth over hers, his lips much warmer than she'd expected.

Ava

She arrived at Stooges at an hour when most people were tucked in bed, dreaming. Even Stooges was starting to wind down, based on the number of cars in the parking lot. Inside, people would be racking up their last round, ordering one last drink before they paid their tab and went home on the arms of people they should or should not be with. If Ian were here, this would be the time to catch him.

Ian and his friends liked to come when people had enough drinks in them to look the other way. They just wanted to play pool, flirt with waitresses, and drink underage. They didn't want to be seen as hometown heroes or hear people's opinions about the season. If there was any place in Worthy that could happen, it was Stooges at 1:00 a.m. on a Saturday morning. She had come there to catch him with his guard down, to ask one six-word question of him: *Why won't you tell the truth?* It was risky, being anywhere near him. Yet she had to take this chance.

She stepped inside, grateful for the dark, smoky atmosphere where she could also go undetected. Stooges was the place in town for the undesirables to congregate. But it was also the place where some of the town's business leaders showed up, anxious for a little "live and let live" themselves. It was a place where you weren't Baptist or Methodist,

Democrat or Republican, white or black. Stooges was Worthy's equivalent of Switzerland. The thought made her smile, and as she did, beside her, a grizzled older man leaned close.

"I'd love to know what you're smiling about," he said.

The smile disappeared from her face as she tried to scoot away, but he reached out his mitt hand and grabbed her forearm. "Now don't go running off and take that pretty smile with you," he said. She was caught like a fish on a line.

Clay had brought her here one night, showing her the one place in town that served alcohol, the "den of iniquity," as his mother called it. They'd ended up playing a round of pool and having a few beers. They'd had, actually, a very nice time. One of the nicest since they got to Worthy. But as they left, he'd warned her never to come alone. That's why she'd gone to ask him to go with her, the one man in town she knew well enough to ask, only to be told to go home. She kept seeing him walk away, getting in Darcy LaRue's car, his actions making her more resolved than ever to go forward with her plan to somehow find these boys outside of school and make things right.

Now she regretted her risk as she scanned the room, no longer looking for Ian—just hoping for someone who would come to her rescue. The man tightened his grip and pulled her closer. He was wearing a white T-shirt with a black leather jacket. His hand on her arm was so completely tattooed that she couldn't see any actual skin color. He smelled of cigarettes, stale beer, and sweat. When he smiled at her, his teeth were a yellowish brown.

"What you need," he said, "is a beer." He reached around to pour her a beer from a pitcher on the table behind him. When he did, he let go of her, and she took the opportunity to flee. "Hey!" she heard him call after her. "You're leaving your beer!"

Her heart pounding in her ears, she charged forward, looking for the door but disoriented by the dark interior and her own panic. She kept moving, narrowly missing a waitress with a tray of drinks, sidestepping into another man and sending his beer right into his chest. "I'm so sorry!" she cried out, raising her voice to be heard over the country music blaring through the speakers. Stooges usually had live music, but she guessed whoever the entertainment was had finished up and gone home. She gestured to the waitress, already a few steps away delivering her drinks. "I was trying to avoid hitting her and hit you instead."

Unlike the first guy, this one was handsome and looked to be about her age. He wore a plaid flannel shirt over a gray T-shirt, now drenched, and a worn-out pair of jeans. The ensemble was, thankfully, absent the requisite cowboy boots that seemed to be part of the male uniform in Worthy. Even Clay had gotten some after they'd been there a few weeks, buying a pair for Clayton as well.

"It's fine," the man said. Unlike the first guy, this one didn't scare her. She took in the way his eyes crinkled at the corners and the one little dent of dimple that formed in his cheek when he smiled at her. Though his hairline was slightly receded, he was handsome and in good shape. If things were different, she might even be attracted to him. She stepped slightly closer, in order to give the appearance that she was with this guy so no other lowlifes would approach her.

He would be a good person to at least stand near as she kept looking for Ian, though she feared either he and his friends had been there and gone or they'd not come at all tonight. Sometimes they didn't after away games. She hated that she knew all that, but he'd told her.

The man held up his now-empty glass. "I'm gonna go get a refill before they stop serving," he said. "Can I get you one?"

"I'll buy!" she said. "It's the least I can do." She began fishing in her purse for money, but he put his hand over hers, a gentle pressure instead of the tight grasp from before.

"I got it." He grinned. "I'll be right back." She nodded and stood alone nervously, trying not to make eye contact with anyone else as she continued to scan the large room, her eyes falling on two kids, though they weren't the ones she was looking for.

She didn't recognize the boy at all, but the girl was unmistakable. It was the girl from her class, the one who knew the three dead girls. She could still picture the look on her face as she'd read Emily Dickinson aloud. While the rest of the class stared vacantly at their desks or out the window, that girl had listened intently, her face a mixture of sorrow and excitement.

Ava had felt sorry for her, losing her friends like that. She'd felt guilty for her mixed feelings about Keary Malone's death, almost as if she owed the girl an apology. She thought of that last morning at the school, of the utter humiliation that followed. She'd been so distraught she'd left behind her leather volume of Dickinson poems, a gift from an old boyfriend she'd once thought she'd marry.

Her new friend returned and handed her a beer. She took a long, grateful sip, wishing it was a shot of stiff whiskey instead, something that would burn going down like she'd grown used to. But beggars couldn't be choosers.

"You from around here?" he asked, as good a conversation starter as any.

She looked at him from over her glass. "No," she said. "I'm from Atlanta." She relished the name of her real home on her lips. "You?" she asked. "From here?"

"Sort of."

"How can you be sort of from somewhere?" She laughed.

He smiled and took a sip of his beer. "I grew up here but got out as soon as I could. I'm just home visiting my folks." He gestured to a woman perched on a barstool, talking animatedly with a mustachioed man wearing a cowboy hat. "That's my sister. She dragged me here tonight." He shook his head and looked into his beer. "She never left."

"The poor girl," Ava quipped.

He cut his eyes over to her with a little smirk. "Some people like it here."

"Aren't you the devil's advocate," she said, her tone flirtatious. It was her default mode around men, a switch her mind and body flipped in unison, in some unspoken agreement made sometime during puberty.

"Maybe I'm just a devil," he responded. He raised his eyebrows at her and waggled his beer mug in her direction. The response from every man was usually the same. It was the currency she'd traded in for so long she wasn't sure she knew how to stop it. It made her feel powerful, in control, desired. It made her feel good—something she could count on no matter what.

"They're about to close up," he said, his face so near hers that she could feel his breath on her cheek. "Wanna get out of here?" He nodded in the direction of his sister. "I came with her but . . . if you have a car . . ."

The word *car* made her think of her husband getting into another woman's, how quickly and thoroughly he'd believed the worst and discarded her. She thought of saying yes to this other man, of walking out of this bar and taking this stranger home, walking him right into her husband's family's trailer, screwing him in their bed. He had no idea who she was; there was no judgment coming from him. And in the morning he would go back to wherever he came from and this would be just another night. She craved the feel of someone else's skin against hers, the warmth of someone's kiss, the feeling of being loved and valued, if only for what was left of the night.

"Sure," she said.

"Seriously?" He exhaled, shocked that his proposition had actually worked. "OK, let me go tell my sister we're taking off." He hurried away as if afraid she'd change her mind if he took too long.

She was left standing alone. She took the last sip of her beer, scanning the room again just in case she'd somehow missed the boys. But the crowd had thinned enough that it would be hard to miss them. She'd struck out in one way but scored in another.

She was putting the empty beer bottle on the bar when someone tapped her shoulder. She spun around, expecting to find the man she was leaving with. A man whose name, she realized, she did not know. But instead she saw the girl, Leah, standing there, unsteady on her feet, her eyes on her but unfocused. She held out a book, waggling it much the same as the man had done with his beer mug. "You left your book," Leah said, slurring her words.

Ava looked down to find the leather-bound edition of Emily Dickinson poems in the girl's hand. She jerked her head back up, confused. She searched Leah's face, but it was vacant. "This is my book?" she asked, though she knew it was. She wrapped her hands around the book as if to take it, but Leah jerked it away.

"I'm gonna get you another one," she said. "I looked it up. On Amazon. I'll pay for it." She clutched the book to her chest like a child might clutch a doll. "I need this one. I've written stuff in it." She raised her eyes, making eye contact with Ava as best she could. Behind her, the boy she was with watched warily, his eyes darting from Leah to Ava and back again.

"OK," Ava said. She used the same gentle tone she used with her preschool-age children. "Of course. You keep it." From the corner of her eye, she saw her companion head toward her, then stop in his tracks when he saw the kid.

"So you don't care if I have it?" Leah asked, a note of hope dawning in her voice.

"It's yours," Ava said, trying to keep her voice light. The boy Leah was with took a step forward, as if to claim her. Ava nodded at him, and he took a few more steps closer, his cautious, uncertain look no doubt matching her own. "Well, it was nice to see you, Leah."

She turned to go, anxious to get away from any student who had ties to Worthy High. She was actually relieved she hadn't seen the boys she'd come to find. Perhaps she'd been saved from a terrible mistake. Even being near Leah had made her feel anxious, as if she could be blamed for something else just by speaking to her. She made eye contact with her new friend and decided she didn't want to know his name. She could use some anonymity.

"Wait!" Leah called, too loud. Ava felt someone grab her for the second time that night. But this hand around hers wasn't menacing. It was desperate. She held up a finger to the man who was waiting for her, asking for one more second. She turned back to see Leah, whose face was surprisingly close to hers. She smelled beer on the girl's breath, a lot of beer. Leah was going to regret this night in the morning. She thought of her new conquest's proposition. If she took him home with her, she might, too.

"I'm sorry for what they did to you," Leah said.

Ava blinked. "What who did to me?" she asked, even though she suspected she knew the answer.

Leah nodded as if agreeing with herself and tapped the book she was holding, uttering a quote Ava recognized. "'It is better to be the hammer than the anvil.' Right?"

Ava nodded slowly, anxious to see what she was getting at.

"Everyone thinks those boys are so good. But they're bad." She squinted at Ava. "And we know, don't we?" She nodded again and smiled, but the smile was more chilling than consoling. "We're the only ones who do."

Leah pitched forward and would have fallen the rest of the way if Ava hadn't reflexively reached out to brace her. She transferred Leah into the arms of the boy with the worried expression, letting go only when she was sure he had hold of her.

He wrapped an arm around Leah, who smiled up at him. "I love you, Talmadge," she said to the boy, who blanched. But Leah took no notice as she turned back to Ava. "Mrs. Chessman, this is Talmadge. You don't know him because he doesn't go to our school."

Ava could see her thinking about this, her thought processes dulled by the alcohol. "Of course, now you don't, either." She leaned forward and crooked her finger to indicate that Ava should move closer. "That's not your fault. It's theirs. Everything is their fault. You won't forget that, will you?"

"Come on, Leah," Talmadge, Leah's rescuer, said, tugging her gently away. "We'd better get you home." He turned to Ava. "I'm sorry," he mumbled. "She's been . . . real upset lately. I thought tonight might . . . help."

She laid her hand on his arm. "It's OK," she said.

Talmadge took a few wary steps with Leah, not progressing very far as she fought against him, her eyes still intent on Ava, like she was close to saying something she couldn't quite express. Ava wished the girl wasn't so drunk, so incapable of making real sense. She hadn't found the boys at Stooges, but she had found something. Or someone. Someone who needed help, possibly more than she did. She began to think of how she could find out just what it was that the girl couldn't say.

Leah

SATURDAY

She awoke in Talmadge's car, her head resting against the car window, gone cold in the night. His jacket was tossed across her, and he was gone. She sat up in a panic, her eyes darting around to take in where she was. She looked in the back seat to find him sleeping there, curled up in a ball, or as close to a ball as his lanky form could make. He wore just a thin T-shirt and jeans. He must've frozen without his jacket. She rubbed the fogged windshield and tried to determine where they were.

She scanned the recesses of her memories from the night before. She'd lied to her parents, said she was sleeping over at Sidney Riggle's house. And her parents, encouraged that she was "making some nice new friends," hadn't asked many questions. She and Talmadge had driven around for a while before going to Stooges, his surprise for her. He'd played for Zig and scored them drinks. After that, the night got fuzzy.

She found her purse at her feet and pulled out her phone, hoping her parents hadn't tried to call her. But there were no missed calls or texts.

She checked the time: 7:28 a.m. She had to pee. She opened the passenger door and looked over her shoulder at Talmadge. He slept on, so she jumped out of the car and dashed into a clump of bushes, squatted, and peed. She pulled her jeans back up, feeling the pee wetting her underpants. A thought occurred to her: Had she and Talmadge *done* anything? She dashed back into the car, shivering from the exposure to the cold morning, and sat back down, closing the door a bit harder to wake Talmadge up. But he didn't stir.

She watched him for a moment, trying to remember more from the night. There was something nagging at her. Something embarrassing she'd done. Something out of character. Something she shouldn't have done. She felt ill. And not just from drinking too much the night before. She fished around in her purse and dug out two aspirin, plucked the water bottle Talmadge always kept in his console, and washed them down.

She leaned her head back and closed her eyes, willing the aspirin to take effect. She tried to picture her and Talmadge fooling around in the back seat, tried to decide if that was something that could actually happen. The thought, surprisingly, didn't terrify her. It actually made her feel kind of nice. She reached back into her purse and extracted a piece of gum. She didn't want hangover breath when he woke up. She closed her eyes again and chewed her gum.

After what felt like hours, she glanced down at her phone: 7:42 a.m. She exhaled loudly and tossed her phone into her purse, then looked to see if the noises she was making had roused Talmadge. But he slept on. Left without options, she crawled over the back seat and cuddled next to him, putting her head up against his chest so she could hear his heart beating out its steady rhythm. "Talmadge?" she whispered. "You awake?" In answer, she felt his heart accelerate. She looked up to find his eyes on her, blinking in confusion.

He leaned up on his elbow. "Hey," he said, his morning smell different from the way he usually smelled. But not in a bad way. This scent—the one she was privy to now—was his most basic scent. It was private, intimate. She scooted closer to him, trying to close the gap he'd created by sitting up. She tugged at him, pulling him back to her, his face drawing dangerously close to hers. They blinked at each other. He shook his head and sat up again, this time all the way, pressing himself against the passenger window as far away from her as he could get without leaving the car.

"No more," he said.

Her heart picked up speed. "No more? No more, what?"

He looked out the window, though she knew he couldn't see much through the condensation. "No more games," he said.

She pushed herself up to a sitting position as well, drawing her legs to her and hugging them, a sense of shame filling her. Shame was a reflex since the night of the accident; it had become her body's default mode. She hadn't always reacted that way to things, but she couldn't remember what came before. It was as if what she'd done that night had altered her forever, changing her body's composition and chemistry. Something niggled at her mind, something that told her Ian and Seth were part of whatever had happened last night, that they were tied to it. They always were.

She buried her face in her knees. "Did I tell you something last night?" she asked.

"We don't have to talk about it if you don't want," he said. "You were drunk. You've been through a lot. We all understand."

She popped her head up. "We all?" She widened her eyes. "Who is we all?"

"Well, I mean, not we all. That's an exaggeration. I should've said we both. Mrs. Chessman and me." He turned his face to the window, took his finger, and drew a line in the condensation.

She felt it coming back to her, the confirmation that something bad had, in fact, happened last night. But not bad as in she threw herself at Talmadge, which was something she was fairly certain she'd been considering at the height of her drunkenness. Before something changed. Something shifted. Now she knew that something was seeing Mrs. Chessman. "What did I say to her?" she asked.

"I'm going to turn the car on," he said. "Warm it up in here." Without waiting for her OK, he awkwardly climbed over the seat, all angles, slid into the driver's seat, and cranked the ignition. He turned up the heat and patted the seat beside him, indicating for her to join him. "Soon's it warms up in here, I'll take you home."

She slid into her spot beside him, leaning in to feel the warm air as it slowly began to fill the car. "What did I say to her?" she pressed.

"We should actually drive around some," he answered. "It'll heat up in here faster."

"Tell me, Talmadge."

He drummed his fingers on the steering wheel. "I didn't really hear," he said. "You were talking to her. I wasn't very close."

She narrowed her eyes at him. "You're lying." She leaned back dramatically, crossing her arms and staring him down. "Tell me, Talmadge. You owe me the truth."

He turned his head toward her, anger flashing in his eyes. "I owe you? The truth?" He gave a bitter little laugh. "Please explain how that is."

"Because something happened last night. Something you know and I don't. As my friend you should tell me."

He pushed on the buttons that controlled the heat to make it go up, but it was already at the maximum setting. He dropped his hand back into his lap. "So we're friends now? Is that what we are?"

She swallowed, the flavor in her gum all but gone. "Yeah. I mean, why wouldn't we be?"

He did not look up. He did not answer, even as she studied him, waiting, her heart pounding with anticipation of what he would say. Flashes were coming to her. She felt the shame crawling back. "Tal?" she prompted. She didn't want to hear it, but she had to. The not knowing, she reasoned, would make her crazier.

"You kind of . . . weren't acting like my *friend* last night." He was silent for a moment, weighing his words. "You were acting like . . . more." He swallowed and looked pained. "More than friends."

She nodded. She remembered wanting him. She remembered holding his hand. She'd thought that seeing Mrs. Chessman had detoured it, but it must've come back. In her drunken state she'd grown brave enough to act. Looking at him, she remembered his hands on the bow that played that violin so passionately. She wanted him to play her, too.

"Sorry," she said, even though remorse was not exactly what she felt.

He looked at her. "You don't remember at all?" The look on his face wasn't anger. It was hurt.

"Did we . . ." This time she was the one to look away. With the defroster on, the windshield had cleared. She watched a squirrel bounce across the land and skirt up a tree.

"We . . . ," he tried to say, but his voice gave out. He swallowed again, his Adam's apple moving in his throat. "You got any more of that gum?"

Thankful for something to do, she reached into her purse, fished out a piece, and handed it to him. She noticed he didn't let their fingers brush when he accepted it. He unwrapped the stick, crushed it into his mouth, and chewed harder than necessary.

He crumpled the wrapper and flung it over his shoulder into the back seat. That told her all she needed to know. Talmadge was usually meticulous about his car. It wasn't a super-nice car like some of the kids at school had, but he was still proud of it, tinkering with it, figuring out the way it worked, detailing it. If things were different, he and Graham might've been friends.

"You can tell me," she said. "I need to know."

"Give me a sec," he said. "I'm thinking." He opened the door and got out, letting in a whoosh of cold air to chill her all over again. She watched him walk into the same clump of bushes she'd already ventured into as he slept. Though the greenery mostly covered him, she could tell by the motions he made that he didn't just need a minute to think. He needed a minute to pee.

He came back to the car and climbed in, still not making eye contact as he shut the door. He switched on the radio, and the jazz station blared from the speakers. He quickly turned down the music, talking to the knobs instead of her. "We kissed, OK?" he said, his voice barely loud enough to be heard. "We kissed, and . . . you don't even remember it."

He gave another bitter laugh. "I don't know why I expected any different. I've waited my whole life to kiss you, and . . . it's like it didn't even happen." He went to shift the car into reverse, but she put her hand on his to stop him.

"No, Talmadge. Not yet. We need to talk about what happened. I still don't understand."

He looked at her like she was crazy. And like he was past caring. "You got drunk. You went up to some teacher and said all this crazy shit to her. Then I tried to take you home, but you freaked out and said you couldn't go home like that, so we drove here because I didn't know where else to go." He squinted at her. "You don't remember any of this?"

She shook her head and looked down to escape his accusing gaze.

"So we got here, and we got in the back seat to sleep, and then you started crying about something. But you wouldn't tell me what it was. It was something to do with what happened with Mrs. Chessman. You said you couldn't tell anyone. Then you just . . . started kissing me."

He was quiet, and she knew he was reliving it, recalling it with a clarity she envied. Not because she wanted to remember it, exactly, but because she hated the hole in her memory. Funny how something not so terrible she couldn't remember, but something awful she could recall with disturbing detail. "Who stopped it?" she asked. Her heart started galloping again as the words left her mouth. "We did stop . . . right?"

He glanced over at her quickly, and then away again. He turned the radio dial, leaving it on a rap song this time. "Yes, we stopped. But you . . . would've kept going." He said it like she'd betrayed him, like he was describing something she'd done with someone else. "You got mad that I stopped us. You said—" His voice cut out on him, and he reached for the water bottle, swallowing a deep gulp. "You said it didn't even matter." He replaced the cap, put the water back. "You said you wouldn't feel it anyway." This time when he put the car in reverse, she didn't stop him.

They drove to her house in silence, stopping a hundred yards away so she could get out and go inside without her parents seeing. He didn't so much put the car into park as shove it, the entire vehicle jolting to a stop. She rested her hand on the door handle but didn't tug at it, sensing that if she did, it might be a long time before they spoke again. She snuck a glance at him, watched his profile, willing him to look back at her. She tried to recall what it was like to kiss those lips, what he tasted like. But nothing came to her. "I was drunk," she said. "I didn't mean it."

"I know that," he said. He turned to meet her gaze. "That's the problem, Leah. You never do. And I'm not sure I can keep meaning it when you don't." He waved at the door, indicating she should get out. "I should go. My folks are probably worried."

She opened the door and stuck one leg out, expecting him to stop her, to tell her to wait a minute, to pull her back to him and kiss her so she remembered it this time. But he didn't say a word as she got out, closed the door, and began to walk home. It was only after he had driven away that she realized he never did tell her what he'd heard her say to Mrs. Chessman, though she feared she already knew.

Darcy

SUNDAY

On Sunday afternoon, she bit the bullet and went by Tommy's condo to give Graham the things Leah had left for him on Friday. She exhaled breath she did not realize she was holding when she pulled into the parking lot and didn't see Angie's Volkswagen Beetle with the ever-present fake flower in that cutesy vase thing that came with the car. Darcy could remember seeing Angie driving that car around town long before she stole her husband. Even then she'd thought that flower was ridiculous. How Tommy took the woman seriously was beyond her.

Darcy was just glad she would not be seeing Angie today. Things had been tense enough without having to be pleasant to someone everyone knew she despised. She would've been nice, of course, because Graham would've been right there, watching. Graham, the boy she would do anything to protect—even let him go move in with her ex and his floozy girlfriend and her stupid flower car.

She climbed the rickety metal stairs to the second-floor condo, wondering just how Graham had managed it with his bum leg. Stairs had to have been difficult for him, if not impossible. *Don't let it worry you,* she heard Clay's voice say in her head. *He made his choice.* But was it Graham's choice? Was it anyone's choice to be where they all were?

She saw their lives like so many dominoes falling, the first one toppling at the moment that Tommy pulled into the stadium parking lot with Graham in that damn Charger.

Winded from the climb (she had to get back to exercising soon), she reached the door of the condo, a place she still couldn't imagine Tommy living, even though he'd been there for months. The place was on the outskirts of town, a little two-building complex some developer built, then promptly forgot about. A place inhabited by people exactly like Tommy, people who were between phases of life: young people between their parents' home and one of their own; the occasional family between houses, needing a quick place to live; and men between marriages. It was not a place to call home. It was not a place her son belonged.

She raised her hand and knocked lightly, heard Graham's voice from inside: "Come in." She turned the knob, and, sure enough, it opened.

"Graham," she fussed. "Why don't you have this door locked?"

"Hey, Mom," he said. "Good to see you, too." He was on the couch playing a video game. He barely even looked her way.

In two steps she was out of the "foyer" and in the condo's tiny kitchen. The sink was full of dirty dishes, and she wrinkled her nose. She never left dirty dishes in her sink; it was a matter of principle. An open pizza box with a withering slice of pizza still in it was on the counter. That Angie was no housekeeper, and she remarked on it aloud before she could stop herself.

"She's not here," Graham replied.

"Well I realize that, but she could've tidied up before she left, couldn't she? She can't expect you to do it. You're injured."

On the TV screen, someone screamed and collapsed to the ground. Graham sighed and threw the controller down on the couch, somehow sending the TV screen to black. She entered the den cautiously, as if Angie or Tommy might be hiding in a corner, ready to jump out at her.

"No, I mean she's not here anymore. At all," Graham said. He patted the couch, which was the only seating option in the room. Tentatively, she lowered herself to sit beside him.

"What do you mean, 'not here at all'?" Darcy asked, even though she thought she already knew.

He looked at her like she was dense. "She moved out."

She had to bite back the smile that threatened to fill her face. She felt her spirits lift inside her: this was the best news she'd heard in a long, long time. Ding-dong the witch is dead. "Are they broken up?"

He exhaled loudly and picked up the controller again. "Jeez, Mom, I don't know." The TV screen came back to life as he began a new game. He was, it was clear, not interested in continuing this conversation. On the screen, a man was running through an urban scene as women dressed like prostitutes looked on.

His attention still on the screen, he added, "She wasn't too keen on my moving in here. They've been fighting a lot. And her shit's gone." He nodded in the direction of the master bedroom. Darcy shuddered at the thought of her husband's things mixed with Angie's, his toothbrush nestled beside hers in a little cup by the sink. Her hair and his entwined on the same hairbrush. Her feminine products under his sink. It was all so intimate, so close. A new wave of betrayal washed over her, surprising her. And yet Angie was gone. So was the betrayal over? And what did that mean?

Don't get ahead of yourself, Darcy, her internal coach chided. She hated herself for even thinking it. She wanted to be one of those women who said, "I don't need him," and meant it. But she'd been with Tommy most of her life—the part that counted, at least—and that was a hard thing to sever. She'd been sawing at it now for a year, but some connections were simply too formed to make a clean cut. She'd resolved that they would remain, and that she would just have to ignore them, for the rest of her life. But now? Now Angie was gone.

A face filled her mind: Clay. She blinked, and he was gone. She turned and studied her son's profile, seeing herself in it, seeing Tommy, too. "Everything good?" she asked, her voice tentative. "You getting settled in?"

A few seconds passed. On the screen, the man was now in a car, racing another man. She almost said he should turn it off, should stop playing it. Maybe they could blame this game if Graham's case ever went to trial. Maybe insanity by means of video game was an actual defense.

"It's fine, Mom," he said, glancing over his shoulder at her, then back at the game. "I mean," he amended himself, "as fine as it's ever going to be." His hand stilled on the controller and, on the screen, the action stopped. He gave Darcy the side eye, then dropped his gaze.

"I killed those girls, Mom." He closed his eyes. She saw a tear leak through the closed lid and begin its descent down his cheek.

She moved forward, clasping her hands together to keep from wiping away the tear, her protective urge stronger than ever. "You didn't mean to, honey. You didn't mean to."

"Maybe I deserve to be beat up, to go to jail, to have something terrible happen to me."

"No," she said, her voice somewhere between fierce and frightened. "No, you do not. You were a kid. You were doing what kids do. They make mistakes. They don't think past the nose on their face. If I had been held accountable for every stupid thing I did as a kid—" She stopped, realizing that Graham wasn't listening. He ducked his head to hide the tears that had joined that first one, wetting his cheeks.

Through his tears, he spoke. "It's the first thing I think about when I wake up in the morning. And the last thing I think about at night." She thought of finding the girls' pictures in his room, hidden like another boy might've hidden a *Playboy*. She'd thought if she didn't address it, he'd get over it, move past it. But this wasn't something he—or anyone else in town—was going to get over. They were just going to have to learn to live with it.

"In time, it will get better. Your heart will heal just like your body."

"Yeah, well, hearts take a lot longer." He gave a little ironic laugh. Mostly, she suspected, for her benefit. She could already see him tucking back into himself, returning to the place where everything was fine. For the first time, she'd seen just how hard he had to work to maintain that.

"Yeah." She made herself laugh, too, and ruffled his hair like he was five years old again. In some ways, he always would be. That was the way it was with your kids. No matter what they did, or didn't do, they were your kids and you loved them no matter what. It was the most extraordinary miracle—that humans could love like that.

"Hearts do take longer." Sensing his need for a subject change, she hitched her thumb in the direction of the kitchen. "I left books from Leah on the kitchen table."

"OK," he said. He thought about it. "Can you drop something off to her, do you think? I've got a worksheet finished that I might as well hand in."

"Good job!" She praised him, her voice too effusive and earnest, trying to make up for what just happened.

He rolled his eyes. "It's a worksheet, Mom. Not a term paper."

She reached over and patted his arm. "Well, I'm just proud of you for keeping up. A lot of students would've let this put them behind."

His answer was mumbled, but she heard it loud and clear. "My grades are about the only thing I have going for me."

She started to argue, to tell him that wasn't true. That he had his good sense of humor, his friends and family, so many things going for him. But she knew it would fall on deaf ears. "Sometimes we don't want to hear your rah-rah speeches," Tommy had said to her in those last days before he left. Once a cheerleader, always a cheerleader, she supposed. She couldn't help herself.

"Can you get my worksheet? It's on top of the books on my bed." He gestured at his leg to indicate that he did not feel like getting up and retrieving it.

"Sure, honey," she said. She stood and walked toward the back of the condo, where the two small bedrooms were. "I'll just swing by Leah's on my way home right now and leave it with her so she can take it in tomorrow." She tried to keep her voice upbeat.

She paused outside the master bedroom door, willing herself not to look in, but of course she had to peek. She saw the tangle of bedcovers on an unmade bed. She smelled the lingering smell of Tommy's cologne, a brand she'd bought him every Christmas since they'd been together. She stepped inside, chastising herself for doing so but unable to stop. She walked over to the closet, pulled open the door, anxious to see for herself if it was really true, if there would be no women's clothing hanging there beside her husband's.

"Mom?" Graham called. She froze as if he'd walked in and seen what she was doing.

"Yeah?" she answered.

"Where'd you go?"

She hurried into his room, snatched the paper from his bed, and rejoined him in the den. "I was just looking at your room. It's so . . . bare. Don't you want some things from home to make it more . . . homey?"

"It's not my home," he said. He turned his attention back to the TV. "This place isn't anyone's home."

She smiled at his profile, letting his words fill her with comfort. And something else, something that resided somewhere deep inside her, in spite of circumstances to the contrary. Something she both hated and loved about herself, the eternal cheerleader. She felt it well up inside her chest, buoyant and irrepressible: hope.

Marglyn

SUNDAY

Every time Mary Claire showed up in one of her dreams, she feared it would be the last time she would ever see her. And every time her daughter returned for another nocturnal visit, Marglyn wished she could go on sleeping forever. But wasn't that what Mary Claire was already doing?

Last night's dream had begun with Marglyn in the yard, watching the driveway as she had the afternoon with Hale when he confessed. She heard a creaking noise and looked over to find Mary Claire just sitting on the swing, motionless. Instead of being too big for the swing set as she was in real life, MC fit in the tiny bucket seat just perfectly. Her daughter was growing smaller. When she tried to move closer to her, Mary Claire began to swing, kicking her feet out so Marglyn would have to back away. There were rules here, Marglyn understood. Rules both of them had no choice but to abide by.

Mary Claire began to talk as she swung back and forth. There was a sense of urgency in her voice with her usual bossiness thrown in. But in the dream, in this new reality, Marglyn didn't mind the bossiness. She welcomed it. She welcomed every part of Mary Claire—even the parts she used to correct and complain about.

"Why haven't you taken Leah the clothes?" Mary Claire asked.

"Th-the . . . clothes?" she stammered. She'd discarded the notion not long after she'd woken up from the last dream. She couldn't possibly take those clothes to that child with no preamble and no invitation. What was she supposed to do, just show up at her house with a bag of clothes and say, *Here*?

"Yes, Mother, the clothes. The ones I picked out for Leah. The ones she needs." She gave a little harrumph at the end that was so familiar and so her it made Marglyn smile.

"What?" Mary Claire asked. "What's so funny?"

"I just miss you," Marglyn said.

"I miss you, too." Mary Claire shrugged and stopped swinging, digging her feet into the ground until her toes made an imprint. "That's why I come to see you."

"Will you always come to see me?" Marglyn asked, her voice rising in hope.

She could see MC pondering the answer. She fixed Marglyn with one of her penetrating green gazes. "I don't know," she admitted.

Marglyn nodded and didn't bother to hide her disappointed expression.

"I hope you will," she said, in case she got a vote. "It . . . helps. To still see you."

"Are you going to the meeting tomorrow?" Mary Claire asked, and her knowledge of the meeting didn't surprise Marglyn. She somehow understood that her daughter was privy to information, that in death her scope of knowledge had widened, that her field of vision was quite large, no longer hemmed in by location or time.

"I wasn't going to," she admitted. The other mothers were going ahead with the meeting, but she'd told Hale she just couldn't go. If she didn't show up, they'd get the point without going through that rigmarole.

Mary Claire's look was both earnest and guileless. "What happened to you, Mom?" she asked. "You used to do things. You used to take action. You were—" She broke off.

"I was what?" Marglyn asked, filled with a desire to know what her daughter wasn't saying. And suddenly aware that Mary Claire was going to disappear again at any moment.

Mary Claire smiled and cocked her head. "You were good at being good."

Marglyn shook her head. "No I wasn't."

Mary Claire yanked on the chains of the swing until they rattled. "Yes you were. And I was jealous. I was jealous of anyone you helped, because I always thought that it was taking away from me. But you know what I've learned?"

Marglyn kept herself from rushing forward to clutch her daughter to her in fear that she would disappear entirely and she would never know what it was she had learned. "What, honey?" she asked, her heart straining forward in her chest, reaching out to her even as her arms stayed still. She could feel it in the space between them, their hearts meeting in the middle. And in the meeting, the barest flicker of healing. "Tell me what you've learned." She smiled at her daughter.

"I didn't have to be scared of you showing love to someone else, of you helping other people. Because love is a renewable resource. The more you give, the more you have." Her smile widened. "But you already knew that, didn't you?"

Before she could answer, Mary Claire was gone, and Marglyn was awake in her own bed, thinking that she had better try to get back to sleep. She had some things on her agenda for the coming day, things her daughter needed her to do.

◆ ◆ ◆

They held the meeting on Sunday afternoon at Cynthia's house, her husband, Ted, greeting Marglyn at the door, his mouth in a tight, grim line as he held it open for her. He glanced at her, then quickly away. It was clear he knew she was the holdout in the group, the one there under duress. She wished Hale had come with her for reinforcement, but someone had to take Robert to his tutoring session. He was failing math, and there was a test on Monday. Sometimes it astounded her, the way they had to keep parenting. The way they had to keep living.

She perched on the edge of Cynthia's sofa, accepting her offer of coffee both because she could use the caffeine and because it would give her something to do with her hands. Holding her cup was better than clenching and unclenching her fists. When she wanted to scream, she would squeeze the coffee cup tighter. It was better than putting her hands around Cynthia's slender neck.

When Leslie arrived, Marglyn greeted her, shifting on the couch to indicate there was plenty of room and to have a seat. Cynthia came back in with the coffee in a delicate china cup she probably received for her wedding and rarely used. She apologized that she'd forgotten to ask whether Marglyn took sugar or cream. Marglyn said she needed neither and took a sip of the strong, dark liquid as if to prove it.

"I can't believe you take it black," said Cynthia. "I just can't drink it like that." Leslie nodded and murmured in agreement.

Marglyn did not tell them that before Mary Claire died she could drink coffee only with extra cream and extra sugar. Hale used to tease her that it was like a dessert. And she would tease back, "So what if it is?" And they would laugh because they didn't have a care in the world, even though they thought they did.

But on the morning after the accident when Hale poured his coffee, she'd come into the kitchen and said, "I'll take some," in the flat monotone voice they'd begun using around each other, zombie voices. He'd nodded somberly, pouring the coffee into a mug, the steam rising up and enwreathing his head. When he wordlessly shuffled over to pull the cream out of the fridge, she'd startled them both when she said, "No. I'll just take it black." She'd drunk the whole cup that way, hot and bitter.

She'd drunk it like that ever since.

Now she sipped her coffee and forced herself through the pleasantries, making small talk about the weather and the team's record and the other things in Worthy that you talked about when you didn't want to talk about the issue at hand. She was grateful Leslie's husband had not come, either. When Cynthia found that out, she sent Ted to watch football, and he slunk off looking relieved. Cynthia sat down in a wingback chair across from them, then said she'd forgotten her own coffee and jumped up to fetch it. Marglyn relaxed a little that it wasn't going to be four against one.

Cynthia got right down to business when she returned, still mysteriously not holding any coffee. Marglyn nearly pointed it out, but refrained.

"I thought of having our attorney here today but figured it might be best if we met just us," she began. She said "just us" in a conspiratorial tone with a little inclusive grin, like they were best girlfriends planning a day at the spa or a surprise party for another friend.

Marglyn thought briefly of what she'd have done if Cynthia had gone so far as to have a lawyer there, the indication that they were ready to proceed. Would she have walked out? Before the accident, she would've suffered through, erring on the side of politeness. But the new her, the post–Mary Claire Marglyn, drank black coffee and did not sit through blitz attacks. She'd said she would meet to talk, not meet to pursue a lawsuit against someone she'd sat next to at a football game two weeks before the accident. This meeting was pointless; she was not interested in suing anyone over an accident. She realized that's what she'd come for—to tell them so in person.

"I just think," Cynthia said, "that there should be some restitution, some acknowledgment on his part." She waited for a nod and got one from Leslie. "A court case will ensure that happens." She raised her eyebrows. "I'm just not sure he's going to have to pay for this the way he should. I mean, he's just walking around, free as a bird."

Leslie nodded again, so agreeable that Marglyn couldn't help but think of her daughter Keary, always so cheerful and kind, eager to please. Just like her. "It'll help us feel like we've put things right," Leslie chimed in, then looked to Cynthia for approval.

Marglyn gripped her coffee cup tighter. There were pink roses encircling the rim against a gray lattice pattern. It was the kind of china a young bride would choose, someone who thinks only of hearts and flowers and happily ever after. It was something perhaps her own daughter would select, had she had the chance to get married. *Don't you know,* she wanted to say, *that this won't put things right? Nothing will ever be right again.*

"Have you all stopped to think about what a court case might do to our girls' memories?" she spoke up. She looked at Leslie. "Your daughter wasn't even a licensed driver. Don't you worry about her culpability in what happened at all?" She thought of those beer cans, carted off to the recycling plant as if they'd never existed at all. But they had. And what role they played, no one would ever know. Not if she had her way.

Her hand trembled slightly as she set the coffee cup down on the table beside her. The clatter of the china against the wood startled Leslie, who had been looking at Cynthia for cues as to how to respond. Marglyn rose as if lifted by an unseen hand. "I'm sorry," she said. She took a step toward the front door, just inches from the formal living room they sat in.

Darcy LaRue lived in a house similar to this one, just a few streets away. She'd been there once, for a meeting to plan the booster barbecue. She thought of Darcy, probably sitting in that house alone right now. She'd heard at church that morning that someone had vandalized the LaRue house last week, splashed red paint on the door like Passover blood. But tragedy had not passed over the LaRue house.

She looked down at the two sets of eyes blinking rapidly at her, the two of them unsure why she was standing or what she was going to do. "I can't stay here," she explained. "I can't pretend what you're discussing is OK." She pointed vaguely in the direction of Darcy's house, seeing her as she'd seen her at the football game not all that long ago. Darcy had come with Graham, who'd promptly disappeared with his buddies, and her friend Faye, who Marglyn also knew. Darcy had spent a lot of time talking to Faye about Tommy, loudly enough that Marglyn had heard a good bit of it.

She'd felt sorry for her that night, and blessed that Hale hadn't done to her what Tommy had done to Darcy. She'd been so overcome she'd looped her arm through Hale's and kissed his cheek right in the middle of the game for no reason at all. He'd looked at her in surprise. "What was that for?"

"For being a good man," she'd said. And he'd leaned over and kissed her back, a big, loud kiss on the mouth, embarrassing Robert so much he'd pulled his hoodie down over his head. Marglyn had laughed and turned her attention back to Mary Claire, who at that moment was turning a flip in the air, head over heels. She'd looked back at Darcy, offered her an apologetic smile. *I'm sorry my life is so perfect and yours sucks.*

She'd been so stupid.

"I won't sue the LaRues. I have my reasons, and I'm not sure you want me to go into them."

Marglyn waited a beat to see if the two mothers would press, would ask if there was something they needed to know, something that implicated their daughters. She saw Keary's mother shift in her seat, the movement barely perceptible unless you were looking for it. She took the shift to mean that Leslie wasn't sure suing was the right thing, either.

She focused on Cynthia. "You do what you need to do," she said. "But if you pursue it, please know I will speak to the LaRues' attorney."

She licked her lips, her mouth suddenly very dry. "You'll leave me no choice."

Cynthia opened her mouth as if to argue, then clamped her lips shut again. Her eyeballs looked like they were going to pop right out of her head. The two women stared at each other for a moment. No one spoke, but she could hear Cynthia's shallow breath revealing her nerves like a poker player with a tell.

"I'll show myself out," Marglyn said. And she did.

Leah

SUNDAY

In her bedroom, behind a locked door, she paused while changing and stood in front of the same mirror she once stood in front of as a little girl. Used to be, the mirror reflected her first attempts at putting on makeup, a glittering tiara on her head, a pretty new dress. But today, it reflected her chest. All traces of summer were gone—no more contrast between white skin and tan skin. She slipped a hoodie over her head and thought of that long-ago sunburn, and then of Talmadge outside the pool that day. Talmadge had been ignoring her texts since early Saturday. She knew she would have to tell him the whole truth and nothing but the truth in order for him to forgive her. She was losing her nerve.

A knock on her door made her glad she'd already put a shirt back on. She heard her mother working the knob. "Why is this door locked, young lady?" she asked, her voice muffled by the closed door. "You know we don't lock doors in this house."

Leah sighed and looked up at the ceiling just like her mother did sometimes. Then she stood up and opened the door. "I was changing," she said.

Her mother eyed her with that look that told her she knew there was more to it but had decided not to push. Leah had been getting that look a lot lately.

"There's someone downstairs for you," her mother said.

Leah wrinkled her brow. "Who?"

"The mother of that boy you've been . . . helping," she said, and sniffed as if she smelled something rotten. Leah's mother did not approve of Graham LaRue. She'd listened to the town gossip and, like so many people, determined that he was at fault in the accident. And yet she was the very one who'd taught Leah to reach out to those in trouble, to extend a hand of kindness to those in need. Leah thought of Graham alone in his house day after day, living under threat of harm, limping in pain from the accident. If anyone needed help, he did.

"Oh, she's probably bringing his assignments to me for tomorrow," she said. As she brushed past, her mother felt like a column, stiff and immovable. She walked downstairs thinking of the power she possessed, power her mother knew nothing about. Power to take an ax to that column, to crumble the house around all of their ears.

Darcy LaRue sat awkwardly at the kitchen table, holding a single worksheet in her hand. She held it up as Leah entered the room, fluttered it at her. "I brought this for Graham. He said it might be good for you to go ahead and hand it in." She put the paper back on the table, and Leah hoped one of her brothers hadn't left something sticky on the surface like they usually did.

"OK, I'll take it in tomorrow." She shrugged. "If Worthy High caught up with the times, we could do all of this via e-mail." She added a little false laugh as punctuation.

"If Worthy High caught up with the times, that would mean the whole town would have to," Mrs. LaRue said wryly. "I doubt that will happen."

Leah rolled her eyes in agreement. "True." They looked at each other for a moment, and in that look were a thousand unsaid words—words about pain and secrets, about judgment and fear. About living in a place where you wanted to be yourself but couldn't—not only because other people wouldn't approve but also because you weren't entirely sure who *yourself* actually was. Leah sensed that Mrs. LaRue felt that just as strongly as she did, and she realized anew that growing up meant growing more uncertain, not less.

Mrs. LaRue ran her hands across the paper in front of her, caressing it. "It gave me an excuse to check up on my son," she said. "So I don't mind."

"He's at his dad's?" Leah asked, feeling odd but also feeling the need to make small talk, since Mrs. LaRue didn't seem especially compelled to leave. It occurred to Leah that the woman had nowhere else to go.

"Yeah. He seems to be settling in." Mrs. LaRue smiled at something, a mere flicker that came and went. She didn't elaborate on what made her smile, and Leah didn't ask. She rose from the table, and Leah felt relieved that she wouldn't have to keep making small talk.

"Thanks," Mrs. LaRue said. She thumped the paper. "For taking that for him. For . . . everything." For one horrible moment, it seemed as if Mrs. LaRue was going to start crying in her kitchen. And then the doorbell sounded, pulling them both out of the moment.

From somewhere in the house, she heard her mother's voice say, "I'll get it." She and Mrs. LaRue eyed each other; the arrival of another person meant they were now trapped in the kitchen together. They listened in silence as the door opened and her mother greeted the visitor.

"Well isn't Leah just the popular one today," they heard her mother say. "You have another visitor!" she called out. "It's Mrs. Miner!" Leah and Mrs. LaRue traded wide-eyed looks and, as Leah moved forward to greet Mary Claire's mother, she wondered who was more startled—her or Darcy LaRue.

Marglyn

SUNDAY

She held out the bag full of Mary Claire's clothes and forced herself to smile at the girl coming toward her, this girl so full of life. But her smile died when she looked past her to see someone else standing there in the kitchen doorway. Someone familiar. She blinked a few times, as if to clear her vision. It was too unlikely, too odd, considering the meeting she'd just been to. Why was Darcy LaRue standing in Leah Bennett's kitchen?

She'd seen her at Brynne's funeral. Everyone had. It'd been the talk of the town, how she'd had some nerve showing up like she did. And yet, Marglyn had quietly understood her dilemma. Show up and she was inconsiderate. Not show up and she was disrespectful. Darcy LaRue was damned if she did and damned if she didn't.

Now they eyed each other as Leah and her mother kept a respectful, silent distance. Marglyn was the first to break the silence, feeling guilty as she greeted her, as if she should also confess that she'd just come from a meeting with two other mothers who were determined to mete out punishment for her son, for her entire family, if they had their way. But she simply said, "Hello, Darcy. I—" She waggled the heavy bag in her hand. "I was just bringing by some things I thought Leah could use."

She looked over at Leah to explain further. "Some of Mary Claire's clothes. Some new things, barely worn. You look about her size." She offered this explanation instead of the real one: that her daughter had come to her in a dream and basically demanded she do this. She had a sudden thought—had Mary Claire arranged this somehow? Had she meant for Marglyn to run into Darcy at Leah's house? She thought of her daughter up in heaven, orchestrating outcomes there much the same as she had here. The thought made her smile, and she turned it on Leah. "I think she would want you to have these."

Leah stepped forward, looking as if she would like to melt through the floor, which Marglyn didn't blame her for. She herself was not far from the same reaction. And yet she was the adult, the example setter. "Thanks," Leah mumbled, and took the bag.

Beside her, Leah's mother asked if she could get her anything. "No, thank you," she replied. The last thing she needed was to join Darcy in the Bennett kitchen, sit at the table, and make small talk, which could lead to larger talk, which could lead to her spilling the beans to Darcy about the other mothers' plans. She thought of her most recent dream, of Mary Claire's earnest, urgent face asking her to take her clothes to Leah. She'd thought her daughter was being kind, but maybe she was being something else: a peacemaker. She had not ever seen MC in that light.

She glanced over at Mrs. Bennett, a quiet, stoic woman who she knew only in passing. She wanted to grab her hand and say, *Don't do what I did. Don't miss her when she's standing right in front of you.* But she kept quiet, her hands empty of the bag now, her mind grappling for something to say, something in summary that would get her safely and quickly out of the situation.

"Well, it was good to see you all," she said.

Darcy said quickly, "You, too." Marglyn gave a little wave and turned to leave, hearing as she did: "In fact, I'll walk out with you." Her heart sank into her shoes, making her feet so heavy she had to stop moving, giving Darcy LaRue time to catch up.

Ava

SUNDAY

The police had made her delete all her students' phone numbers. "Don't want you to be able to text any more young men," the wiry one had said, licking his lips as he leaned forward and lasciviously watched her delete each contact in her list marked "English class." Satisfied that she'd done as told, they had let her keep her phone. They didn't know about the piece of paper she'd had the kids write all their numbers on that first day, just in case. She doubted the kids even remembered they'd done it.

Now with trembling hands, she fished the paper out of the drawer, her eye falling on the one number she needed, the name written in girlish curly script: Leah Bennett. She'd spent all weekend telling herself not to follow up, to let it go, to let the chips fall where they may. But she sensed that if she did that, the chips would fall on the side of her life ruined forever, those boys going on with their lives while hers was derailed. She kept recalling Leah at the bar, eyes glazed over, the alcohol in her bloodstream working like a truth serum.

She had to know what Leah knew. And it wasn't likely Leah was going to tell her on her own. She retrieved her phone from her purse and sat down on the couch to enter the number. There was a missed call, and she hoped for a fleeting moment that perhaps Clay had called. But it was the guy from the other night, a text saying he'd enjoyed meeting her, and while things hadn't worked out that night, perhaps they could see each other? Some part of her nearly texted back, the same part that had caused her to respond to Ian's tactics. The same part that had let him get close enough to her to ruin her life. Because when a guy showed her attention, she felt seen, known, loved, appreciated. She let them give her what she didn't have herself, as if the only way that validation could be obtained was if someone else—someone male—provided it.

She had to stop that thought pattern from repeating itself inside her brain, inside her heart. That pattern had echoed throughout her life in big and little ways. She had to figure out how to feel good about herself apart from what a man thought of her. Without letting this stranger— or even Clay—have the power to dictate her happiness. It could start with deleting his text.

She swiped her finger across the screen, pressed the red "Delete" button. The text disappeared, and she felt a little surge of something that seemed like power, like hope. Maybe she didn't need a man to make her feel valuable. Maybe she could just decide that for herself.

She entered Leah's number and typed a few words, just a short plea, one she hoped would reach her without getting Ava into any more trouble. Maybe, she thought, instead of getting her into more trouble, it would get her out of it.

Leah

SUNDAY

She stood at her window peeking from behind the blinds at the two women standing on her driveway, talking. She studied their postures, the set of their chins and shoulders, the looks on their faces, trying to determine what they were saying to each other. Neither of them seemed particularly happy, but it did not look like they were angry, either. Sad, maybe. But not angry. She watched as one—Mary Claire's mother—reached for the other, and, for the briefest moment, they embraced. Forgiveness. That's what she was seeing. Without really understanding why, tears sprang to her eyes.

She walked away from the window, flopped onto her bed, and hugged a throw pillow to her. It was one she'd made in Vacation Bible School years ago, a T-shirt cut into a square, stuffed, and sewn shut. She'd kept it on her bed ever since. Now she studied it, trying to determine whether it was a T-shirt or a pillow. She saw both when she looked at it—the thing it was before and the thing it became. The one was always a part of the other.

There was a knock at the door. "Come in," she said, her voice muffled by the pillow.

Her mother entered the room, carrying the bag of clothes Mary Claire's mother had brought over. "Do you want to keep these?" she asked. "Or should I donate them to the church? I'm sure there are some less-fortunates who would like to have these nice things." Her mother's voice sounded shaky, uncertain. Her mother's voice sounded afraid.

"I'll keep them," Leah said. "She wanted me to have them." Though who exactly wanted her to have them, she couldn't say for sure. Was it Mary Claire's mother or Mary Claire herself? If it was MC herself, how could her mother know that? It wasn't like MC knew she was going to die and made her final wishes clear. She tried to recall what MC's mother had said, dangling the bag of clothes in her direction. Was it "She wanted you to have them" or "I think she'd want you to have them"?

Her mother set the clothes down in front of her closet and peered inside. "If you're going to keep those things, then maybe you should get rid of some of these other clothes?" she asked hopefully, as if this gift could spark some organization. Leah's mother loved things to be orderly, neat, just so. She usually steered clear of Leah's room.

"Sure," Leah said. Across the room, her phone, plugged in on her desk, pinged, letting her know she had a text. She thought one word: Talmadge. He hadn't gone this long without being in contact since she'd blown him off to hang out with Mary Claire, Brynne, and Keary. She didn't like the silence between them, but she didn't like what she'd have to do to get him talking to her again.

She saw her mother frown at the phone. At least she assumed she was frowning at the phone; she could've been frowning at the volume of Emily Dickinson poems the phone was on top of. What her mother had against Emily was unclear, but she definitely didn't care for her.

"When you feel like telling me," her mother said, now back in the doorway, her empty hands clasped together, looking as awkward as Mary Claire's mother had looked when she walked in and spotted Darcy

LaRue, "I'd love to talk about . . . everything. I know—" She stopped talking, searching Leah's face as if the answers might be written across it.

She took in a deep breath and continued. "I know there are things you're not telling me. Things you think maybe I wouldn't understand. But I—" She paused, as if waiting for Leah to supply the words she was grasping for. When Leah kept silent, she finished in a rush, words tumbling over themselves. "I understand more than you know. And I'm here. If you need me. OK?"

It was the most her mother had said to her in weeks. It was the thing she'd dreaded. But now that it was upon her, it wasn't as ominous or scary as she'd thought it would be. It actually felt kind of . . . good. She could see that her mother cared, that she wanted in. And maybe that didn't have to be a bad thing. She nodded and watched as her mother visibly relaxed, her shoulders lowering, her pinched mouth going slack. "OK, Mom."

She waited until her mom left, then hopped up to check her phone, finding a text from Mrs. Chessman of all people. She read:

I'm sorry for texting you like this. But I'd love to hear more about what you were saying Friday night. I think it might help.

Leah shook her head and put down the phone, her eyes straying to the clothes nestled there in the bag where her mother had left it.

Right on top was a shirt she remembered MC buying. She'd tried it on for them, doing one of her "fashion shows," as she always called it, standing in front of the mirror and eyeing herself with a confidence Leah didn't have, one she could only watch and envy. But Mary Claire didn't have confidence anymore. She didn't have anything. She was gone, and the shirt was in Leah's possession. Maybe that meant her confidence was up for grabs, too. Maybe in wearing MC's clothes she could borrow some of what she needed.

She slipped from her bed, knelt beside the clothes, and inhaled the scent of her lost friend, a floral, powdery scent that was so Mary Claire it was as if she were standing in front of her. "I know what you'd do if you were here," she said aloud. "I know what you'd do if you were in my shoes." She gave a little laugh at the thought. Mary Claire would've never been in Leah's shoes. She was too smart and strong for that. Maybe with some luck and the right wardrobe, Leah could be, too.

"Thanks for the clothes," she whispered.

She walked back over to the phone, picked it up, and started to text Mrs. Chessman back, but she wasn't ready for that yet. She put the phone down and picked up the volume of poems underneath it instead. Mrs. Chessman's poems. She opened the book of poetry just like she used to open her Bible, letting it fall open, willing her eyes to fall on just the right words, words that would bring her comfort, direction, something. Her eyes lit on the word *hope* and then she saw the word *feathers*. It was as if Emily herself was nudging her toward the lanky violinist who'd turned handsome when she wasn't looking.

She thought of the anger in his eyes the other morning as he'd dropped her off and driven away. She thought of how hopeless she'd felt after that, yet according to Emily, he was hope. He was the thing with feathers. He was Talmadge Feathers, and she had to go to him, to tell him the thing she'd been unable to say since the night the girls died. She couldn't put it off any longer.

Marglyn

She arrived home expecting to put her feet up and rest. But the minute she saw the police car in her driveway, she knew rest was still a ways away. She entered the house to find an officer sitting on the couch with Hale, both of them looking ill at ease, like two suitors waiting for their dates. The first thing she thought was that one of the other mothers had done something after she left and he was there to tell them so.

Her heart sank as she thought of her conversation with Darcy just moments before. "I don't fault you. I don't fault him. Accidents happen." She'd said those words, and she'd meant them. As much as she wanted someone to blame, there was no one. Except maybe herself.

"Is this about the accident?" she asked, sliding into the spot next to Hale, open as though he'd saved it for her, because wasn't that what marriage was? A permanent place next to someone, a place always reserved for you right by his side? She thought of Darcy, left with that spot beside her, open and bare. She reached over and took her husband's hand, clasped it tight.

"No ma'am," the officer said. In looking at him, she could see that he was a young cop, green and squeaky. He probably wasn't much older than Mary Claire. He would not be involved in the investigation into the accident. That was for the senior officers. He was more likely to cover lesser offenses. An awful thought came to her mind. "Is this about Robert? Did he do something?"

She thought of something her mother had said once, after Mary Claire was born and she was still trying to have a relationship with her, still hoping she would stop drinking. Her mother had looked at the bundle of pink in Marglyn's arms and said, "All kids are good for is breaking your heart."

Turned out, for once, her mother had been right.

Hale's laugh in response was his blustery "huh-huh-huh" laugh he did around other men. He let go of her hand to pat her knee. "It's not about Robert." He pointed to the cop with a grin. "He's here about the girl, the one you were with . . ." He didn't finish the sentence because he didn't need to. Ginny. The one she was with the night their daughter was killed.

The officer began explaining, tipping his chin down and dropping his voice a level. "She was picked up today. For shoplifting. She confessed and, in questioning her actions, we discovered a connection to you." He looked from Hale's face to Marglyn's face and back again. His voice went up an octave. "And, well, it was just . . . odd. If you could've seen her face, she just seemed . . . guilty, but of something more than shoplifting. Like what she was confessing was bigger than what she was brought in for. And I just wondered if you've had any trouble out of her, or ever felt threatened by her, or . . . anything?"

Hale shook his head. "I told him other than the one time she came to dinner I've never seen the girl."

The officer ignored him. "It was like," he continued, "it was like she'd done something terrible to you all. It bothered me so much I just had to come by and do a welfare check."

"Where did you arrest her?" Marglyn asked, a theory beginning to form in her mind, one that would explain why her name had come up. "Was it at Peabody's?"

The officer's eyes widened. "How'd you know that?"

"I took her shopping there the night . . ." She glanced over at Hale and back at the policeman. "The night our daughter was killed."

"I heard about that," he said, ducking his head in deference, his voice sinking low again. "I'm sorry for your loss."

"Thank you," she said stiffly. She was so tired of hearing those five words. She knew it was what people said, but she didn't care if she ever heard it again.

"What did she take?" she asked, anxious to get past the condolences, to focus on the issue at hand.

He reached into a folder he held on his lap and handed her a printout. She looked down and saw that it was a list of the items recovered. *Ginny,* she thought as she scanned the list. *Why?*

She rose from her seat and left the two men sitting there. She could feel their eyes on her as she crossed the house and disappeared down the hall. She let herself into Mary Claire's bedroom, now a little emptier after taking the clothes to Leah. But the bag Ginny had returned to her was still on the bed. She picked it up and carried it back to the den, handing it unceremoniously to the cop.

"Are these the items?" she asked, her voice croaky and stiff. She watched as he dug through the bag, nodding all the while. She felt exhaustion overtaking her, the kind of exhaustion that isn't solely physical but emotional. The kind that settles into the middle of your chest and radiates outward, the kind that comes from reaching out to someone when it would've been easier to walk away. But she was in it now. And so was Ginny. To the best of her ability, Ginny was hanging on in the only way she knew how.

"How'd you—" the police officer began, but he broke off, realizing, she guessed, that some things were best left unexplained.

"Is she in jail?" she asked.

He nodded. "It was her third offense. We had no choice."

Marglyn nodded, remembering the night she had Ginny over for dinner. She glanced at the dining room table. She'd had such high hopes for how it would go. She thought perhaps Ginny and Mary Claire would connect, bond, whatever girls that age did. She'd wanted to be the conduit, the link between them. One day they'd tell the story of how they'd met, she'd daydreamed. They'd say they had her to thank.

Instead, Mary Claire had glowered through dinner, making snarky comments, critiquing the food, and texting the whole time, which was forbidden at the dinner table ordinarily. But Mary Claire had known that Marglyn wouldn't push the issue in front of Ginny. She'd most likely used the phone to summon Brynne to rescue her, the car horn sounding from the drive just as they were finishing up. Mary Claire had leaped from the table and waved at them all as she called out some excuse over her shoulder about having to leave and rushed out the door. From her place at the table, Marglyn had watched Brynne's wheels kick up dust as they sped away.

Later, in the kitchen, Ginny had helped her wash dishes, and she'd tried to apologize for Mary Claire's behavior, her words halting and uncertain. "Oh, don't apologize, Mrs. Miner," Ginny had said, her voice taking on a wistful, dreamy quality. "I'm sure she's got so many important things to do." Marglyn was glad Mary Claire had left; it was probably better for all of them. If Marglyn saw her, she'd say things to her, things about being selfish and awful. Things akin to what Mary Claire said to her the day she died. So much anger and strife and tension. So much heartbreak, just as her drunk mother had predicted.

She felt tears prick her eyes. Being angry at her daughter, having rules for her, scolding her about being sassy or texting at the table or staying out too late. It was all such a luxury. It had been a gift, and she hadn't even seen it.

"If you'd like to take these clothes to the store and offer them in exchange for what she took, perhaps they could drop the charges?"

Marglyn said. To save, to soothe, to make right was a compulsion she couldn't quite squelch.

The cop shifted nervously. "Oh, ma'am, I think we're past that now."

"Please," Marglyn said. "I'd consider it a personal favor. It's—well, this is just all a misunderstanding."

He rose. "I'll see what I can do. But I'm not making any promises. I was just making you aware of the situation." He nodded at Hale. "Thank you for your time. I'll just be getting out of your way, then."

He nodded at Marglyn, shrugged. "There're just some things we can't make right," he said. He held up the bag. "But I guess we can try." Marglyn saw him to the same door Mary Claire had once been so eager to run out of.

Darcy

SUNDAY

Her phone was lit up with calls when she got back in her car after talking with Marglyn. Her first thought was of Graham. He'd fallen down while alone or forgotten some important paper she'd need to come back for or the angry boys had found him at Tommy's. Her heart in her throat, she'd lifted the phone to find that all the missed calls were from Clay. Odd. He didn't usually call her over and over again. Something must've happened with Ava. Something he could share only with her.

She put the car in reverse, anxious to get away from the Bennett house and aware that she was likely being watched either by Leah herself or her uppity mother. She hit the last number called and listened as the phone rang and Clay answered. "Darcy?" His voice sounded panicked.

"Yeah?" she asked, beginning to feel afraid. "Is everything OK?" Maybe something terrible had happened. Maybe Ava had killed herself. She wouldn't blame her if she had. The woman basically had nothing to live for. She chided herself for thinking such things, but the truth was every time she felt hopeless or desperate, she thought of Ava, comforted by the notion that at least she wasn't her. No matter how bad things get, her mother used to say, there's always someone worse off. In Darcy's case, that person was Ava.

Clay sighed, and she could see him shaking his head as he did. She'd seen him do this many times when they'd discussed Ava. "The first time I called you was because I could see what was building, and I thought maybe if you showed up it wouldn't. But I couldn't get ahold of you, and then things just got . . . worse."

Graham's name popped back in her mind again, unbidden. But he couldn't be with Clay. She'd left him in that tacky walk-up condo an hour ago, safe and sound. "Clay, what's going on?" She heard the panic in her own voice.

"It's Tommy," he said. "He showed up here for lunch and hung around when he shouldn't have. There was a . . . meeting that was taking place here with some of the kids and coaches about . . . what happened. And Tommy kind of insinuated himself into the middle of it and . . . well. It got ugly."

"Ugly how?" she asked. She thought of Tommy, standing up for Graham the only way he knew how. With his anger and his posturing and his drive to protect what was his. She thought of Tommy, alone now that Angie had left him, letting Graham move in even though he had to have known that would push her right out the door. Tommy, who was not her husband anymore but who'd been the love of her life for as long as she could remember. She felt sick.

"A couple of guys asked him if he wanted to take it outside, and . . . he said he did." He exhaled, his breath a rush of wind in the phone. "I called the cops, but they still got in some good licks before they got here to break it up. He was . . . It was three against one." He paused, waited for her to say something. She was too intent on finding a place to turn around so she could get to the hospital instead of home. "I'm sorry I didn't try to help," he added, his voice weak.

She thought of Tommy out on the football field when they were in high school, strong and tall and godlike, raising the football like a scepter. He'd never realized he'd stopped being that boy a long time ago. But now he was alone, and hurting, and broken. And so was she.

"It's OK, Clay," she said. "I appreciate you calling."

"Can I call you later?" he asked. And she could tell in his voice he knew the answer.

"I might be busy with . . . everything," she said. She gave a little false laugh. "Sounds like I'm going to have two invalids on my hands."

"Yeah," he agreed. He paused, and in that pause she could feel them moving away from each other, the slightest shift, the merest correction, but enough to change the direction they'd been going in.

"You remember when we saw each other at the church the first time, at the funeral?" Clay asked.

She hit her blinker to merge onto the highway that would take her to the hospital, accelerating to keep up with the flow of traffic. "Sure," she said.

"Remember we talked about making the coq au vin?"

She moved over into the fast lane, passing other cars. She'd made this drive so many times when Graham was in the hospital, she could almost drive it in her sleep. "Yes," she said, feeling anything but sleepy. Feeling alive.

"I told you I didn't know why I remembered making that coq au vin. But I did."

Don't say it, she thought. *Oh, please, Clay, don't say what you're about to say.*

"I remembered because I fell in love with you that night." He waited a beat, then added, "I guess I'm still sort of carrying a torch."

He said it, she thought. And she laughed. She laughed out loud. She composed herself. "I'm so sorry, Clay, I shouldn't laugh. I'm a mess." She hoped he heard the rueful tone in her voice. She hoped he knew her well enough now to know she didn't mean to—would never—hurt him. Not on purpose.

"You have every reason to be," he said. She could hear him smile, and she felt relief flood her body. "It's been an honor, Darcy LaRue, to walk through this mess with you. I don't know what I would've done without you."

She passed the exits, counting them down as they blurred past. "Me, either," she said, and meant it.

"I guess we both need to tend to our own messes now, huh?"

She nodded, and tears filled her eyes, turning the other cars' lights wavy. She realized he couldn't see her nodding and said aloud, "I guess we do."

She saw the sign that said **Hospital: Next Exit** and slowed slightly.

"I hope that we can still be friends," he said.

She smiled. "I'm sure we will be."

She hung up feeling relieved, as if she'd just gotten the right answer on a test she'd been sure to fail. She thought of the fake blood on her front door and the fake blood on the wedding dress, how in a way it had all come full circle from last year to this, bringing Tommy back to her, bringing her back to herself. She reached the exit, hit her blinker, and pushed harder on the gas, accelerating toward her idiot ex-husband who didn't deserve her. But it was rare that anyone got what he or she deserved in this life, for better or for worse. Which was what made it so awful and amazing at the very same time.

Leah

She stood in her mother's bedroom doorway and observed her for a full minute before her mother realized she was there. She raised her eyes, regarded her silently. Behind her eyes, Leah could see the million things she was not saying. Instead she just said one word, a question. "Yes?"

"I need to go somewhere," Leah answered. Even just saying that made her heart pick up speed. She felt vaguely nauseated, which would only get worse before it got better. One step at a time, though. The first step was getting to Talmadge.

"Where?" Her mother put down the book. It was one of her Christian romances, which was, Leah felt, a misnomer. Mrs. Chessman had taught them about misnomers. At the thought of Mrs. Chessman, she went from vaguely nauseous to stomach churning. One step at a time. That was for later. This was for now.

"I need a ride to Talmadge's house." She looked down at her feet to escape her mother's disapproving stare. "I need to talk to him, and I can't get him on the phone."

"Is that who you were with? The night of the accident?" It was as if her mother had been waiting for the open door to ask.

She shook her head. "No." She gave a little ironic laugh. "I wish."

"Are you ever going to tell me what happened that night?" her mother asked as she rose from the bed and smoothed her clothes.

"Part of me being able to tell you at some point means I need to go see Talmadge now. I can't really explain it more than that, Mom." She met her mother's penetrating gaze. "I just need you to trust me."

She expected a lecture in response, her mother warbling on about how trust is something you earn, not something you expect. Instead her mother reached out, brushed her hair off her shoulder, and then rested her hand there, the warmth and steadiness of that hand giving her something she hadn't realized her mother still could provide—security, comfort, reassurance. "OK," she said.

"OK you'll trust me, or OK you'll give me a ride to Talmadge's house?"

Her mother smiled. "Both."

"Thanks." She smiled back. She turned to go and get her things, but her mother tightened her grip on her shoulder, halting her.

"I trust you, Leah," she said. "And I hope, when you're ready, you'll trust me enough to tell me . . . whatever it is that's been going on." She blinked a few times, debating saying more. "The truth shall set you free," she added.

Leah closed her eyes and nodded, hoping that were true. There was so much she needed to be free of. When she opened her eyes, her mother had already turned away.

◆ ◆ ◆

Her heart sank when they pulled into Talmadge's drive and his car wasn't there. She should've called first. But he wouldn't have answered. She turned to her mother to tell her she was sorry, that they should just go home. But before she could open her mouth, she saw a flash of movement. The front door of his house opened, and Talmadge stepped outside, a cat weaving in and out of his legs as he stood on the stoop and blinked at them unbelievingly.

"It doesn't appear that anyone else is home," her mother said, her voice anxious as she scanned the front of the house.

"Mom, it's fine. I just need to talk to him." She turned to look at her. "That's all. I give you my word." Her parents had taught their children that phrase since they were little, how giving your word is serious and powerful. And honorable.

She turned to make eye contact with Talmadge. She was going to give him her word now, speaking the truth she'd been unable to say. She recalled an Emily Dickinson line: *Truth is so rare that it is delightful to tell it.* It was almost like the verse her mother had quoted. She hoped God and Emily were both right.

"OK, honey," her mother said. She reached over and patted her hand. Leah looked at her mother one last time, and, as she did, her mother winked, the movement so quick she wondered if she'd imagined it. "It'll be just fine," her mother said, nodding in agreement with herself. "You'll see."

Leah found herself nodding, too. Her mother turned her attention back to the windshield, signaling it was OK to go. She stepped out of the car and heard as, behind her, her mother shifted into reverse and backed out of the drive.

She lifted her hand. "Hi," she said.

Talmadge stood there for a moment, hands in pockets, debating what to say. The cat wandered away, off toward the barn. He pointed to the disappearing car. "I can't believe you got her to give you a ride here."

She grinned, thankful he was making a joke. She'd feared he'd extend the silent treatment, tell her she might as well go home. But this was Talmadge, who would never turn her away. She looked around, taking in the silence and stillness. Usually there were Feathers family members milling everywhere, but not today. "Where is everybody?"

He shrugged. "All over the place. Dad had to use my car because Mom had to take the kids somewhere. So I'm just chilling here." He gave her a rueful grin. "I was asleep on the couch when I heard you pull up."

She rolled her eyes. "Must be nice." She didn't say that she hadn't slept much at all since he pulled away and left her standing on the curb with a decision to make. "You didn't take my calls," she said.

He shrugged again, looked down for a moment before raising his eyes to meet hers. "I can't solve your problems for you, Leah."

She wanted to argue with that, wanted to say, *But you can! You are the solution! When I'm with you everything else gets easier. When I'm with you I don't hurt so much.* But that was too much, too soon. Instead she simply said, "I'm not asking you to."

He leaned back against the doorframe and studied her for a second. "Then why are you here?"

"Because you asked me to tell you something . . . if we were gonna . . . still be friends." She felt stupid. Exposed. Vulnerable. All things she hated feeling. And yet, there was no way around it. Talmadge had made up his mind, issued his ultimatum. To be with him was to open herself up to feelings she wanted to avoid, to truth she wanted to ignore.

He stepped away from the doorframe and held his hand out like a maître d', inviting her inside. She nodded and headed toward the open door. Just before she walked inside, he put his arm down, like one of those bars that prevent access. She looked up at him, startled, afraid he'd changed his mind and was just going to send her home. "You don't have to say anything at all," he said. "Just that you came here willing to is enough."

A smile filled her face as she studied him. Yes, she decided in that moment, she loved Talmadge Feathers. *Hope is the thing with feathers.* She looked into his eyes, saw kindness there, acceptance. Maybe that's what everyone in the world was searching for—someone who, when they felt vulnerable and exposed and afraid, would meet them in the doorway with a look of love so pure it made all that other stuff fall away.

"No," she said. "I want to tell you. I need to tell you." And as she said it out loud, she realized it was true.

He pointed her to the couch in the small den just inside the house. "Then have a seat."

She did, gathering herself into a little ball, pulling her knees to her chin and wrapping her arms around her legs as he sat down on the other couch cushion, keeping a respectful distance, his eyes intent on her.

"Do you want to, like, talk about the weather or something first? Ease into it?"

She laughed. "Nope. I'll just blurt it all out if that's OK."

He nodded once. "Sounds good to me." He wiped his palms on his jeans. "Go for it."

She took a deep breath, like a child about to go off the high dive for the very first time. She exhaled. "So," she began. "You know who Webb Hart is, right?"

He rolled his eyes. "Duh." Talmadge may not have gone to her school, but even someone who lived under a rock in Worthy knew who he was.

"Well, one day Brynne came to me and asked me to . . . do something. For him. For the school." She swallowed. "For her." She felt tears prick her eyes and promised herself she would not cry. There would be time for tears later. She glanced at him. He nodded, looking worried.

"She'd already done it, and she told me it was . . . no big deal. She said it was this inevitable thing, and it would be better to get it over with this way. Because it would, you know, mean something. Like for a greater good. Or whatever."

She paused, thinking she heard a car coming. She scanned the window in front of them, but there was no movement save the cat stalking something outside in the grass. "So. She kind of . . . convinced me. To do it. And I don't know why, or how."

231

She thought of Brynne that day. She'd been wearing shorts and a T-shirt and the weather had turned cold, but she'd been too proud or stubborn to accept Leah's offer of her sweater. Leah should've known then not to follow this girl, that she was no leader. But then, oh then, she had seemed to be. Leah would've followed her anywhere, and she did.

Sometimes she wished they could've talked about it after. She wished she could've told Brynne how wrong she'd been. She wished she could've asked her why—if she were her friend, she would've put her in that position. But the truth was, it was only through the tragedy of Brynne's death that she'd gained the courage to ever say those things to Brynne. Had Brynne not died, everything would've stayed the same. She shivered, even though the wood-burning stove was hard at work just across the room.

"You OK?" Talmadge asked.

She nodded, rested her chin on her knees, and continued. "Webb had this . . . idea. This . . . I don't know what you'd call it. He saw some TV thing about the Muslim martyrs who supposedly get however many virgins when they get to heaven." She glanced at him. "You know what I'm talking about?"

He raised his eyebrows and nodded. She knew he wanted to say, *Duh*, again but was holding back because he could tell this was nothing to joke about.

"Well, he started saying that those guys were stupid, dying so they could get virgins. That he'd already had some and could have more any time he wanted." She could feel her heart picking up speed, threatening to beat right out of her chest if she said too much too fast. She took a deep breath. "He said, 'I'm fucking Webb Hart. I don't have to die to get all the virgins I want. All I have to do is win football games.'"

She looked at Talmadge, knowing he already knew where this was going. There was a moment of complete silence in the room. The kind you have when someone dies. With his eyes, he told her to go on. So she did.

"After that, it just became this . . . thing. This secret pact thing between Webb and his stupid minions, Seth and Ian and those guys. They put the word out that after every win, Webb wanted a virgin basically delivered to him. They thought it was funny, or cool, or . . . I don't know what they thought it was. But they got other people." She looked up at him. "Other girls," she corrected herself. "To do it."

"And Brynne was one?"

"Yeah, apparently everyone knew she was still a virgin because she'd taken some big vow at some church thing in middle school or whatever, so everyone teased her about waiting till she was married. Somehow Ian and Seth—" She shuddered, thinking of Ian cornering Sidney at school, how small and scared she'd looked. She thought of how ridiculous it was that she'd looked just as scared to be exposed as she'd been to go through with it. This town. These people. They needed shaking. She thought of Mrs. Chessman, how she could shake things up. How she could be a start.

She remembered herself. "Sorry," she said. "I was just thinking."

He held out his hands, palms up. "Take your time."

She picked up where she left off, trying not to picture Ian's and Seth's faces as she spoke their names again. "Somehow Ian and Seth convinced her that that was stupid. That what Webb wanted her to do meant . . . more." She looked at Talmadge, willing him to understand. "I wish you could've seen her face. The way she talked about it. Like she'd joined a cult or something. She'd get all dreamy-looking and say that I just had to do it, that it was . . . this life-changing thing."

"She was in love with Webb," he said.

She shook her head. "No, it wasn't like that. She truly believed in . . . in . . ." She saw Brynne's face in her mind, the way her eyes had pled with Leah. She'd hardly had to say much to her. It was mainly the look in her eyes. She thought of a vocabulary word they'd had in her

SAT prep class: *implore*. Her eyes had implored her to go along with the plan. She thought of another word, a church word. *Beseech*. Brynne's eyes had beseeched her to be the next girl. She'd looked at Leah as if her very life depended on getting this yes.

"He manipulated her," Talmadge went on. "He figured out she had feelings for him, and he controlled her by using those feelings." He raised his eyebrows. "Think about it. I bet she became the main person doing his recruiting. I bet you weren't the only girl she got to do it."

Leah felt her heart beat harder, pounding against her rib cage as if it wanted out. She thought of Brynne's mysterious absences those last weeks, how they teased her about where she was going, who she was spending time with. She always said she had to help her grandmother, but once they drove by her grandmother's house and her car wasn't there. "I bet she has a secret boyfriend," Keary had breathed. Keary loved anything romantic.

She wondered if Brynne was working on Keary to be next. She wondered if, after she'd dropped Leah off for Webb, Brynne had sidled up to Keary and whispered the first little snippet of the plan, drawing her in with promises of doing something for the team that very few girls could do, with talk of being truly worthy to be the team's cheerleader. Just the way she had with Leah.

She thought of Keary's face, learning the truth, learning what Leah was out doing. She tried to picture the depth of shock and disappointment that would register there if she knew Leah had handed over her virginity to a stupid football player with a God complex and some seriously misplaced ideas about world religions. Keary was sweet and innocent and lovely. Keary wanted to be swept off her feet with chocolates and champagne and rose petals. She would've been horrified. Maybe so horrified that she couldn't think straight while driving. So horrified maybe she drove straight into the path of an oncoming car. What if that was what had happened that night?

She thought of Graham, receiving threats. Of Darcy LaRue's face when she saw Mary Claire's mom. What if, by telling the truth about Webb, she could prove that Keary caused the accident? Or, if not prove exactly, she could sure make it sound like it. Enough that maybe she could save Mrs. Chessman *and* Graham.

"Leah?" Talmadge prompted beside her, his voice gentle and the slightest bit afraid.

"Yeah," she said. She laughed a little, feeling joy and hope. She thought of her mother's words to her, "The truth shall set you free." What if that truth had to be embellished a little? "I'm just thinking." She picked at a string coming loose in the seam of her jeans. "About options."

"Options are good." He got that Talmadge look on his face, the one that reminded her how much he liked her, how he was her biggest fan. How had she forgotten that so much that she'd let herself get talked into doing what she did? With time, perhaps, she could forgive herself for that. The wondrous thing was that Talmadge, she could see, already had.

"I wish I'd exercised my options that night," she said, determined to finish. And, now that she knew what came next, not so afraid to finish anymore.

"But you didn't," he said, making it easier for her. "You went through with it." She nodded. There was more to the story, of course. There was the part about Ian and Seth, the part she would save for Mrs. Chessman.

He slid over to her, close enough that his leg lined up with hers on the couch. She could feel the heat of his body through his jeans. He slid his arm around her and pulled her to him. He kissed the top of her head in a way that was comforting, fatherly, even. "I wish that hadn't happened to you," he said. "I'm sorry I wasn't there."

"Me, too," she agreed. She leaned into him, letting him pull her even closer. "That was my fault."

"It's gonna be OK," he said, unknowingly echoing her mother's words. Words she'd needed to hear then, and now, and probably for a long time to come. "I'm glad you finally told me."

"I was so ashamed. Because it was my choice. I . . . went along with it, even though I knew I shouldn't." She was quiet for a few moments, thinking of Ian and Seth, of their role in making sure she did go through with it. "I was so ashamed of what I did that I didn't feel like I had a right to say anything. But then with everything else that has happened, I think maybe . . . I should. Tell what I know. Maybe it'll help . . . things."

"If you feel you should, then you should," he said. She could tell that he was trying to sound more stalwart than he was, more certain.

She licked her lips, gone suddenly dry. "Can I have a glass of water?" she asked.

Talmadge nodded and leaped up to get it. She watched him walk away, trying not to see what she was seeing in her mind: Seth and Ian that night, their hands on her, pushing her back into the room, calling her names, their spit hitting her as they shouted at her, saying such awful things. She'd seen drawings of demons in church books. But none of them had looked like Seth and Ian. And yet, that night, they had been as evil as anything she'd ever encountered.

Talmadge returned, handed her the water, and she drank it gratefully, feeling it work to dislodge the lump in her throat. She'd told the worst of it, and now there was just a little more to go. Exhaustion flooded her body, pulling her down from within. She handed him the glass, still half-full.

"Can you take me somewhere?"

He knitted his brows together and pursed his lips. "Sure. Where?"

"To Mrs. Chessman's. It would be easier on me to tell this once." He started to say something, but she held up a finger. "I just need to close my eyes for a minute first." As if on cue, she yawned. "All of a sudden I feel like I'm going to pass out. I need . . . some rest."

"OK," he said. He patted her shoulder, as nervous and awkward as a middle school boy. She smiled, remembering when he was just that. When he was just her friend. But he wasn't anymore. She leaned forward, pressed her mouth against his.

"Thanks," she said, and gave a little half smile at the look of surprise on his face. She turned away from him to lie down on her side, pulling her knees up, wrapping her arms around a throw pillow that smelled like the wood-burning stove, like his house. Like him. She felt him cover her with a blanket. Then she fell quickly and totally asleep.

Ava

Sunday

She tried not to move too quickly or breathe too deeply or lean too far forward. She kept her hands still on her thighs, bracing herself as she listened to the girl sitting in front of her. A girl who'd once been her student. A girl she'd not really paid much attention to. A girl who didn't demand much, or anything at all. She watched Leah swallow, the skin on her throat moving against the muscles there. She was a tiny thing, frail, even. But, looking at her, Ava knew that she was strong inside. She suspected that Leah was figuring that out about herself as well.

"So I went there, like Brynne asked me to do," Leah said. She'd already explained, in a rush of words, Webb Hart's plot to deflower as many virgins at Worthy High as he could, playing the only card he had, but a card the town valued above all. He was a god on the field. And gods got what they wanted while mortals acquiesced.

Ava saw how Leah was keeping her eyes on the boy sitting across from her. He was the same boy who'd been at Stooges that night. Something existed in the air between them, an unseen but powerful current pulsing. Ava felt it there and was jealous. She'd never had that with anyone in her life, though Lord knew she'd tried to find it. It was the thing that had left her always open, always wanting, always searching. She'd tried to create it many times with strangers, with boy-friends, with the man she married. But, she realized, sitting there, it was not something one could create. It either existed, or it didn't. The realization didn't make her feel sad, but hopeful. Maybe she could still find it. She envied the two kids sitting there with something between them so precious, so rare. She hoped they knew what they had.

"Brynne drove me straight to the party after the game," Leah went on, "and basically said, you know, get out, or whatever." She paused. "So I did."

Ava saw her inhale, look to the boy for strength. He nodded, his chin barely dipping, his eyes closing slowly, then opening again. "But I didn't intend to go through with it." Leah looked straight at Talmadge as she spoke, as if speaking to him only. For a moment Ava felt as if she were intruding.

"I was going to talk to Webb, tell him how he shouldn't be doing this, that it was wrong. I just didn't want him to be mad at Brynne. I thought—" Ava watched as Leah took a few deep breaths in and out and feared she would stop talking altogether. She forced her hands to keep still on her lap.

"I thought I could talk sense into him, be the voice of reason. I thought we were sort of, you know, friends. We ate at the same table at lunch and stuff, and we'd talked a few times. I thought maybe that would make a difference or something."

She glanced over at Ava this time, and in her eyes Ava saw the pain and the truth and the residual fear. "But it didn't work," Ava said, prod-ding Leah to finish her story.

Leah shook her head, and a tear leaked from her left eye, leaving a track in her foundation as it traveled the length of her cheek. "Ian and Seth were there, too. I . . . didn't . . . expect that part." She rolled her eyes, trying to add some levity. "I don't know what I expected. When I tried to leave, they . . . stood in front of the door so I couldn't get out.

They called me names and told me I had to do what I'd said I would do. That I'd promised. I tried to get out the door, but then I finally just—"

Leah buried her face in her hands, and her shoulders moved up and down, up and down with the effort of keeping her emotions inside. Ava knew this was a defense mechanism. She knew that, in order to get through the story, Leah could not break down. By telling the truth about that night—and those boys—she would get part of herself back, the part that was lost that night. Maybe not all of it. But some. And some, as she told her kids, was better than none. Some was a start.

"You gave in," she said.

"I just wanted it to be over," Leah said into her hands. "I wanted to go home." Ava watched as she lifted her face from her hands and found Talmadge's face, the home she'd wanted to get to. He got up and crossed the room with his lanky gait, falling onto the couch and covering her with his arms, hiding her from Ava's sight. He rocked her back and forth as she cried. When his eyes met Ava's, she saw that he was crying, too. And so was she.

After a few minutes, Leah sat up straight and wiped the tears from her eyes. She looked right at Ava and asked, "Is my mascara a mess?"

Ava couldn't help but laugh in response. "I'll get you a washcloth so you can fix it."

Leah nodded, and Ava could almost see the relief run over her like a fountain. She'd done it. She'd told the truth. It was the first step on a long path, but she'd begun it. "I'm proud of you," she said. "For being brave and coming forward like this." Talmadge squeezed her in agreement.

"Those boys aren't angels like everyone makes them sound," Leah said. "Just because they wear the jersey and win football games. They're not worthy of the respect people give them."

"I don't want them to get away with what they did to you," Ava said, her mind already churning with thoughts of punishment and retribution. Suddenly she was more concerned with Leah's case than with her own. It felt good to think of someone else for a change, to be concerned with something beyond her own set of problems.

"I want you to tell the authorities. But not for me. For you. They should have to answer for what they did to you. Don't worry about me."

Leah rewarded her with a tight, brave smile. "I want to stop Webb from hurting any more girls. I know I wasn't the only one." Her face got serious, and Ava suspected she was thinking of other girls at school, other victims. "Girls who are too scared to tell." She folded her hands as if in prayer and rested her chin on her knuckles. "So call your lawyer," she said. "Let's make it happen."

Darcy

SUNDAY

She watched from her chair by the bed as Tommy's chest rose and fell, rose and fell. It was déjà vu—same hospital, same floor, perhaps even the same chair with the plastic seat pad that squeaked every time she moved. Other than her son's birth and a few visits for minor emergencies, she'd never spent time in this hospital. She'd made up for that since the night of the accident.

Tommy roused, his eyes seeking her out before he was even fully awake. He gave her a brief smile of relief upon finding her still at her post. "You stayed," he said.

She nodded just once. "I did."

"Thank you," he said, his words barely more than a mumble. He leaned forward to reach for his cup of water on the tray table nearby. Reflexively she hopped up to fetch it for him, cursing herself as she did at how natural it was, this instinct to serve him, to fuss over him. To care about him. A stronger woman would let him get his own damn water, would sit stoically as he pawed at the air trying to reach it.

"Do you need some ice?" she asked. She shook the pitcher that had held fresh ice hours ago. "This is melted."

He took a sip of water, sucking through the bendable straw. She didn't think she'd ever seen Tommy drink from a straw before. It made him look childish, weaker. She watched with interest. "This is fine," he said. He handed her the cup. She put it on the table and returned to her chair.

"They said you can go home in the morning," she said, making conversation.

"I guess that means I'm not pissing blood anymore," he quipped. But she could see the shame on his face as he said it.

She shrugged to appear nonchalant. "I didn't ask many questions. I'm sure the doctor will tell you when he comes by to officially discharge you."

Tommy fussed with the blankets so as not to look at her. "Yeah. I'm sure he will."

Several minutes of silence passed. Outside she could hear an announcement droning on the intercom, a piece of machinery being pushed past, the squeak of rubber-soled shoes on linoleum. The sights, the sounds, and the smells had come back to her so quickly upon entering the place. In the weeks since they'd been home, she'd blocked it from her mind, convincing herself she could leave it behind. But you didn't forget this place. It lived in your subconscious forever.

"So I guess I'll go and check on Graham," she said. "And then I'll come back for you in the morning?"

"You don't have to do that," he responded.

She squinted at him, cocked her head. "If I don't," she said, "then who will?"

He gave her a rueful look, one that was so Tommy she could believe—apart from the black eye and laugh lines she saw now—that no time had passed, that he was the same Tommy she'd always known and loved. The Tommy from before, the one who would've never betrayed her. "I'm sorry," she said. "That you got hurt trying to defend Graham."

He dropped his gaze back to the blankets, wadding and releasing them in his bandaged hand. A few seconds of silence passed as she waited for the response he was clearly forming in his head. He didn't look up when he answered. "I wasn't."

She didn't understand. "You weren't what?"

"Defending Graham," he said, turning his attention to the IV in his hand, tracing the tubing with his other one. She feared for a moment he was going to yank it out.

"I thought—" she said. "I thought you got in a fight with some of the football players who were threatening him."

"Who told you that?" he asked.

Clay had lied to her, or told her his version of the truth, one he could live with. Wasn't that what everyone did when push came to shove? Create a truth they could live with? Hadn't she done the same with Graham? She didn't know which man to believe. She realized it didn't matter.

"N-no one," she stammered. She could lie, too. "I just . . . assumed. The threats, his moving in with you . . ."

He looked up at her finally. "No. It wasn't them. I mean, yeah, that's the way it started, but it ended with Chessman and some of his friends. He . . . said something. About you." They blinked at each other, an acknowledgment that there was something between her and Clay. She thought of the kiss in the car, how she'd told herself this could be her new life.

"I said to him, 'Hey now, that's my wife.' And he said—" He stopped, winced. She let him pretend it was because he was in pain, but they both knew that it was not the physical kind. He continued. "He said, 'Not anymore she's not.' And I just—I just took a swing at him. I thought—who is he? Who is he to tell me you're not my wife anymore? Who is he to even say your name?"

"Did Clay—" She gestured at him, there in the hospital bed, bruised and bandaged. "Did he do this?"

Tommy gave a little scoffing laugh. "Coupla his staff jumped in on his behalf, defending his honor like he was some woman." He shook his head. "It was like all of a sudden all the anger I'd been feeling—about the accident and the threats and—" He looked down again. "And Angie moving out. It just all came roaring out."

His voice got quieter. "And then to hear him talk about you like he had some sort of claim on you? Like he knew you at all?" He looked at her with apologetic eyes. "I felt like you were the one good thing I had left, and in that moment, he took it away somehow. I . . . just flew into a rage. I don't think I've ever been that angry in my life." He paused, remembering, she knew. "It was like I couldn't even feel anything; I knew they were hitting me and kicking me. I knew I needed to give in, but I couldn't. There was something in me that wanted to just keep on fighting."

He looked at her, and she felt it, whatever was in the air between them that had always been there, way back since that moment when he was on the field and she was on the sidelines and their eyes met and something passed between them. Something powerful and connecting. Something that was created in that moment and had held all this time. She'd told herself it was gone, broken. But just like that, it was re-formed. "I didn't want to stop fighting . . . for us."

"Tommy—" she started to argue. She wanted to add, *You're only saying that because you're hurt, you're confused, you lost your girlfriend, and everything sucks right now. I'm your safe place, I'm your sure thing, I always have been, and you need me to be again. Tommy, don't do this to me. It's not fair.* The words were on her lips, all of them.

"Don't say it." He stopped her, holding up the hand with the IV in it, the tube snaking from it. "You don't have to." He lowered his hand and began to smooth the blankets on his lap. "It took me years to wreck our marriage. And it'll take me years to rebuild it. But I intend to try." He looked up. "And you can't stop me." He smiled as he issued the challenge. He was still so good-looking, so charming when he smiled. *Damn it,* she thought.

"Try all you want," she replied, working hard to keep a straight face. But she failed, and the smile that was inside her emerged so that they both sat there grinning like idiots. It was all so absurd that it made her want to laugh. So she did.

Leah

MONDAY

She told the story. First to Talmadge, then to Mrs. Chessman, then to her mom, which was probably the hardest of all. But she had to tell her so she didn't hear it from anyone else. Her mom had waited long enough, longer than anyone.

Her mom cried, then thanked her. She didn't get in trouble at all. Her mom said she'd had enough trouble without her adding more on top of it. "Thank you," her mother said after, her voice thick with tears. "Thank you for trusting me enough to tell me. I'm not sure I deserved it. But I'm going to try to, in the future. I want to always be someone you can come to. OK?"

Leah said OK, and then she cried, too. And when her mom hugged her, she felt all her mom's love going inside her, filling her up. Her mom held her for a while and was quiet, and Leah knew she was praying, which was OK by her. She could use the prayers.

After that it was time to tell the story to Mrs. Chessman's attorney, who would then decide how best to proceed. Mrs. Chessman drove her to the office, looking so pretty that Leah could see why those boys chased after her, why they thought she had something they needed. She studied her former teacher's profile as she drove, tried to imitate the determined jut of her chin. Mrs. Chessman would've said she was no role model, but to Leah, she was. She was showing Leah how to stand up under the crushing weight of shame.

She'd been too filled with it at first, because she had gone through with what Webb wanted. She had done that. She could blame Ian and Seth for barring the door, blame Brynne for goading her into it, blame her parents for raising her the way they did—she had a million excuses. But at night, lying alone in the dark, the memory came to her of her and Webb together. And that memory couldn't be blamed on anyone else. It was what kept her silent for so long. But not anymore.

Each time she told the story, she felt lighter, and stronger after. And whenever she thought of keeping silent, she remembered Sidney Riggle and Emily Dickinson's words. By telling her story, she could stop one more heart from breaking. She would not live in vain. And then the fact that she'd lived and her friends didn't would make some kind of sense.

She wore another of Mary Claire's outfits to the attorney's office. Wearing her clothes gave her the courage she needed to be someone different than she'd been in the past—someone braver and stronger, like Mary Claire had been. Someday she might not need the clothes to help her be that person, but for now, she supposed it was OK to use them. She had a suspicion that Mary Claire approved.

They drove a few miles in silence as she internally rehearsed what she would say to the attorney. And then the police if necessary. Her stomach roiled at the thought, but she would not back off this new plan, especially the part that would set Graham free, the part that involved a bit of a lie. But Leah believed the accident really could've happened exactly the way she was going to tell it—no one knew what really happened that night, after all. Brynne could've called her to tell her that Keary had found out and was upset. Keary could've been so distracted that she caused the accident. Truth or lie, it didn't make the girls any less dead. And Graham had his whole life ahead of him.

She told the attorney, who said to call her Nancy, the story. About Ian and Seth being there. About how Brynne had loved Webb and thought if she did that for him, he'd love her, too. About how badly Leah wanted to please other people, how twisted and ugly it had gotten in her mind.

Mrs. Chessman and Nancy listened, and then Nancy dabbed at her eyes with a tissue and told her she was a brave girl and that Nancy had some phone calls to make. Then they told Leah she could go home, and Mrs. Chessman said there was someone who wanted to take her home, and he was waiting right outside. Mrs. Chessman and Nancy began throwing words around: *coercion, statutory rape, exoneration.* And Leah left them to it.

Outside the attorney's office, she found Talmadge waiting in the parking lot, standing in front of his car and holding his violin. As she approached, he put the violin under his chin. When he held up his arm, she saw the tattoo, the one that had sent her running in the other direction months ago.

When she could, she decided, she would get one, too. A feather on her shoulder or back or someplace only he could see. She felt something course through her, something raw and hungry, as she thought of being naked with Talmadge Feathers, of being tangled up with him. And for the first time since everything happened, the thought did not terrify her.

"Forgot something!" he said, and gave her a brilliant grin. He lowered the violin, walked over to the driver's side door, and extracted the poetry book. He handed it to her, gesturing with his elbow at a page marker sticking out from the top as he put the violin back in position. "Open it," he said.

He began to play, the music unfamiliar, beautiful, haunting. She opened the book, grateful to have somewhere to look other than right at him. She felt his eyes upon her as she read, "Hope is the thing with feathers / That perches in the soul / And sings the tune without the words / And never stops—at all." He had underlined the part about the tune without words, the tune that never stops at all.

The song ended—his tune without words—and she looked up at him. "I wrote that for you," he said.

"It's beautiful." She closed the book, held it to her chest.

"I'll never stop at all," he said.

Tears filled her eyes. "I know that now," she said. She began to cry. "I'm sorry I didn't for a while."

He held the violin with one hand and pulled her to him with the other. He kissed the top of her head. "You do now," he said into her hair. "And that's what matters."

They stayed that way for a long time. She breathed in, inhaling the moment, feeling it go down inside her where it would live, she knew, forever. She thought the words *I love you* but did not say them aloud. She figured Talmadge could feel them anyway, that her feelings had always and would always be entwined with his, carried inside him in the place where his music resided. The last safe place she knew of in the world. Besides, there would be time later to tell him she loved him. There would be time for all of it. She'd lost something that night, but by not being in that car, she'd gained something, too: life, and the chance to live it.

Ava

Tuesday

January 12

"If you sign right here, you'll be accepting your plea agreement," Nancy said, sliding the paper across the desk to her. "You can read it if you like, but it's pretty straightforward, what we talked about." She lifted her chin in the direction of the paper.

Ava nodded, keeping her face appropriately serious when what she wanted to do was jump up and down in sheer relief. Leah's story had shaken everything up, even though it hadn't led to a big court battle like they'd originally thought. Instead, it had come down to a quiet meeting among the boys, the coaches, their parents, and the lawyers. When the district attorney was reluctant to press charges—Leah had consented; a few other girls, like Sidney Riggle, denied anything had happened—Nancy had only smiled. "I know Worthy. Where legal recourse ends, decorum kicks in. We'll appeal to a higher power." She'd winked at Leah and Ava. "It'll work; you'll see." And it had.

The higher power Nancy had alluded to hadn't been God—they hadn't had to go that far. Once the parents and coaches got wind that Leah planned to go public with her story anyway, they'd urged the boys to do whatever it took to make it go away. The adults didn't want their championship season tainted by scandal. And the boys didn't want people to know just how despicable they'd been. That kind of thing can follow you for the rest of your life.

When it was all laid out, everyone agreed to do what Leah asked. Ian and Seth owned up to their part in what happened with Leah that night. Ian also admitted that he'd sent the pictures of Ava to himself after finding them on her phone. And Webb stopped his campaign to deflower virgins. He had no choice now, really. In Worthy, someone was always watching.

In that moment, Leah had won. She'd won for all the girls the boys had wronged. She'd won for Ava, too. When Ian apologized to her, his father had been gripping him by the arm, holding him there until he'd gone through with it. She hoped he'd squeezed tightly enough to leave a mark.

While it wasn't jail, it was something.

The terms of Ava's plea agreement for the texts were reasonable: six months' probation, the charges reduced to one: contributing to the delinquency of a minor. It was a punishment that befitted her crime of being stupid, not thinking beyond the moment she was in. She could live with that.

As soon as she could, she was leaving Worthy, moving to Macon. She would find an apartment the kids could come to, get a job, blend in to the crowd there. In Worthy, she knew, she would always be whispered about and doubted. She would always be an outsider. But in Macon, she could start over with a new life, one far enough away from all that had happened here.

She accepted a pen and poised it above the line intended for her signature, hovering for just a moment as she thought of how lucky she was that Leah had done what she did. She'd never thought of herself as a lucky person until now. She put the pen to the page and signed her name.

Marglyn

She stood in Mary Claire's room with a box of trash bags in her hand. She'd done this every day for the past three days, unable to go through with the task. With the house on the market, she had to address the issue of what to do with MC's room. Hale thought it would be better if they gave away Mary Claire's things, boxing up a few precious mementoes but otherwise erasing her. As if she'd never posted hand-drawn **KEEP OUT** signs when she was nine or begged to paint the walls Pepto pink when she was six or tried to crawl through the window to sneak out when she was fourteen.

Marglyn walked over to the bed and placed the box of trash bags there, a step. The only one she would make today. She wasn't ready to let go, and she didn't know if she ever would be. She would talk to Hale about it, tell him she had to go slower. Her eyes fell to the file folder the young guidance counselor had brought by. She reached for it. If she wasn't ready to clean out the room, at least she felt ready to read whatever was inside that folder. Surely that was progress.

Inside the folder was the beginning paperwork for college admissions, a handwritten list Mary Claire had submitted with her top choices. UGA was first on the list, and MC had drawn stars around it. She pictured her as a little girl, dressed like a UGA cheerleader for Halloween, three years running, blonde ponytail bouncing high on her head, the red-and-black ribbon tied around the elastic, so huge Hale said it looked like helicopter blades.

She blinked away the tears and flipped through the pages, looking over the answers to questionnaires, reading the list of activities MC had participated in to beef up her application, glancing over the names of the people she intended to ask to write a recommendation for her. It was all there—a whole life ahead of her, one she'd planned to live to the fullest. Sometimes the anger over the unfairness of it all shook Marglyn so hard her teeth rattled in her head. She was about to toss the whole thing back on the bed when she saw a full page of MC's handwriting, the last page in the file. She sank down onto the bed to read, still shaken, only this time for a different reason.

Affixed to the top of the paper was a sticky note that read:

Essay rough draft: Please read and let me know if it's OK!!

Mary Claire had drawn a big smiley face next to it. Marglyn pulled the sticky note off so she could read what the paper said:

Prompt: Tell about someone who inspires you.

Last night my mom invited a stranger to dinner. She'd seen the girl walking down the street in the cold rain and given her a ride home. While they drove, my mom asked the girl questions about her life, learning of the struggles she has just to get to and from school, to have food and clothing, all things I take for granted.

My mom told me that her heart broke for this girl, so she invited her to dinner. She didn't just give her a ride. She didn't feel bad but went on with her life like most people would, thinking she did her good deed for the day and that was enough. She did something about it. She took whatever action she could take, doing her best to make the world a better place one little effort at a time.

My mom and I don't always get along. And sometimes her do-gooding gets on my nerves. Sometimes it's inconvenient and embarrassing to me. I know how selfish that sounds, and I want to be better than that.

I want to look for people who need help and do something for them. Not just say, "Oh, I'll pray for you," like lots of people do. Not just pretend I didn't see them and go on about my business. Not get busier and busier so I'm too busy to notice. My mom cares, and she acts. I think that's the difference that makes the difference.

My mom is my hero. And though I've never told her this, some-day I hope I get the chance to be like her. Maybe the difference I can make right now is to tell her how proud I am of her. And that she should keep on doing what she's doing. And that, someday, I hope to be just like her.

Marglyn held the paper to her chest and whispered into the room, "Thank you, honey." Tears rolled down her cheeks as she rocked the paper back and forth, cradling it like she wanted to cradle her daughter. She pictured her there, wrapped in her arms. She smelled her rose-petal scent, felt her soft young skin, saw her there just as she would be, just as she should be. She hugged the letter, thinking it was perhaps the most precious gift she'd ever gotten, a missive from beyond the grave, a miracle that the last words MC said to her actually weren't the last words at all.

She stood up and collected her purse and her car keys. She got in her car and drove, stopping by Trout's for a bouquet of flowers along the way, making the drive out to the cemetery as she often did, especially now that her dreams of her daughter had come to an end. "You'll want to have a place to go," the funeral director had said. And he'd been right. At this moment, that spot by the lake was calling to her as if Mary Claire herself had arranged a meeting.

She grabbed her little last-minute bouquet and quietly, reverently made her way along the path to the spot where the girls were buried. She saw movement up ahead and froze, fearing that one of the other mothers was there. She'd avoided them ever since that terrible lawsuit meeting. Childishly, she glanced around for a place to hide before she was spotted. But as she peered ahead, she saw that it wasn't one of the other mothers at the girls' graves. It was someone at Mary Claire's grave. In a fraction of a second, she knew exactly who it was. A sprig of fake flowers—the kind you might find at Dollar General—lay at the base of the grave marker. And over it, looking down, her lips moving as if she was saying something, was Ginny.

Marglyn stepped forward, the rustle of the leaves making enough disturbance that Ginny startled and whirled around to face her. When she saw it was Marglyn there, she blanched and began to apologize, taking steps backward. "I'll go, I'll go," she said. She turned and began to walk away quickly, all but fleeing.

"Ginny!" she called out, her voice carrying through the trees and over the lake beyond. It was an unseasonably warm January day, with the kind of impossible blue sky she loved, the kind with no clouds, just a straight view to heaven. She looked up, hoping Mary Claire was watching, was cheering for her. "You don't have to go!" She waved her arm, motioning for her to come back.

Ginny stopped, paused, and studied her for a minute, looking wary. She began walking back toward her, her steps plodding and hesitant. They met at the foot of Mary Claire's grave, both of them falling into silence as they did. Together they stood as if waiting for MC to join them. But Marglyn knew she already had. She'd been with them all the time.

"I was wondering," Marglyn said, "if you'd like to come to dinner." She thought of Mary Claire's favorite dinner, the one thing she could get her to indulge in no matter how much she claimed to be dieting. Spaghetti and meatballs. She would make that. She would set the table, and this time the flowers would go in the center of the table instead of on a grave. She would leave Mary Claire's seat empty, reserving it for her forever. But she could pull up another chair for Ginny. There was always room for one more.

The Girls

After

It's opening night of a new football season. Not everyone who was there last year is back this year. But that's OK. We are still Worthy, just a different kind.

They can't see us there, among them. And that's OK, too. We stopped expecting to be seen a long time ago. Instead we are in the breeze that has just a hint of fall crispness to it. We are in the music the band plays, the voices raised in elation or despair, the thud of bodies colliding on the field. We are all around, still as much a part of the town as we were before.

The people of Worthy know this. They feel us there. They know we are, always, a part of them, cheering for them like we always did. Just from a different place. We have watched as they've all gone on with their lives. We send them love, the kind we've found in this life apart, the kind that never ends. Brynne sends out the most love of all, because she knows what it feels like to need it. There are things you don't forget about Worthy, and this is what Brynne will remember most of all—how she got love all wrong. And how happy she is to get it right now.

Ava Chessman isn't in Worthy anymore. She moved to Macon and got her kids back full-time thanks to her lawyer. She got a job working for her lawyer, too, and she likes it. She's even thinking about going to school to be a paralegal. Her divorce is final, but she's not dating anyone. We agree that maybe that's for the best, at least for a while. Mrs. Chessman is getting to know someone new, someone she didn't know so well before: herself.

Clay still runs the restaurant. He and Darcy aren't really friends anymore, but they're cordial when they see each other, even if he and Tommy still bristle around each other, emitting testosterone into the air so that everyone can feel it. Sometimes when Darcy and Tommy come to Chessman's for dinner, she and Clay will catch each other's eye. They look at each other for a fraction too long, both remembering their kiss and wondering what might have been. But it never goes any further than that. And it never will. Darcy is Tommy's girl. Always has been, always will be. Though they're not living together again, they can feel themselves moving toward it. And that is all the progress Darcy needs for now.

Talmadge started school at Worthy High this year with Leah. He's already asked her to homecoming. She and her mom are going shopping for a dress in Atlanta, and her mom isn't even saying things about how sinful dancing is. Leah is glad Webb, Ian, and Seth are gone. We all are. They're playing college ball; they are another town's problem now.

Graham escaped prosecution after Leah told the police that we'd called her that night just minutes before the crash, that we'd told her that Keary was distraught because she'd found out what Leah was going to do. How she was out of her mind at the thought of Leah going through with it. Leah told the police that she'd begged Keary not to drive, that she'd feared something might happen. Even though that is not what happened at all.

We never called Leah because Brynne told us she was busy and we would see her later. But dying made us all just short of saints, and there was no reason for the police to check our cell phones, no reason not to believe Leah. The way she saw it, it was a small lie, but big enough to get Graham LaRue out of any charges in the crash. We agree with Leah: Graham deserves a second chance. And we get a second chance, too. We get to go on being the town darlings—Worthy's lost princesses who died tragically through no fault of our own. Though that's not exactly true.

Every few weeks Leah goes to our graves to put out fresh flowers for us. She leaves the cemetery feeling grateful she's not there with us. Sometimes her new friend comes with her. Her name is Ginny. Mary Claire's mom introduced them. And though it should be said she's nowhere near as good a friend to Leah as we were, she'll do just fine. There's so much to look forward to, so much ahead for Leah. We can see that from where we are.

Sometimes we talk about what really happened that night, the part everyone in town still guesses about but no one gets quite right. We recall driving down Mary Claire's driveway with Keary nervous and jumpy. Keary wished Leah was there to drive, and she intended to push Brynne on exactly why Leah wasn't there. But first she needed to tell her secret. She chose the moment we were nearing the end of the driveway to do so. She just couldn't keep it to herself any longer.

"I saw Ian and that sub Mrs. Chessman hugging during halftime when I went to the locker rooms to get some aspirin." She blurted it out, then glanced over her shoulder to make sure we'd heard. She added, "They were hugging like boyfriend and girlfriend." Just to make sure we fully understood what she was getting at.

Brynne and Mary Claire laughed. "Quit lying!" we said. "Ian would never hook up with some old woman! Not when he could have any girl in school!" Up until the week before, Ian had been Mary Claire's boyfriend, so she was especially defensive. We laughed and laughed until Keary's face burned with embarrassment and something else—rage.

She turned to look at us, her eyes flashing in the dark car. "I'm not lying!" It was so typical that we wouldn't believe her, so like this town to think that the great Ian Stone was better than that, above it all. But she knew what she saw, knew the caught look on Mrs. Chessman's face when their eyes met, the hungry look in Ian's eyes.

She turned back toward the windshield, forgetting in her frustration and lack of experience to look both ways before pulling out, her angry foot heavy on the gas pedal, launching the Civic out onto Main Street. Right into the path of a speeding car driven by a boy we all knew, a boy who, until that moment, was winning his race.

ACKNOWLEDGMENTS

This book was finished after an accident that left me without the use of my right hand for a time. Being right-handed and a writer, this was awful and hard and left me feeling like perhaps this novel would never be finished.

I am thankful to all the people who stepped into the gap the accident left in my family's life—friends, family, and neighbors—who brought meals and sent treats and prayed and encouraged us along the way. There are too many of you to name, but you know who you are.

I'd also like to thank the medical professionals—most notably my physical therapist, Susan Aiken, who didn't give up on me regaining the use of my hand and who also read all my novels, which is above and beyond the call of physical therapist duty. Susan, you once told me that hands are a specialization that some therapists don't want any part of. I'm grateful every day you did.

Thank you to Curt, who listened to me cry about how I might never write again. Then let me know that you believed I would, giving me the strength to believe it, too. Every good marriage moment I write about—in this or any book—is based on what I've experienced with you.

Thank you to my kids—Jack, Ashleigh, Matt, Rebekah, Brad, and Annaliese—who make me proud and remind me that if I never write another novel, my greatest accomplishment is already achieved in them.

Thank you to my mom, Sandy Brown, who believes in and supports me without fail or falter. I am blessed among daughters.

Thank you to Liza Dawson, for being the agent I always wanted, not to mention needed. When I needed you this time, you showed up big. I won the agent lottery.

Thank you to Jodi and Caitlin, who make me look far better than I am. I couldn't have asked for a better team working their editing magic on my behalf.

Thank you to the team at Amazon Publishing. You had my back with my last novel, and I felt the support big-time. (Think we can do it again? Yes, let's.)

Thank you to Nancy Malcor, who served as legal adviser and also cousin. Not many authors can say that.

Thank you to Jeanice Fashimpaur, Michelle Jensen, and Erica Baxter Cole, whose stories inspired me.

Thank you to the artists whose music served as my writing soundtrack this time around. They include (but are not limited to) Bob Seger, Lady Antebellum, Kenny Chesney, The National, and Taylor Swift. A special thanks to Damien Escobar, whose incredible violin arrangements inspired Talmadge's music.

Thank you to the Authors out of Carolina: Kim Wright, Erika Marks, and Joy Callaway, who listened and advised about this novel as we logged oh so many miles all over the Southeast.

Thank you to Ariel Lawhon, because of all the reasons. Mostly for listening to all the bleating. And for helping me up when I fell. (Literally and figuratively.)

And always, always, thank you to Jesus: For You alone are worthy.

ABOUT THE AUTHOR

Marybeth Mayhew Whalen is the author of several novels, including *When We Were Worthy* and *The Things We Wish Were True*. She speaks to women's groups around the United States and is the cofounder of the popular women's fiction site www.shereads.org. Married for twenty-six years, she and her husband, Curt, live in North Carolina with their six children, ranging from young adult to elementary age. Although Marybeth spends most of her time in the grocery store, she occasionally escapes to scribble some words and work on her next novel. Visit her at www.marybethwhalen.com.